WISP

a novel

BY

Elizabeth Mostyn

First edition 2022

Copyright © Elizabeth Mostyn,

Licensed to P'kaboo Publishers

ISBN 979-8-88526-484-6

p'kaboo
publishers

www.pkaboo.net

P'kaboo Publishers would like to thank and acknowledge the following people who were instrumental in the completion of this title:

Paul Thompson for organizing the submission, agenting and also text edits, and for the photographs of St Andrew's that constitute part of the cover image;

Beta readers, for their valuable feedback:

Rebecca Stoll, Jessica McFarland, Sadie Byrne, Laura Muetzelfeldt;

Early beta readers:

Leslie Noble, Robin Rossouw;

Layout and formatting: Faizan;

Also thank you to Robin Rossouw for her artistic input on the cover design.

To my sister Linda

W
I
S
P

Table of Contents

1982

"Bloody hell!" she shrieked, "How could you do such a stupid, brainless, thing?" She tried to dust the infected mosquito off her arm. It was anchored by its tiny mouthparts, so small she couldn't feel them, so efficient that she couldn't get them free.

He was at her side in a moment, his big hand ripping the insect off, dropping it on the laboratory floor, stamping on it hard.

There was blood on her arm, not much.

"How on earth did you do that?" she asked, "How many times have you done it before?"

He looked shamefaced; he was rarely careless. He had been decanting the mosquitoes from their dirty tank into a clean one. It wasn't even his job. And it was usually straightforward, with enough time to stop an escape between the tanks. Not that day.

"Where is Mickey, anyway?" she asked, her voice shriller than usual, trying to keep the panic down.

"Don't know," he said, "He's always cleaned before this. Maybe he's ill."

"Why the flaming hell did you have to start cleaning anyway?" She gives his cleaning cloths and disinfectant a nasty look, "What's wrong with you? Haven't you any of your own work to do?"

He doesn't reply. She knows why. He can't cope with mess, and he won't allow their animals, even the infected mosquitoes, to be kept in less than pristine conditions.

The two virologists stared at each other for the longest time. The mosquitoes are infected with ZIKV, the Zika virus.

✦

2014

Ben Furness, a Professor of Microbiology

The draught from the roof knifes through his thick coat and the woolly scarf he has wound around his neck, and he looks up to see the cold stars through the broken beams, though most of the joists and plaster lie in heaps on the floor.

He first realises it is happening again when he catches the familiar smell.

It's all the same as before: a deep gold musical sound, not like a cello or anything he can think of, coming out of nowhere but deeper, rounder, fuller than any music he has ever heard. His heart begins to change its beat – not faster, slower: not harder, softer. As his legs begin to feel boneless, he slips gently down the wall onto the filthy floor and sits there waiting in a warm haze of expectation.

The rainbows and the snow start together, large soft flakes falling through the split light, softening the piles of building rubble. He feels the golden sound taking up the space around his heart, warming his whole body like a down comforter.

He focuses on the disturbance in the air about a foot above the ground and five feet in front of him, his damaged eyesight begins to clear. There is gold here too and colours the like of which are not normally available to human sight. He has stopped trying to clarify it: it is peacocks and birds of paradise, orchids, and poison arrow frogs, all the rainforests of all the world. It shines with heat and the million colours have incredible brilliance. A flash and a sparkle, and then a mist like dry ice, starts to funnel out from the centre. Now, there are sounds one could call music, but no music Ben has ever heard before; new, original music; refreshing, calming, uplifting - but spare, unfussy.

There is a rush of wind as a figure forms in the mist and becomes solid but still somehow transparent.

It's the man, brown as a berry and dressed in a rough wool robe. His head is partly shaven and he's gangly and thin. His brown eyes twinkle out of a face strong with laugh lines. His calloused hand is wounded, and two drops of bright blood make their way down his wrist. His mouth is open, although no words come from it. Ben takes a deep breath and finds a voice in his parched throat. He asks, as he has before,

"How can I help?"

The apparition has never answered, and it doesn't answer now.

It stands slightly above the ground and smiles at him. It looks as if it is speaking but there is nothing he can hear except the music getting louder, louder. The split colours of the light begin to spin around both Ben and the figure and the wind comes back from somewhere, catching-up everything within the room. The music is splitting, now, into disharmony: the colours begin fragmenting into moving mosaics that make his eyes sting with heat and pain.

Ben is snatched up on the wind and the rainbow, up into the storm, buffeted around and around, knocked this way and that by whatever is in his way. The whirling comes into his head and the cold comes back. It's the hollow black cold of Scottish winter and, at that minute, becomes unconsciousness. The glorious smell is the last thing he remembers.

PART ONE

MICHAELMAS TERM

Once more, after the vision, Ben felt he should telephone Professor Reilly, the Dean of Divinity. When he had consulted him on the first of the previous two occasions, the Dean had asked Ben to call him if anything like that happened again. He did not think, however, that Reilly believed what Ben had told him: he had been too softly spoken, too keen on humouring the old man.

Ben had gone to him because he supposed that such a person would know something about this religious stuff. Ben didn't he'd never really been interested. He was a scientist and believed in what he could see with his eyes, hear with his ears, feel with his hands, smell and taste too. He wasn't un-spiritual, though, he thought. He was convinced of the existence of *something*, although he didn't know what it was: goodness perhaps. The study of mycology had formed a large part of his life.

However, the more he studied the world and all its wonders, the more he felt the awe which he thought of as spirituality. It was a part of his personal code to celebrate the magnificence of the creation, even if no one had actually created it.

The Dean of Divinity, despite Ben's up-front declaration of atheism, had told him, on that occasion, to go away and pray about it. Ben didn't even know how to do this, although he had, gamely, got down on bended knee in St Salvator's University Chapel, and managed to get as far as, "Dear God..." That had been all, and it had sounded to Ben as if he was taking the name in vain. There wasn't any more he could say in conscience. He'd have been talking into the void of his disbelief. Not scientific; not logical. Not anything, really.

The visions, of which he'd had four now, were always similar; not like the other thing, the thing which had happened in the late summer. He'd called in at the Police Station about that. It was only the sense of weirdness which connected the two experiences. At least he hoped so.

*

That other time, he'd gone for a walk. It had been a bit cold, late at night, for walking but he'd felt the need. He walked most nights. The difficulty was in stopping. He kept telling himself, "Just as far as that lamp post; just as far as those trees; just as far as that farm gate", always extending it a little more and a little more. Walking was good for him. He was addicted to it. Since Free went.

That night, he was deep in the country, still on the road but it was very boring. He had a torch in his pack and there was, anyway, a full moon, so he would deviate a bit, go cross-country to the road on the other side. A large field lay between him and the other road. It had been slightly chilly during the day, but it hadn't rained. He wouldn't get too muddy; and his boots would cope.

He found a break in the wire fence. The field had already been cut for hay and there was only short stubble left. He'd caught a few stray strands around the fastenings of his boots and stopped to pull them off. When he stood-up he found he could see a long way.

The country was becoming ever more minimal at this time of year. Hay in, not much stock hereabouts; only the trees standing in the moonlight - and many of them starting to lose their leaves, exposing the tall conifers as sentries over the land. No people either: his main reason for walking in the night. No one could ask him how he was. He didn't have to say he was fine; didn't have to pretend to be cheerful; didn't have to avoid saying Free's name.

He'd spent much of his life with her, why should he avoid saying her name? He knew the look on their faces if he should inadvertently mention her name. They'd look sorry and ask him if there was anything they could do. Bring her back, he wanted to yell. If you can't do that, you can't do anything. And don't tell me you understand. You don't.

He walked on, feeling the emptiness inside, feeling it digesting him like a parasite. Odd how it sometimes occurred to one, the physical effects of a psychological state. He felt his gut rubbed raw by emotional pain. Someone had once said that all her skin had been rubbed off by the pain of a failed relationship. Couldn't remember who.

He was wrong, though, there were people. Well, there was some movement over there. It could be an animal, but he felt that it wasn't. A child, he thought. But what's it doing out here on its own at this time of night? He tried to see it again, down by the hedge between the fields. No, he couldn't see it. Maybe his eyes were deceiving him. Not likely: they were still pretty good for middle age. He peered for a few moments and then looked away completely. He'd often used this technique in the field: sometimes one could catch sight of movement when one looked back.

His eyes swivelled back to where he had first seen something and, sure enough, there was another movement. A child? Trying to blend into the scant foliage? He moved in that direction, slowly and as soundlessly as possible. He had halved the distance between himself and the child when it saw him and tried to melt further into the hedge. He started to move more quickly, and the child detached itself from the bushes and began to run. It did not run well: Ben saw that there seemed to be something wrong with its legs. It was only 10 yards away from him when it fell and started whimpering.

Ben crossed the intervening space quickly, preparing to pick the hurt child up. It was curled into the foetal position, its shoulders raised, its arms around its head. He saw that it was female and wearing just a cotton shift, torn and dirty, and that she had scrapes and blood on her skinny arms and legs. He bent down towards the little girl and spoke gently.

"Hello, my dear. What are you doing out here on your own in this cold - and without a coat, too?"

She didn't respond, except to tighten her arms around her head and cringe away from him. He could see, in the bright moonlight, that her legs and arms were misshapen as well as being bruised and the skin torn away as if by fence wire. He reached out to touch her and she suddenly uncovered her head and a narrow face, tiny eyes, a huge nose, came up towards him.

Ben stepped quickly back, stunned at her appearance. The very large nose was partly a visual effect because the skull was much too small and underdeveloped: the rest of her torso seemed small but reasonably normal. Her eyes held only panic. He could not have told her age from her strange face, but the rest of her was about the right size for 7 or 8 years old. He was still reeling from her appearance when she thrust out her fist and punched him hard in the gut. Her arms and legs might be twisted but she had enough strength to do some damage. As he doubled over in pain, she jumped up and sped away; still limping but showing a much stronger turn of speed than could Ben, even had he not been winded.

Looking into the hedge, he spied an old blanket, where the child had been nesting. He sank down on it until the dizziness and pain receded. He was feeling a sense of profound shock underneath the dizziness. He puzzled as to why it should affect him so badly.

*

He'd gone to the Police Station the following morning and reported that there was a child wandering around somewhere to the north of the town. He'd walked around, himself, for some time before he came home but hadn't been able to see any further trace. She'd vanished like a dream. No, not really like a dream. He knew the difference quite well. No, more just like the vision - but he'd had that before, the vision, nothing to do with seeing the child. He didn't feel he could tell the police about that.

He'd been worried, though. She'd have parents who were

looking for her; people who wondered where she'd got to. Someone had probably found her: he'd decided during the night, someone would have spotted her and taken her home. He told himself that he would have gone to the Police Station then, if it had been open. There was only a daytime police presence in St Andrews: town and gown joked that, if one wanted to commit a crime, one had to telephone Kirkcaldy first. He didn't see how large and black the bruise on his abdomen was until next morning.

*

The police, in the morning, had been kind and taken down all the details he'd provided about the child. They'd been a bit sceptical about the physical description, the sergeant had never heard of such a thing. Ben assured them that such did exist; they said they'd be in touch. No one had reported her missing, they said, which was a little alarming. Oh, well, he'd done what he had to - he could forget about it. Hadn't been able to. It had come back to him occasionally, like tonight, when he'd had a repeat performance of the holy vision.

Now, after the vision, he decided not to call Reilly about it after all. It was past midnight anyway and the old boy would, presumably be in bed. A naughty little thought came to him as he wondered who Reilly would be in bed with... There was absolutely no reason for that, he thought, he probably has a perfectly respectable marriage. Ben didn't know. Not being much curious about such things, he didn't much care.

✦

Ben's undated diary entry 1 –
some time at the end of summer

I haven't kept a diary in years; too much to do, busy living life instead of writing about it. Anyway, why would my comings and goings be of interest to anyone else? Naturally, I could remember them, so I didn't need to write them down for me. I have noticed a little slippage of memory over the past week or two – and I feel I should make a few notes to kind of keep track. I think, as well, that it might be a good idea to reflect on something that happened a couple of days ago.

I saw a child out in the countryside - where I'd been walking late on; not being able to sleep. It has been like this pretty much since Free went. Free was my wife of many years. Her real name was Frederica, but she hated it; had always hated it. Free seemed appropriate at the time - because she was the most free-spirited person I have ever met. One never knew how she would react to anything; she considered being called unpredictable a great compliment! Except at the end, of course. She wasn't free then. I lost her. I loved her. I love her. I took care of her; I did everything I could.

The child, back to the child. I don't mean our child; she's grown and away. It was the child I saw when I was walking. I've said that already. Only old folks repeat all the time; I'm not there yet.

It was a wee girl and she had something seriously wrong with her. She had a very small head, her nose looking large in comparison. Her arms and legs weren't right. She was wearing just a thin shift - and it was quite cold. I tried to speak to her, but she ran away. She punched me and ran away. It hurt. The bruise was huge and didn't go away for two weeks.

I didn't go straight to the police. Somehow, I wanted desperately to get home, to my own place. I suppose I wasn't feeling too well, I needed comfort. I dropped around to the police station in North Street the following morning. I know the desk sergeant thought I was daft. He hadn't had anyone reported missing anyway. Put it down to an old fool's fancy. I don't know why I didn't show him the bruise.

✦

Belinda Fleming, University Principal & Vice-Chancellor

Belinda was very tired; the blasted meeting had gone on all day. Three weeks in Switzerland had lulled her irritable bowel but it was screaming again today. The pressure of the Development Board had induced severe pains in her abdomen. She had doubled up, twice, in the ladies' lavatory, and found it hard to straighten to her full five feet three. It was days like this which made her wish she still worked with yeasts in biochemistry and did not have a sign on her door saying, "Principal and Vice- Chancellor".

Now it was time to check her outgoing mail, sign it, and hand it back to her secretary before leaving for the night. Hazel had placed the out-tray precisely parallel to the edge of the cherry-wood desk: the crop of university-crested letterheads settled snowily in place. Belinda picked up the first one and cast her eye over it. It was some admin matter of no interest. She signed it with the best flourish she could muster and carried on to the next and the next.

It doesn't take very long at all when you can't be bothered to read them.

She rose from the chair and shrugged into the smart, waisted, blue tartan jacket which she had sloppily stretched over the back of the chair, instead of bothering to find the coat-hanger provided for it. Lifting the out-tray, she took her briefcase in the other hand and went into the outer office. Hazel was franking mail - mail, obviously, which didn't require the revered signature.

"I'm putting this on your desk, Hazel," she said, "And I'm going home!" Hazel said goodnight just as she passed through the door. It took Belinda exactly two minutes to reach the porch of the Principal's Residence next door. Mark was home; his neat-but-dull grey Nissan Micra parked on the gravel in front of the residence. He'd have fed the kids already. Yahoo, she thought.

✦

Minerva (Minnie) Latimer, a Psychiatrist

In her first-floor flat in North Street, Minnie was just waking up. She had been rising at precisely 7am for the last thirty years. She reached out her clawing left hand to turn off the alarm button. She might have said that the alarm had never had the opportunity to ring in those thirty years, but it wouldn't be true: the clock was only two years old, all her previous ones having become frustrated with not being allowed to do their job and packed it in the day after their guarantees expired. Minnie put her feet to the floor, straight into the old-lady tartan slippers.

"What have I come down to?" she said out loud, as she did every time, she saw the detestable things as she did when she forced her feet into the latest round of orthopaedic walking shoes. At arthritic fifty-four she was no longer able even to wear the modestly heeled lady-doctor shoes she had favoured since she was fourteen.

She stumped across her bedroom and painfully took the rose-pink dressing-gown from the hook behind the door. Polly, the compact black cat, wound around her legs purring. Minnie opened the door and Polly sprinted down the steps into the street in search of adventure. The letters dropped through the letterbox into the front hall. Minnie looked over the high banister, trying to guess what they were.

There were four envelopes, she could see. One was large and plastic junk. Why did the Royal Society for the Prevention of Birds think she might want to join it? Two were what used to be called foolscap, business size that is; one brown, one white. The brown would be the plumbing bill. Minnie sighed.

Hardly anyone ever wrote letters these days, including her. The last envelope was white and windowed. Another bloody appointment with the bloody rheumatologist in bloody Dundee. She turned around and went, as fast as she could, to put the kettle on. Her usual breakfast of gluten-free granola was easy to pour into a cereal bowl, but, oh, how bored she was with it. Not quite as bored as she was with working part-time because of the difficulty of moving with arthritic inflammation. How can you practice psychiatry part-time? Although she did have other things to think about.

Michaelmas Term

*

Ben watched the spider wire-walking on the strand, light just catching the filament strung above his bed. Arthropoda, he thought, Arachnida... the rest trailed off in a humid oil painting. The deep glossy greens and bright scarlets of the rain forest, the creepers, the screams of monkeys in the treetops, the deep silences surrounding the mobile and the lethal - and the smells, they were what he always remembered best: heavy, cloying perfumes, exotic strong scents from the flowers making a frantic statement to attract hurried insects during their own single day of life.

And all of it underpinned and undermined by the stink, plants and animals decaying on the forest floor. Rot, fungus, mycology.

He thought of the heat and immediately shrank under the duvet: St Andrews on an October morning was not the place to get drawn into tropical memories from years back. Ben had no need to get up yet: it was just after 7.30, and one of the many advantages of living in St Andrews was that everywhere was close to everywhere else. But his bladder was full, and he had to attend to it. Like all ageing things, it was getting a bit of a nuisance these days. Behind the bathroom door was a piece of paper torn from his reminder notebook - stuck to the door with a bit of Sellotape. In thick red felt-tip it informed him that today was the first day of term, beginning of Week One, end of Freshers' Week.

He tried to recall what time that meant he should be in the department - should have written it down, fool, getting just a bit absent-minded. What was he thinking when he was writing the note? He must have written the note; it was in his writing, and he'd lived alone since Free went.

He did what was necessary in the bathroom and hurried back to bed. The heating would kick in in a minute; a bit longer to laze, then. He crawled back under the downie, into his own warmth. One of life's rare wee pleasures.

*

The dream didn't announce itself as a separate thing, it was joined into something else - he couldn't remember all the complications when he awoke. But he remembered the main one, the dream about Wisp. They always had a special quality. She had grown up, and was very beautiful, with smooth, freckled, skin and auburn hair, just like Free's, right down her back, catching the sun, although she had brown eyes like his own. Somehow it was always sunny when he dreamed of Wisp.

She was wearing trousers, or jeans, he supposed, like all the young people did, but smarter than most. Well, of course, she would have inherited her mother's good taste. A nice dark blue, covering long legs. He thought she was probably taller than him by now. A loose Indian-style blouse; white, with fancy coloured embroidery, bright green sandals with a flower on the strap, just like those he had spotted in Hogg's window the other day.

He'd thought how much Wisp would have liked them then.

Beautiful, slim hands, she had, like a musician, maybe. He had heard music in the background. Did she like music, he couldn't recall. It was one of his own favourites he heard; the Debussy *Images*, impressionism for piano, he thought. Wisp was saying something, but he couldn't hear above the music – which was getting louder. He woke up, wishing he could have talked to her; his lovely, lovely girl. What might he have said to her?

Jake Ellwood, a Neuroscientist

Dark burgundy silk dropped from an alabaster knee, and he realised she wasn't wearing stockings. No tights either, though, her elegant burgundy, very high-heeled shoes, were melded to bare feet. He was amazed for the second time since six o'clock this morning.

The first time had been when he had opened his office door and found her already sitting there at his desk, in a locked corridor, in a locked building. For a scientist in early middle age, divorced, jaded, and rarely surprised by anything, Jake was finding this all a bit much. He rubbed his eyes with the heels of his hands and did a second take.

She stood up and towered over him: she must be at least six feet tall, maybe a little more. She extended a cool and creamy, ringless hand, palm down and he realised, with a jolt, that he was expected to kiss it. He took hold of it awkwardly and shook it lamely. Neuroscientists from Inverness don't do hand kissing.

"Good morning, Dr Ellwood," she said quietly, "I'm so sorry it's really early, but this is the only time I could be sure of getting half an hour to ourselves."

She spoke with an English accent, upper class; a woman accustomed to having her wishes carried out. Preferably yesterday. She stared past him into the glazed corridor, the steady brown eyes taking in the space running along the side of the whole of the second floor – to another locked door with a yellow and black sign. Jake could almost hear the Sam Spade commentary, but he was far from a down-at-heel gumshoe. He didn't say anything; waited for her to tell him who had been murdered and what she expected him to do about it.

Jake came out of his daze, not before time. The gorgeous woman with no stockings had settled in the chair, where he usually tried not to bully his students. Jake tried to prise his mind away from this obsession with female legs; via the curiosity about whether she normally wore tights – he had been told by Kate, before she left him, that they were more comfortable, and that no modern woman would wear stockings willingly. He craved legs in real stockings. He forced his mind to attend to what she was saying. He hadn't caught her name - could prove a problem eventually. This was something of a recurring thing with him. At some stage it becomes too late to ask.

"I am very concerned," she said, "Not about the way he is behaving in general, he seems fine by all accounts, but this thing... well, it's just beyond anything. It's crazy, he's crazy. Things like that just don't happen!"

Well, here goes, thought Jake, find out what she wants.

"Miss, er, er, perhaps you could tell me what you want me to do about it. Perhaps, er, you could tell me what *exactly* you want from me?"

She looked at him as if he had crawled out from under a particularly damp stone. What Kate used to call the Joan Bakewell look as though her feet were inadvertently soaking in a bowl of dirty water.

"You are the expert," she said, crisply, "You know about temporal lobe damage, that's what you published in *Nature*: a paper about the experience of god." She said it with a small "g," frosty, like the October day in St Andrews, cold, sharp, brightly polished. He decided that he should, until he could let the information he had barely heard, sink in sufficiently to work out what the hell she was talking about, offer her a coffee.

She rapped out "black, no sugar" as he rose to switch on his personal kettle; the one which the departmental safety officer had cut the plug off – *no auto switch-off, pal, Health & Safety*. Jake had the cord stripped back and the plug re-attached before the officer was back in Animal Behaviour where he belonged.

"Tell me about it from the beginning," he said. He tired easily of messing about pretending to be Joseph Bell. He liked puzzles though; liked finding out. She performed a slow, deep, sigh and closed her eyes. He noticed how long her lashes were, black and silky, and pulled himself back again from fantasy land.

She started by telling him that her uncle was a senior member of the university, a few years from retirement and working fewer hours than normal because writing a book. St Andrews is a place which grips its community to its fifteenth century bosom so they can hardly get away; where you find emotionally stunted PhDs wrapping veg in shops. "He's a mycologist," she said, "A lifetime interest in fungi."

The story which emerged from then on in was nothing to do with mushrooms, although Professor Furness had worked in microbiology for a long time. Widowed, he lived a quiet, though slightly eccentric, life but now...this foolishness. He had reported seeing what he described as a "Holy Vision" – at least he thought that was what it was.

"I think," she said, "That he's going senile or something." Jake wondered aloud why she was here, talking to him, instead of in St Mary's talking to the Dean of Divinity. Or talking to an actual medical doctor.

"That's just it," she sighed. "They might believe him, mightn't they? Religious maniacs, aren't they? Isn't this what they're looking for?"

Her voice quavered for the first time on the last sentence. Jake detected a pale pink blush over the bridge of her elegant nose and his Sam Spade sense rang a tiny bell in the back of his head. There was a lie here. He filed it for future cogitation.

"Visions aren't very common round here," he said, "Which is surprising considering the history of the place. There's been lots of religious thrashing and screaming in the past, though, so hysteria's not all that far under the surface. There are all kinds of things under the surface here". He hesitated and put his elbows on the desk.

"I'm not a psychiatrist, you know, I'm not qualified to comment on sanity".

"I know, "she said sharply, "I'm looking elsewhere for that. I want you because you can show that the spiritual sense comes from processes going on in the brain; that lesions in the temporal lobe led sufferers to see God." It was quite a big "G" this time. Definitely.

*

It had been one early morning in late September, in the Genetic Engineering Department, when they had discovered that one of the subjects was missing. James Florrie had run an investigation, as he was required to do, but he had found no obvious breaks in the system. It could not have escaped through a window or any of that shit. It had to have got out **with** someone, but who?

Not someone who had done it deliberately, he felt sure. It must have been up behind the person and so small that no one had seen it. Son of a bitch! Anyway, it was his fault. He was the Night Security Superintendent and it had happened on his watch. Who was to blame was irrelevant. He was responsible.

Mervyn Adams' work group had combed the countryside. Luckily, its weak legs couldn't have taken it too far. The shocking fact was that it had managed to get almost eight miles away before they recaptured it: it was no shock that it had taken three men to subdue it.

✦

Christabel Furness, a Secret Agent

Christabel came across her uncle at the bottom of South Street, on her way back from the pet shop. The little dog obviously thought Ben was very exciting, wiping her muddy paws all over his pants. He didn't care; he greeted the dog before acknowledging his niece.

"Hello, wee girl!" he laughed. "Where did you come from?" He rubbed her behind her disreputable ears and remarked on her smiling wee face. Then he straightened up and said hello to Christabel.

"Good morning, Uncle," she said as if she'd seen him yesterday rather than three years ago, when she'd arrived without notice to tell him her dad was dead.

"How are you today? I see you've met my dog. I was just buying her a collar and lead: can't keep using my stockings."

"Where did you get her from?" he asked. "I thought you couldn't keep a dog, with travelling so much." Christabel smiled, an illuminating smile, like Ben's own.

"Ah, well," she said, "Mary Jane and I are getting married – so we've decided to come back to the UK. We've bought an ancient country cottage in Surrey!"

Ben blinked: not only had he not yet got his head around the idea of same-sex marriage, but he had had no idea Christie was gay. She went on.

"It'll be nice to have a sweet little dog," she said. "MJ likes them too, although she's insisting on having at least a couple of cats as well. And, bizarrely, she has a most peculiar soft spot for ferrets…"

Ben gulped, imagining the rural idyll and the ferrets. It was all too much. He slipped gently sideways into the Mustelids.

"There was a time," he said, "When I was interested in small predators. The weasel family is fascinating. You won't hunt them, though, the ferrets, will you?"

"God, no, MJ's vegan, and I'm moving that way too. I do know, though, that you have to keep ferrets in pairs, or they die. I've done a bit of research – and I managed to get a book from the New York Public Library. Unfortunately, it had a lot of rabbit recipes in the back, so I didn't let MJ see it. It was good, though. Apparently, they make excellent pets – even come to meet you when you come home!"

The only thing Ben could think of to say was "Ah."

Michaelmas Term

*

Minnie limped painfully, relying heavily on her stick, along North Street, going toward the shops in Market Street. As she passed the archway into St Salvator's Quad, she saw Ben Furness coming out of the university church. She wondered what he was up to, making for the University Chaplain. He wasn't religious - but there he was, now talking earnestly. She noticed that his shoes were very wet. She wondered, not for the first time, whether he was looking after himself properly. No obvious interference, she instructed herself sharply. Absolute discipline.

The town sparkled under a pale, bright sun and, although there was a definite snap in the air, it could be classified as a nice day. Continuing students had mostly returned over the weekend, parents with Volvos trundling up the M74 with personal effects piled up to, and on, the roof.

This morning, it was business as usual for returning students - and their teachers – but there were still bejeants, wandering round in scarlet gowns looking for lectures they should probably be attending.

Ben, leaving after a word with Mary Ellis, the University Chaplain, nodded as he passed Dr Latimer, and went next door into Biochemistry & Microbiology. He said a bright hello to the janitor at the front desk and took the dangerous stone steps two at a time to the second floor.

Seemed like more steps up to Micro. this morning: getting harder, he thought; comes to us all in the end. He chuckled, thinking of the times he'd joked about how useful it would be to have a chaise-longue on the half-landing, so old codgers could recover their equilibrium before giving the children the benefit of their wisdom. He didn't say it again to Lucille, sitting at the desk - only real old codgers repeat all the time.

Lucille Moreton was the middle-aged bleached blonde who ran the department. If not for Lucille, there would be no exam questions, or results. Like all good administrators, Lucille had made herself indispensable. She stepped over to a trolley parked against the left-hand wall and poured two cups of coffee. She took her time adding milk and sugar and then presented Ben with one.

"Professor," she said. Shaking the hand without the coffee cup, she gave his hand a peculiar little squeeze and smiled at him, showing a gap where a canine tooth had been in the Mesozoic era.

"Could you see John Malley this morning?" Lucille said. "Doctoral student with a first in toxicology from Edinburgh - work something to do with alkaloids... Do you recall?"

"Ah," said Ben, with half-recognition - he did seem to be getting a bit vague. And he'd never been that type of teacher, ever. He looked around.

"Will I be in here?"

"No," said Lucille, "The seminar room is free down on One. I've put him in there, and you'll be handy for his lab too."

They drank their coffee and talked about the weather. Ben wondered why she kept wrinkling her nose at him. Did she fancy him? Surely not. He felt a giggle coming on and suppressed it - what would Free say? Have said? His stomach felt odd thinking of Free and he realised he was hungry - the emptiness was obvious when one thought about it. He took a nice chocolate biscuit from the secretary's plate, and covertly slipped another in his pocket for later.

When she'd escorted the professor to the first-floor room where John Malley was doing some of his reading, Lucille placed a 'phone call to Paul Grant, Chair of the department. He promised to come down in five minutes.

She hadn't been worrying for the whole weekend because she'd hoped that the talk the Prof had had with Ben during the long vac might have done the trick. Ben had taken to coming in to teach again each morning of the final couple of weeks of last Whitsun term.

Lucille was always kind to him: she had, after all, twenty-five years' experience of baby-sitting gifted but strange academics, including the current Principal, when they were both girls in the department. Ben Furness, after all, was mostly fine - and, as today, she was still able to fudge the difficulties by aiming a postgrad, working in one of his areas of interest, in his direction. She felt she owed him that because of his past tragedies.

Last month, coming back, in heroic mood, from a study trip to South Africa, Paul had decided to take the bull by the horns and confront Ben. Ben had been very gracious and understanding, had accepted that he was not expected to come in to teach every day, but just to run seminars, do a little research, and supervise the occasional PhD student in his special areas; a reduced load, on the premise that he needed time for finishing his book.

Lucille, listening at the door, had been concerned at that turn of events. It seemed a bit likely to make the older professor feel unwanted. The Chair and Ben had parted on excellent terms; had gone for a drink in the Castle. Paul had come back to the office with a pink glow on his face. He'd reassured Lucille with one word. "Sorted!"

Wasn't.

*

Felicity was waiting for Jake in his postgraduate teaching laboratory, holding a bright green folder against her ample chest, her scrubbed face particularly shiny this morning. She wasn't the sort of postgrad who was amenable to having her long hair freed and her glasses taken off, producing a highly intelligent stunner. Not that she wasn't highly intelligent, naturally, but her white lab coat clutched her plumpish figure somewhat tightly and she had no legs to speak of.

That wasn't nice, was it? Jake felt faintly saddened by his chauvinist pig-voyeur thoughts. He was better than that, not an old-style pig, not even a piglet. He just had this penchant for legs. He always had a slight rush of disappointment when he saw Felicity and thought, wistfully, how handy it would have been if she'd had nice legs and the ability to seduce him. It wouldn't be very difficult, in his depressingly celibate condition, - but without the necessary legs, it was no go. Unfortunately, he suspected her of being a bit in love with him. She tended to blush rather easily when in close proximity.

"Jake," she was saying, "I've been looking at the results and it looks as though the damage *was* in the mid-brain as you thought..."

Told you, he didn't say. Sometimes Felicity was a bit too clever for her own good. There had been an obvious clue in the clinical description. The man had had a classic "fencing" posture at the end of his life - and his having been a boxer was a fair give-away.

The flexure: curling and stretching of opposite arms and legs,

27

suggested contusions in the region around the cross-over of the nervous system. He asked to see the sections and looked into Felicity's binocular microscope. This sort of thing had become a regular part of their workload since the NHS had been outsourcing some of its scientific work to the universities. The payment was helping to support Felicity's PhD.

"Fairly straightforward then," he said, straightening up and checking the request date in the green folder, "Get Vinnie to write a note to Professor Carlson: he'll be wondering why we've taken so long. Why *have* we taken so long?"

"We haven't, really," said Felicity, blushing charmingly (or it would have been if she had had legs). "Dave had a bad reaction to something in the frozen section room and no one could find out what it was. He hadn't finished the sections, so we were stuck."

Jake felt anger surging around his throat, the acid was coming in every day recently.

"Why in hell didn't someone else do it?"

Felicity became raspberry and started to say, "Er..."

Jake slammed down the file and said flaming bloody hell – which was as near to blasphemy that his memories of his wee Highland Maw would let him go. He already knew precisely why no one had done Dave's work - they were short of technicians and the university had an agreement with those they did have that teaching staff and postgrads were forbidden to do technician's jobs.

He walked over to the wall where there were several pieces of equipment plugged in: he wanted to use his good old-fashioned monocular microscope to check some of Felicity's slides in the good old-fashioned way. That was the way he had been taught histology, and he knew he was quite capable of distinguishing confusing artifacts of staining without error. The plug of his microscope was wedged in behind the adaptor, which was carrying a power bar with five other plugs in it. His large fingers couldn't reach the switch. One of these days, the whole place would explode in a giant fireball.

"Felicity," he shouted, "Bring your clever wee hands over here and turn this on for me, will you?" She came over and clicked the switch without difficulty, her hands accustomed to delivering lambs on the farm since her girlhood.

After he had looked at the slides (and hadn't found anything of interest) Jake went back to his own room. He felt disgruntled about life in general: the beautiful but strange woman sitting in his locked room, her very peculiar request about her batty uncle, Felicity not having legs, and now the possibility of a nasty argument with whomsoever was Shop Steward this week. He could do with-bloody-out it.

A light scent lingered in his office, her perfume. He didn't have a clue what it could be, but it smelled flowery, and it worked its magic on his developing headache. Ah, if only. He sat down at his cluttered desk and, leaning the chair back against the wall, put both his feet up the edge of it. Felicity's perfume was eau de acetate; Kate had objected, ethically and politically, to any kind of perfume at all.

Christabel Furness was rather more than a touch of glamour; she was a whole lorry-full, all on her own, and he had the overwhelming but pleasant feeling that she could run him down if she felt like it. He had promised to talk to her uncle, that was all, and telephone her in London

– he knew he wouldn't see her again. He sighed.

Life is so far from how it should be.

*

Professor Furness had kindly agreed to meet with Jake on Tuesday at 5pm. The older man had said that he had to supervise a practical with some undergraduates until then; he always liked to take an interest in the welfare of the younger ones, although he hadn't lectured honours classes for some time. They'd decided on Jake's room in the Medical School, although Jake was surprised to find that the Prof still had one in his own department. Exquisite Christabel had said that he was semi-retired.

Still, Jake supposed, perhaps they keep the old boy around for the look of the thing. This was that kind of university; damned hard to get rid of anyone because you met them in Market Street all the time when you were coming out of Tesco's.

Until Tuesday teatime, then, Jake had time to have a think about this odd situation and consider whom he might talk to about it. Christabel had said she didn't want anyone to know about Ben's strangeness: it was all around the Divinity School, so it was unlikely to stay out of the public domain for long, but she'd rather know what she was dealing with before the scientific establishment started to laugh. Uncle was rather well known. Jake could hear her beautifully modulated voice in his head.

Jake picked up the nearest copy of his god-book, the chartreuse dustjacket making it easy to see in the chaos he always pretended was organised. He traced his index finger over the raised silver title,

"Hallucination, Illusion, and the Experience of God" and opened it to the index to remind himself of the page numbers of the section specifically about Holy Visions.

When Jake had checked his memory against what he had thought, several years ago, about hallucinations, illusions, and the experience of God, he made a phone call and arranged to take the Dean of Divinity to lunch at Southgait. The Staff Club did a decent midweek lunch at a reasonable price: prudence precluded any of the real restaurants in the town.

It was slightly after one o'clock when Reverend Professor Martin Reilly turned up, jangling his man-jewellery. He was very smart for any kind of academic, especially for a Dean of Divinity. He would rather have died in a ditch than wear a sports coat with leather patches. Jake felt a little underdressed in his jeans and tatty grey tee-shirt with the alien on the front: it wasn't often that he suffered nostalgia for his gown. The Reverend Professor Martin Reilly was, of course, wearing his. Along with the bracelets.

Jake stood up and got the Rev Prof seated. They had met before at the odd university function, but Jake didn't actually know him. The Rev Prof had, though, written a blistering attack on Jake's book in *The Scotsman*. Jake felt a slight chill on his neck as he recalled the phrase "this arrogant and juvenile trifle". There had been something personal as well, he rather thought – a hint about too many late nights and illicit (and possibly unnatural) sex.

When they had collected their lunch and done with the pleasantries (skirting around the question of unnatural sex), Jake asked Reilly about Ben Furness: had he heard this thing which was going

31

around, did he know the microbiologist, what did he think?

"Well," said Reilly, tucking his napkin neatly into his collar, "I'm keeping an open mind, at the moment, of course. It's easy, isn't it," he smiled palely, "To say the man's past it and gaga – but when you think about it, they thought St Teresa of Avila was a loony too... of course, she *was*... in many ways, although holy, obviously,"

He quickly got into his stride, and it didn't seem to have occurred to him to ask why Jake needed to know. Confidentiality didn't seem to feature in his theological toolkit.

"Of course, when it started, he came straight to me. I've known him for years; we used to be on Convocation together. He was an unbeliever in those days – *I* assumed he still was. He was very worried about it, but I was able to reassure him that it was nothing dangerous. These visions don't tell him to kill himself or anyone else. In fact, they don't say anything at all. Most peculiar, don't you agree?"

He didn't wait for a response, continuing to pick at his lamb chops with his knife, hesitated without tasting them and then liberally doused them with salt and pepper.

"If you're asking if I believe in them, I suppose I'd have to say that I probably don't. I take a 'just in case' position really. Surely if some saint or other felt like appearing to someone round here, they'd at least choose someone who isn't an out and out atheist? We are up to our necks in good Christians - Sister Honoria, at the Catholic Chaplaincy, for instance, is frightfully holy. Do you think that the Holy Spirit would be so inappropriate?"

Jake felt a long way from being competent to comment on that and kept looking at Reilly, who had started to ram down his chops and chips between sentences, reflecting on the definition of 'holy'. He asked the Dean how often Ben had had these visions. Reilly thought they'd probably stopped now because Ben no longer came, worriedly, to tell him about them; he seemed to have had about two or three in the period between last Christmas and the middle of Whitsun Term. Reilly had only seen him in the distance since then and they had not spoken.

Jake stopped himself from enquiring as to why a fit, senior member of the university had not felt it reasonable to follow up on the clearly strange Professor Furness in case he was unwell. Obviously, the policy was out of sight, out of mind. Instead, he asked what Reilly understood to be the content of the visions.

The answer was that there had been all kinds of music and scents and effects; a 'son et lumière'. It seemed that there was a man, who might be a saint, who appeared in the middle of all this. And this only happened when Ben was alone and well away from anyone else.

"As is usual with these things, there is never anyone else around to corroborate them," Reilly's voice was business-like but thin in tone, not the pleasant baritone which would be nice to hear in church.

Jake had occasionally been to concerts in the chapel. The university offered excellent music and, although he was not religious, Jake enjoyed good music, with a marked preference for plainchant. He couldn't imagine Reilly chanting anything, plain or fancy.

The Dean was quite laid back about the whole thing involving Professor Furness and appeared to want to let the thing die away gently – treating it as just an aberration of advancing age. It seemed that he had not thought of trying to set up a controlled experiment; but then, he wasn't a scientist.

He laid aside his knife and fork and began picking each chop up in his napkin to gnaw at the last traces of the meat. There was gravy on his moustache. Jake remembered how much he hated facial hair. There was something faintly odd about the hair on Reilly's head too. It was lush, with a well-defined widow's peak. It was so black it was almost navy blue.

"I thought," said Reilly, "That you were an atheist too. You published that... book. Didn't you? The thing about religious people being nuts?" Jake noted the well-defined pause preceding "book".

"Professional scientist," said Jake. "Healthy scepticism, empirical knowing..." He let it trail off, in the manner of an academic who has no intention of justifying his work. He stared down at his plate and picked up the last trace of crispy crumb plaice with his fork.

A dowdy, middle-aged female academic Jake didn't know, wearing a putty-coloured dress and jacket, came flouncing over to the table, ignoring him, and bending to kiss Prof Reilly on his forehead. Her high, girlish voice informed him that she hadn't seen him for simply an age, darling, and she dropped down, like a sack of coal, into an empty chair.

After a time during which they chatted aimlessly, Reilly remembered to introduce Jake and the woman. Her name, it turned out, was Dr Pat Porno (couldn't have been, could it?) and she lectured in St Mary's. When they fell silent, clearly wishing to be alone, Jake made his excuses and left.

*

The seminar room was on the ground floor of the Biochemistry Building, possibly the nicest part of it – the building a brooding presence on North Street, hunched against the University Chapel, looking too big for its space.

The room had a set of windows onto the street, bringing in much needed light from a bright autumn day. It was a big room for seminars, could hold thirty students. Today it held only twelve.

Professor Furness was taking the Tuesday undergraduate seminar on antibiotics because Dr McShane had broken his leg falling off his bicycle. They were ready to start when Ben saw Paul Grant, the Chair of Biochemistry & Microbiology, sneak quietly in and perch on the table at the back of the room, without speaking to anyone.

It occurred to Ben that Grant could, with his wriggle-bottom, mess-up the handouts Ben had placed there so that the students could take them as they were leaving, until that thought faded in favour of wondering why he was there at all.

Ben called for order, the children had been talking among themselves, and mentioned that they were fortunate to have the Chair of Biochem with them today. They all turned around and Paul oozed up, acknowledged them, and sat back down again on the table.

Realising that the Prof didn't intend to say anything, Ben began his introduction.

"Ladies and Gentlemen," he said, "Today's lecture is an introduction to antibiotics, structure, use, and problems. You will find handouts on the table at the back, under-neath Professor Grant. Please collect them as you leave."

Starting with the apocryphal story of the Dirty Petri Dish, he explained how penicillin had been discovered by Alexander Fleming but put aside for ten years until New Zealander Howard Florey investigated it systematically and introduced it into clinical practice. It, and its relatives, had since saved many hundreds of thousands of lives.

"By the way," he said, "What do you think of Heads of Department and other *hiheedyins* who put their names on the work of their students?"

The group discussed this for several minutes, while Prof Grant looked uncomfortable.

Ben wanted to draw a bacterium on the whiteboard but hadn't yet made up his mind which one; whether it should have flagellae or not. He rather liked flagellae; Salmonella *typhi* would do fine. He drew it and told them the tale of Typhoid Mary Mallon, the Irish American cook who had been thought to have infected fifty-one people, of whom three died, though she remained asymptomatic herself.

"It's likely, though, with hindsight, that she only actually infected three people. It's surprising how history changes with time!"

He talked about typhoid for a while, discussing the faecal-oral route and, then asked what would have to change to stop the spread of typhoid in a developing country. A young woman at the back said "Public health!" while a young man shouted "Wash your bleedin' hands!" Everyone laughed, except Paul Grant.

Ben drew another diagram, illustrating how resistance works, with bacteria changing the proteins in their coats to sneak past the immune system, and speaking about the difference between narrow- and broad-spectrum antibiotics.

It was time to close, so Ben thanked them for listening, reminded them that he would be setting a question in the term exams, and that they should pick-up a copy of his handouts at the back. And read them.

When everyone had gone, Paul Grant oiled his way up to the front and told Ben that it was a long time since he had attended an undergraduate seminar.

Ben knew enough never to ask a department head how he'd enjoyed anything and stood by waiting to be praised or panned.

"Do you think the stories are helpful?" asked Grant.

"Don't you? I think it helps them to remember. Works even better if you make them laugh!"

"Do you really think so? I wonder if we are giving the students short-change if we give less than the maximum of information. After all, they are relying on us to give them enough for them to get a good job when they graduate."

"Is that all?" asked Ben, "I thought we were giving them an education."

"Of course, of course," said Grant, "But I do think that stories are all very well if we have time…but perhaps not in a seminar. I was wondering whether you might feel that you should stop teaching now. You're getting older and, perhaps, not quite as quick as you used to be? What about taking the rest of term off – it's only a short time. You can have a think about whether you want to retire completely – I'll see about arranging an early retirement package. You can make a start on your book!"

He left with a jolly wave, leaving Ben reeling, surprised that the Chair had known that he hadn't yet put pen to paper.

*

Major Makin was a regular sight on the streets of St Andrews: he preached frequently, in various places around the town; trying to bring the residents and Godless Students back to Almighty God. Most people shuffled past in an embarrassed way: the Director of Field Studies in the Department of Divinity marched her candidates for the ministry round to listen and learn. Major Makin was a very good preacher.

Ben was aware of the Major as he turned the corner, slightly anxious about what Paul Grant had said. Makin's voice was powerful: one could often, if one wanted, hear him three streets away. Ben's policy was to cross the road and pretend that the Major wasn't there. There was a difference this morning, though, Ben was hearing the rich, musical voice, but also what it was testifying.

The text, that morning, was something about waiting on God – to tell you what to do or some such thing. Ben found himself wondering if God would tell him eventually what He wanted him to do about the visions. He'd talked at some length, with various theological types who had been very little help. Perhaps there was direct access to God: maybe he didn't *need* human intervention. There was an original idea. He sighed deeply and crossed the road.

On the opposite pavement, coming out of the bank, was Dr Latimer. She had been fun when they had taken that Art History extension course together. She was a good old girl; he was fairly sure that he'd known her for a long time.

"Good morning, Doctor!" he raised his voice against the prevailing wind. She turned in to him, as if sheltering behind his large frame.

"Hello Ben," she gasped. "What a wind! I can hardly breathe!"

He regarded her rather nice, freckled face, which was reddened with the latent heat of the Royal Bank of Scotland, followed by exposure to the usual blizzard. She asked about his health, he said he was fine. She invited him for a coffee.

"I'm just going to have one, failing a G & T at this time of day," she said, "And it better be a big one."

They walked down the close to Brittles, the latest of the transient coffee shops of St Andrews, this one specialising in really sticky cakes.

"I saw you yesterday," said Minnie when they were seated and warming cold hands on big fragrant mugs. "I was surprised you were a chapel-goer..."

"No," said Ben, "Not really. Just wanted a word. That new Chaplain's quite a nice girl."

"Ah," commented Minnie on a sigh, "I'm still surprised a woman got the job – this is such a male-oriented place!"

She wished that he would say something else, and he really looked as if he was going to, then changed his mind. They sat quietly for a few moments, both trying to think what to say next. Like a date, Ben thought, chuckling to himself – haven't had one of those for a long time.

There was a blast of wind as the street door opened and another customer came in. Ben looked up and felt slightly alarmed. Christabel, here? Why? Minnie followed the direction of his gaze to the extremely tall, fair-haired woman, willowy and striking, who had just come in.

She came straight over and asked if she could join them. Her voice was pleasant but precise: perhaps she was another scientist? There was a trace, too, of a transatlantic accent superimposed over polished English vowels.

Ben had half stood when he first saw her. He now stood all the way and held a chair for her. The tall woman pecked him on the cheek and said, "Uncle Ben", very softly. He introduced Minnie as "my friend Dr Latimer"; Christabel as "my niece". They all sat and looked at one another for what seemed like ages. Christabel was on a short visit, to see if her uncle was OK: she had to be back in New York next week.

"Do you stay in New York?" asked Minnie. "I've always thought that must be very exciting!"

"Noisier, anyway," replied Christabel. "I thought I'd gone deaf when I got out of the car here".

Minnie was saying that it was that kind of place, quiet on the whole. Christabel was conversing with Dr Latimer, rather than chatting; much as she had been taught in Diplomatic Circles.

The doctor, asked how long she had lived here, where she qualified, what was her special interest, was unused to being conversed with under the blazing spotlight of someone else's personality. The interrogative boot was usually on the other, arthritic, foot.

Ben's brother Charlie had been a career diplomat and, in Ben's opinion, an extremely shifty character and very likely a spy, who had met

Lady Jane Markham at Oxford where they were both reading PPE as undergraduates. They had married the day after graduation. Perfectly, in nine months, perfect Christabel had arrived. When she reached three months, the whole family decamped to the British Consulate in Calcutta. Several postings and two miscarriages later, Lady Jane ran off with a New Zealander and Christabel became the very young mistress of Her Majesty's Governor General's Residence in Wellington. Despite her youth, she was very good at this.

Ben wondered what she was doing now: Charlie had died two or three years ago in a perhaps accidental shooting in Buenos Aires, the two branches of the Furness family had communicated only over distance for many years with just one visit from Christabel at the time of her father's death. Minnie had now forcibly slanted the light back on Christabel and was asking what she did for a living. Ben brought his thoughts back to the present with a jerk.

"I work at the UN," she said, "Just helping maintain security for the British delegation, things like that. It's quite a pleasant job and we have a very nice apartment nearby."

Minnie asked a question about concerts and theatre: Christabel began telling her about all the music she had heard, the plays she had been to. Minnie's frustrated internal adventurer thought it sounded wonderful; her own adventures tended to be those of the mind. Christabel turned, eventually, to her Uncle Ben and asked him if he really was well – or was he just saying that?

"I could always ask your doctor, I suppose," she said, looking again at Minnie. Minnie made a dismissive gesture with both hands.

"Ah, not me," she said. "I'm a shrink, part-time in the NHS. I have to say, though, your uncle seems quite well to me; he gets about a lot, and I've hardly ever seen him with a cold or 'flu..."

"I sometimes have headaches," claimed Ben, feeling overwhelmed with all the femininity.

"I heard," said Christabel, "That he wasn't so well; just getting on a bit I daresay, not so mobile, getting forgetful. I daresay that would be something you would know a lot about?"

Ben began to feel irritated by the girl. How dare she say such things in front of his friends – even if they had only been friends for three quarters of an hour?

Minnie decided to do a double take for comic effect. Ben was becoming a wee bit bothered.

"Because I'm not so mobile and getting forgetful myself?"

She laughed as she said it.

Christabel froze and flustered that she hadn't meant that, it was the psychiatry… then she laughed along with Minnie and Ben joined in, self-consciously aware that he had missed something.

"I think we'd better go home", he interrupted. "Don't want to bore the good doctor with family stuff".

They were almost onto the street, back in the roaring wind, when he remembered to thank Dr Latimer for the coffee and say, "See you later." He popped back before Christabel whirled him back to South Street as if he were thistledown floating on a strong wind.

✦

Ben's Diary entry 2 - Tuesday night, Week One of Michaelmas Term

What a full couple of days! This time of term always is. Had a nice chat with Lucille yesterday - as well as a couple of biscuits - and a bit of a seminar with Jim, John? that young postgrad. He's got quite a lot of interesting ideas about ergotamine and its derivatives. I think he'll do something important eventually. We talked a bit about psilocybin, too, he'd read my book about alternative consciousness. We're getting some good postgrads these days; enthusiastic and full of stamina. Don't think I was ever that energetic!

I went to chapel Monday morning. I'd never been to Morning Prayers, but it was quite comforting in a funny sort of way.

The chaplain said a couple of little prayers and a postgrad, probably from St Mary's, did a kind of wee sermon. It was about working hard and being upstanding, I think. Something like that. There wasn't any hymn singing, thank goodness! I said hello to the chaplain on the way out. She's new but seems very nice. She asked me who I was and where I worked. I told her I was in Microbiology. I was on the way to see young Jim, even if most of my time is supposed to be spent writing that book about thing, and I haven't done as I was told and thought about early retirement yet!

After I'd seen John, I went out and had a coffee and a think at Halfpenny's. It's a bit scruffy these days; almost no students. I hope they were all at lectures anyway.

Christie came today, joined us in the café, goodness knows why. She seemed concerned about me, but I don't know... I'm fine. Asked a lot of stupid questions when we got home - she interrupted a nice chat with Minnie Latimer I was having in the other coffee shop. That's where all the students have gone; it was absolutely packed! No idea what Christie was after... odd.

*

"Do you mind if I am completely frank, Professor?" asked Jake, pouring boiling water into two mugs with a teabag in each.

The Professor was sitting in the student chair, where his niece had been when Jake came in yesterday. Ben was looking quite relaxed, as if he got a summons from some unknown academic in the Medical School every day.

His rather threadbare knee supported an envelope file - a dull blue one with a large label stuck on the front. Jake had been trying to sneak a read at what it said but had failed miserably. He was good at reading inverted type, but the elegant, black-inked copperplate was illegible upside down. The Professor was nodding, yes, of course, be completely honest.

"Truth is," said Jake, "I feel a bit embarrassed about this – and it was so good of you to come in to see me. As I told you on the phone, my research is biomedical; mainly about brain structure, especially the temporal lobes – my last book concerned the idea that some brain lesions in that area can lead people to have special feelings of meaning – some even feel called by God. I'm told that you have had certain..." he let the ellipsis lie between them for a minute.

44

The Prof was looking interested and scholarly. "Experiences..." another ellipsis, hanging there, almost in sight.

Ben shifted in his chair: just making himself more comfortable, no sign of anything else. He smiled; a nice smile, a room-brightener.

"Yes," he said cheerfully, "I have. Had another one just the other day. Rich and strange. Is this something to do with Christabel?"

His voice, in the question, sharpened with a touch of danger. Jake fished the tea bags out and balanced them on the top of his overflowing wastepaper basket. He'd been having the bit of a clear out he'd not got around to last term.

He added milk and brought the mugs over to the desk. Handing the Prof one, he took his own to the other side. He was still uncertain how to proceed - he'd even had a crisis about whether to use the desk or armchairs and a coffee table pinched from the postgraduate lounge.

"You know it is."

"Didn't you think that perhaps dear Christie should sort of mind her own business?"

Jake, who would never have dared to say that to Christabel, thought uncle had a point.

"She's worried about you," he said, with a slightly nervous smile. "They get like that, relatives. So I'm told. It's the main reason I didn't go into clinical practice. Too hard for me to deal with. She came to me because she'd had an article of mine pointed out in New York - the fact I was at St Andrews etc. – didn't know who else to talk to".

"She thinks I'm nuts, then?" Ben asked, "People do, I know.

Even people who should be open to this sort of thing; people who should know better. I've been speculating a lot about this stuff. You know, I think that if Jesus Christ had been born now, he'd probably have been crucified." He smiled gently, regretfully.

Jake thought that was a joke but wasn't sure enough to laugh. It was most bizarre, sitting here, trying to find a way of approaching this peculiar subject: he'd been worried about talking to Furness. How did he, scientist, magician, and general good guy though he thought himself to be, find the right words to talk to a world-famous fungus man who thought he'd discovered God? I'm not a theologian, he thought, I only believe in empirical evidence. Difficult this. To his own amazement, he had never even considered disobeying the divine Christabel.

The Professor went on, "If they believe what they say they believe, surely they should accept that miracles happen? They seem to think that all that kind of thing belongs to the past. Martin Reilly actually said to me that human beings were no longer worthy of the appearances of God or His Blessed Mother."

Jake was surprised to hear the Capital Letters in this; he had never come across the sign of devotion to the Mother of God except in Roman Catholics. He asked Ben if he was Catholic.

"God, no," said the Professor, with a contrived shudder. "Not a religion for grown-ups, I've always thought. Just superstition. Not into religion at all really. Used to go to chapel for University Service sometimes - part of the tradition, academic procession, gowns, Pier Walk, everything traditional. Quite enjoyed it, and my late wife was a lightweight Presbyterian, she liked sitting with the academic wives on the other side."

He sighed and, folding his hand over the blue file, waited patiently for Jake to say something else. Jake noticed Ben's hands were well shaped, with long fingers and nicely kept nails. No tremor or other physical indications of neurological impairment.

Jake referred to the scrappy notes he had made when Christabel had been here - as well as one or two things he'd copied out of his book when he'd re-read the relevant chapters. He took a long swallow of tea and looked at the other man. He found himself liking him: he wasn't sanctimonious or pretentious, and he was surprisingly relaxed about his weird experiences. There was a quiet puzzlement, though; not quite sure what he should be doing. If he ought to be doing anything at all.

"One of the things I came across when I was re-reading some of my own stuff," said Jake, "Was my reference to Dean Hamer's book *The God Gene*. He says that you're either born with it or not; that Jesus, Mohammed and the Buddha would have had it but some people, who turn out not to be interested in that sort of thing, probably haven't. He doesn't think that being brought up in a religious atmosphere has any bearing on it at all."

"Just an exercise in retrospective research, then? One of my bugbears I'm afraid. Just nature, then", said Ben, "No nurture?"

"Um," Jake raised his mug and took another sip. "The sub-title of Dr Hamer's book was *How Faith is Hard-Wired into Our Genes* - but I think there was a lot of feeling, at the time, that the title was mainly a stunt to boost sales. You remember the re-branding of some titles as 'Templar' after the big success of *The DaVinci Code*? Something not dissimilar to that. Hamer kind of shot himself in the foot, anyway, when he came up with a 'sequence of genes coding for male homosexuality'

47

back in 1993.

"Have any members of your family ever been particularly religious?"

"Don't think so," said Ben, reflecting, "There was a great aunt; Margaret, I think, who was never away from church - a bit obsessed, possibly with the vicar. But no one else that I know of. The family did its hatching, matching, and dispatching at the C of E - but I don't recall hearing God or religion ever mentioned at home."

"Can I ask you a few personal questions?" Jake asked. "Not a full clinical history – just an overview; one or two things about where and when and suchlike? Then we can go on to how you feel in general and when something happens? I want to ask you, very seriously, what *you* think all this is – what you think it means. Would that be all right?"

"Of course," said Ben. He would be delighted to talk about it with another scientist – he'd only gone to the Divinity School because he thought they would be more familiar. He was well aware of the scepticism of many natural scientists; he was profoundly aware of his own. Jake shifted slightly on his chair and said the most dispiriting thing any patient or job candidate ever hears.

"About myself?" asked Ben, "I wonder what I should tell you…" He, too, eased into his chair as if settling in for the long haul. His gaze moved around the room, taking in Jake's untidy bookshelves and the piles of papers on the floor. The computer was right at the back of the desk, as if it had been pushed out of the way by someone who didn't really like them. There was a plastic model of the brain on the window ledge and half a dozen used coffee cups. He thought he'd mention a putative microbiological experiment, before he left, as a joke. He cleared his throat and began.

"Born on the Wirral (that's in Cheshire) 57 years ago, educated at Harrow and Trinity, Cambridge (BSc hons microbiology), Liverpool (PhD – growth patterns of novel fungal systems), came to St Andrews for an MPhil in virology (met my wife here), UC Berkeley for postdoc, some time at Columbia, New York, then St Andrews up till now. My curriculum vitae – that what you want? Travelled a fair bit in the Americas... in the spaces between things."

Jake shrugged his shoulders and Ben went on.

"Quite bright on the whole," he said, "Don't take things too seriously, pretty honest, fairly skeptical, reasonably unsentimental, determined. Bit stubborn, bit arrogant. Enjoy a nice single malt and like dogs. Don't like chemical air fresheners, fish of any kind, cyclists, holy rollers or geographers."

He took a deep breath and added that he was the younger of his parents' two children and, yes, he was aware that his parents were dead. As a last addition, he mentioned that he married Free when he was 25 and they had waited a year before Wisp was born.

"Well, her name isn't really Wisp," said Ben. "She's called Lucy Elizabeth but, when Free was expecting she didn't have a huge bump, so we referred to the baby as Wisp; we thought she'd only be a wee wisp of a thing. It stuck, like these things do."

He went on to say, sadly, that his daughter had disappeared into thin air when she was just a girl and the police felt she had run away, probably to London. He stopped and sniffed and went on to say that his wife had 'passed on' a few years back too: he and Christabel were the only close members of their family, "And goodness knows we aren't close in space or time!"

Jake paused to see if the professor wanted to continue talking about his wife and daughter, but he appeared to have moved on from these painful subjects. Jake had a few headings scribbled on the white postcard he'd picked up from the desk and started to go through them systematically.

"You mentioned liking a single malt, Prof," he said. "Not a bit too fond, are you? There seems to be a fair bit of drinking in *my* department. I sometimes think that it's in inverse proportion to the level of project grants…"

Ben laughed and said that he had nothing really against the drink; he just kept it for what he called the "gentle" occasions.

"Like when I come in after a hard day's digging out at the undergraduate coalface," he said, "Not to relax or cheer me up or help me cope or anything. Just one of those rare wee pleasures. If I drank more, I wouldn't appreciate it nearly so much. Don't understand what people get out of getting drunk. I want to hang on to as many of my brain cells as possible!"

"So, not deluded because of the drink then," said Jake. "What about delirium? Have you any particular illnesses, I should know about?"

Jake asked about his general health: any operations or serious illnesses? Ben said that he had always been pretty well. A touch of malaria when in South America – recurring afterwards of course.

"Seems to have burnt out now, though," he added.

"I'm thinking delirium due to infections, injuries, stuff like that?"

"Don't think so," answered Ben, thoughtfully, "Never had an operation; get the odd bit of a cold. The flu jag's great, though. Don't get the dreaded lurgi every autumn any more. That pig flu jag was a swine, though, a few years back. Had a sore arm for days! Fell on the ice once. Didn't bang my head. The occasional headache..."

"How's your imagination? How much do you live in your head?"

"A bit," admitted Ben. "Don't you think most scientists do? If they are creative anyway? August Kekulé dreamed about the structure of benzene being a ring, didn't he?"

"Come to that," said Jake, "What about dreams? Do you have vivid ones? Do they sometimes persist into daytime? Are you a lucid dreamer?"

"What's a lucid dreamer?"

"Someone who is aware he's dreaming and, sometimes, can control it. You can learn to do it. I found it quite hard, but I managed in the end. It was research for something I was interested in."

"Well, no, then. I do sometimes recall what I was dreaming about but, generally, they seem to me to be remarkably unremarkable. Usually sparked by things during the day, added to memories. Have you read Freud on dreams? I tried years ago but found it impossible. I kept reading it in a cod Viennese accent in my head!"

"Thinking about Freud and Mesmer etc.," said Jake, "Ever been hypnotised?"

"Not as far as I know," said Ben, "Although I read an article in some magazine or other about people sometimes being hypnotised without their knowledge, and not knowing it had happened. Sounds a bit like brainwashing to me. Not very ethical…"

"I think that's probably a conspiracy theory thing, don't you?" said Jake, "So we can probably discount it. Do you believe in ghosts? Or the occult?" Ben didn't give those the courtesy of an answer; just shook his head and made a rude noise.

"Ah, how can I put this? It's a bit embarrassing because I don't want you to be insulted," Jake stopped, and Ben waited, wondering what was coming next.

"I need to have an idea about the sort of person you are… That's an important part of this interrogation," He looked up at Ben, from regarding his crib-postcard, "Have you ever been the sort of person who tries to allocate blame to other people for things you have done wrong yourself?"

"No," said Ben.

Jake made a clear cross against something on his postcard. "How impulsive are you? And what about magical thinking?" Ben didn't know what that was either; Jake gave him a worked example.

"Imagine for a minute," he said, "That you examine your horoscope in the newspaper every day, just for a bit of fun. Would there be any time you might think that it was correct? Is there any time you think that it's right too often for there not to be some truth in it?"

The professor looked at him in wonder.

"No," he said, "You've got the wrong one there, lad! I have a big streak of evolutionary thinking. Nothing, in the past, present, or future, happens without chance. It must or there would be no material for natural selection. Horoscopes are included in that. Naturally. How silly, anyway!"

Jake said OK and told Ben that he was going to ask him a short series of questions about 'magical thinking'.

"Just say whether you agree with my statement or not. Yes or no. If I think too much about something it will happen,"

"No!"

"Life is nothing but a series of random events,"

"Yes!"

"You should never tempt fate,"

"Fate?"

"I do something special to avoid bad luck,"

"No such thing!"

"Well done! You seem to be remarkably un-superstitious."

"Good," said Ben, smiling, "But what about me knowing how to beat the test? Because of being a competitive type of cove?"

"Did you?" asked Jake, "Are you?"

"'Course I am, aren't you? But no, I answered truthfully. You should have told me to, though!"

Jake admitted he should have; it was an easy mistake to make in informal conditions. Ben was sitting, thinking. Then he smiled craftily and said:

"You're from Inverness, aren't you? I'm picking up something of the accent..."

"I am," answered Jake.

"Do you believe in the Loch Ness Monster?"

They both laughed.

"When," asked Jake, preparing to make a fresh set of notes on an A4 pad, "Did you first have what we might call an unusual visual experience?"

"About a year ago," he said, "But I don't want you to think that it's to do with my wife. I have never seen her. And she promised she'd come back if she could. Just to let me know, you know."

He added that his experiences weren't just visual.

"Smells are very common," said Jake, "Where brain lesions in the temporal lobe are involved anyway. Not necessarily in visions. What is the smell, actually? Is it some-thing nice or nasty?"

"It's wonderful," said Ben, "One of the best smells in the entire world. When I was in South America it was the thing I missed most of all. I used to wake up in the night with a craving. With the thing we're talking about, it doesn't make me crave it. It stimulates and satisfies at the same time. It's bacon!"

Jake made a note, and then added an exclamation mark. He wasn't sure whether it called for one or not.

"I just need to ask a few questions about upbringing and that," said Jake, "To tick the box. Did you have a happy childhood? Was your family OK?"

"Yes," said Ben. We had all the things people seem to think necessary, my brother and I. We lived quite a nice lifestyle in a large house near Sandbach. I was a bit younger than Charlie. We never really got on that well. We were very different."

"Were your parents good at treating you both the same?"

"Oh, yes," said Ben, "They were scrupulous about it. They were very big on equality! They treated us absolutely equally!"

Jake spotted the change in Ben's facial muscles when he said this. His zygomatic major raised the inner half of his eyebrows, his frontalis, and pars lateralis raised the outer half of his eyebrows. This signifies fear, anguish, distress. Jake made a mark on the page – and would consider what the lie meant later.

"And so," said Jake, "To the last thing. How does it make you feel? The Vision? Try not to over think it: just say whatever comes into your head."

"Feel? I feel confused, I suppose. Awed. Privileged. Curious. Bewildered. I want to know what it's FOR!"

*

It was getting dark when they emerged into St Mary's Quad, a wintery evening, even though it was so early in the term. North-East Fife can be like that. The two scientists walked down the front stairs together and wished the janitor good night in unison. As they strolled through the gate onto South Street, Professor Furness turned back and looked up at the legend displayed over it.

"Hum," he said, "'IN PRINCIPIO ERAT VERBUM' - In the beginning was the Word. Do you think they'd recognise it if they heard it, Jake?" He sounded sad and older, not something Jake had really noticed during their two-and-a-half-hour conversation. Jake could only shrug his shoulders. The Prof had given him a great deal to think about and he needed to get a Chinese and get home.

They parted outside the gate, the professor walking off, dejectedly, down South Street, Jake through to the *kerry-oot* in Market Street. He couldn't decide whether it was chicken chow mein he liked best or sweet-and-sour. He was suddenly overcome with a deep desire for bacon.

✦

Ben's Diary Entry 3 - Thursday night, Week One of Michaelmas Term

I am having a lot of interesting talks lately and I think that one of these times, I'm going to get to the bottom of things. Today's was a chat with Jake Ellwood, the neuroscientist in the Bute. He wrote a book, apparently, about the experience of God and religious things being due to disruptions in brain function. I haven't read it yet, but he gave me a copy today. It's bright green! I'll start it tomorrow - it's too heavy to read in bed. And I do like to read in bed; one of my rare wee pleasures. Should be interesting, the book. Not that I think there's anything wrong with my brain. Christie does though. Easy to catch her out. She thinks I'm a senile old fool.

Young Jake asked me a few questions but nothing too prying. He laughed when I turned the magical thinking tables on him. I asked whether he believes in the Loch Ness Monster – lots of people from Inverness-way do, or say they do. He suggested that I see my GP so I shall try to make an appointment in the morning. Goodness knows when she'll be able to see me, though. They seem to take longer and longer these days. You'd almost think that you must make an appointment to be ill!

*

The dream of Wisp comes again when Ben gets home. He is dozing on the sofa, feeling very tired after the meeting with Jake Ellwood. He feels as if he has been given a good going over. Like a viva, he thinks, finding out exactly what I know; whether I'm an expert in me! He's put a couple of cushions behind his head. He's rapidly dropping off.

They are at the seaside: somewhere tropical, with white sand and palm trees. The water is translucent turquoise. It is nowhere they have ever been before. Free is stretched out on a beach towel, wearing sunglasses and a chocolate brown one-piece bathing suit, her red hair shining in the sun. Ben recognises the serious ex-swimming champion costume: she never wears a bikini. He supresses a chuckle.

Wisp comes out of the sea, crystal water cascading from her. No nonsense about one-piece bathing suits for their daughter: she is wearing a blue and green two piece, with narrowest gold piping on the edges. She looks fabulous and he knows that he'll have to keep on glowering at all the young men in the hotel dining room tonight. She is far too young. How old is she anyway? He can't work it out and, suddenly, wakes up on his sofa, in St Andrews.

*

"Thing is," Ben Furness had said in Jake's office, "I don't know what I'm supposed to do about it." Now, Jake was lying flat on his back, with his legs hooked over the arm of the sofa in the Warden's flat at Montgomerie Hall, where he lived because he couldn't afford a house when he'd paid Kate's rent. He had finished his Chinese and checked to see there was nothing he desperately needed to watch on the telly. This was his thinking position; this was where he had his best ideas. He recalled when he had asked Ben about dreams.

Ben had mentioned Kekulé, the German chemist who was said to have dreamed a structure for benzene – a circle of six carbon atoms, with enough hydrogen atoms attached so it would work chemically.

It was elegant, of course, although not quite correct – the charge was now thought to be generalized as an electron cloud rather than alternate single and double bonds between the carbons. He was thinking that Ben Furness seemed as rational as, well, anyone else in this university. If ivory towers didn't tend to host much of real life, the stones of the wee grey city tended to host less. He'd certainly met people with less grip on it than Ben.

Ben had talked about the last time he'd had an "experience" – very much in inverted commas. It had been when he was having a period of being very sad about losing Frederica. He'd found walking helped and, some days, he went miles without even realising it. It had been on the way home, though, that he'd come across the tumble-down farm steading and heard a distressed sheep.

He'd followed the sound inside one of the buildings and, although he'd never actually found the sheep, that was where it had happened. "No," he'd said, "I didn't see Free. I never saw her after she'd gone – although I felt her often. Still do." Jake had talked about people who hallucinated their dead partner. It was surprisingly common. Ben was not to be persuaded that he had ever seen his wife.

"I don't think it was anything to do with Free – except that I was walking to deal with the feelings of despair I was having about her leaving me." He had stopped there and was clearly thinking about that. "Unless," he said, slowly, "It happened because I was in such an emotional state – maybe I was open to it?" He said the last bit a little tentatively, as if he had just thought of it.

When Jake had asked him if he'd considered that it was an hallucination caused by longing, the slightest expression of annoyance flitted briefly across Ben's face; gone before it could be established.

"I've thought about that recently, although I didn't at first. I honestly can't see how it can be anything at all to do with that. It's not Free, it's not sad or even giving comfort after my loss, it's religious – which is completely out of my usual sphere of interest – and it doesn't even *touch* what I'm going through."

The last phrase was uttered in such an aching and defeated way, Jake's heart went out to the man. How must it feel to love someone that much? How must it feel to be loved that much? He was entirely sure that he would never know.

The thing Ben had been most concerned with, though, had been that he didn't know why he had been having these "things." He didn't mean why in a clinical sense – with which Jake might have been some help – but in another sense altogether. He had been wondering what the vision, or the Man in the Vision, or God, or something, wanted of him. What was he required to do? There had never been any kind of conversation; no one had told him to do anything.

"Am I supposed to guess?" he had asked Jake, "I can't even fathom a mechanism for that – apart from asking 'How can I help?' which I've done every time except the first. I was too stunned then." That had seemed to be the end of it as far as he was concerned; he had told his story and posed the question which was worrying him. That was it. Simple. Then he said:

"It's odd, though. Each time I've seen him, he's been a bit more distinct, a bit more lifelike. The smell and music and all the rainbows and things have been just the same, but the main man has sort of cleared – perhaps as if there was glass in front of him but now it's gone; or I'm seeing more clearly through it. Something like that. And the last time I saw him, the blood from his hand was dripping onto the floor."

They'd left shortly after that, Ben asking Jake if he wanted to do tests or anything. Jake had muttered something about having a think and promised to pop around and speak to Ben the following day.

*

Jake was, in fact, baffled. Solving problems is to do with making connections and leaps of intuition. There seemed to be no connections to make here – and intuition seemed to be away on a beach holiday. Illusion, delusion, delirium, hallucinations, visions. He needed another mind to bounce off, that might be a step forward.

He wondered about Christabel. Obviously, she was intelligent, from an intelligent family. And she had the legs to distract him when he needed a break. Deciding to ring her in the morning, he went to bed to dream of St Thérèse of Lisieux and rose petals cascading down. Odd how some dreams are so real you can smell the roses. Thérèse was reputed to have said that she wanted to spend her heaven doing good on earth. Had she supposed she'd get a choice?

Need to get him an MRI, though, Jake thought. There could just be a brain tumour.

*

Christabel proved to be "out" when Jake telephoned the London contact-number she had given him. The secretary was astringent.

"I am unable," she said, "To give you another number at the present time. Miss Furness will be unavailable for a few days at least. We are not able to contact her." That was a definite conversation-closer and Jake didn't feel he could do anything except say thank you and hang up.

He spent a few minutes, still eating burnt toast with pâté, running through various colleagues in his head, until he realised that none of them would do. He wondered vaguely about staff in the Divinity School, but he knew very few of them. Martin Reilly certainly wasn't suitable, nor was the lovely Pat Porno. Think again. Must be someone. He wondered if Ben had any good old friends still hanging around the university. Most St Andrews academics did.

*

Christabel wasn't in London, nor was she in New York. She was still in St Andrews, staying at the nicest hotel, with her little dog. It had been the task of a minute to look in the telephone directory and find out where Dr Latimer lived in North Street. She walked the dog for half an hour on the West Sands, took her back to the hotel, dried her on a fluffy towel, settled her back on the bed. Changing from running shoes to killer heels, she left with a "See you soon, pet, I love you!" The little dog smiled happily from her comfortable nest.

Minnie was surprised to hear Ben's niece's beautiful vowels when she answered the buzzer. She had opened the door as Christie crisply clicked up the gently curving front staircase.

She had come to pick Minnie's brains about Ben and psychiatric matters; she was quite upfront about it and Minnie, while the cafetiere was brewing, had to say that although she would be happy to speak in general terms, anything directly about Professor Furness would be out of bounds. She was not his doctor, had never been his doctor, and was not prepared to intrude on any other doctor's patients.

Christabel showed no sign of being disappointed about this, even though she had hoped that an older female might be sufficiently embroiled in local gossip that she would have something interesting to contribute. When she had heard that Minnie was not only an old friend of Uncle Ben's but also a psychiatrist, Christie had hoped to kill two birds with one stone.

Minnie depressed the plunger and began to pour the coffee into tiny, delicate, china cups.

"I can talk to you about dementia," she said, handing her visitor one of the cups, "And how it has affected people I have treated in the past. I can even tell you what little I know about altered consciousness, alternate brain states, especially dissociative disorders, about which I know a fair amount from professional experience. But we must be clear that it is only general information which you could get from various websites, especially the Royal College of Psychiatrists. I really must emphasize that this is just to save you having to do all the research yourself. Save time. Whatever."

"That's very kind of you," said Christabel softly, "I'm really very grateful."

"Is there anything particular you want to know? In general, of course…"

"Yes. I was wondering whether you'd ever had any patients who had visions: any kind, I think, not especially religious ones. And whether you found out what caused them? And if the patient got better?" She put her coffee cup down and lifted the cafetiere and her eyebrows, asking if another tiny cup was in order.

Minnie had slightly detached from their conversation and was thinking how pleasantly domestic this was – two concerned women having a civilised cup of coffee together. She wished she had baked something nice. If I'd known you were coming… She clicked back into conversation mode and reached for what the younger woman had been saying.

"I have treated quite a few psychotics," she said, "Schizophrenics mostly, a lot of them young adults. They tend towards hearing voices, usually. I recall one young man who had an extracampine hallucination – sorry, that's something which isn't actually seen but is believed to be there, a special variety of delusion. This one was of sharks, lots of sharks, coming towards him. It happened when he was walking along the street; no water was involved. He was terrified, as you would be. That, I have always felt, was an entirely normal reaction to his delusion. In an abnormal situation, abnormal reactions are normal."

"Dear God!" blurted Christabel, "That's awful!"

"Most people don't realise what it can be like," said Minnie, helping herself to a second cup of coffee. "How can you unless you have it in your own family or among your friends? Or if you do it for a living, of course!" She went on, saying that there had been little research done on why these things happened although it was possible that trauma could play a part.

"Not necessarily big, horrible traumas like abuse but, perhaps, ordinary ones which are deeply meaningful to the individual: being brought up in grinding poverty, having to hide when the window-cleaner wants his money or when the man comes to read the gas meter, being the least favourite child…

"Thoreau said, 'The mass of men live lives of quiet desperation.' The other part of that, most people get the sense of it wrong, is that they still die with a song in their hearts – it was Thoreau's paeon to the indomitability of the human spirit. But, anyway, I've always thought that the first part was rather tragic. And we by no means treat everyone who has a psychiatric problem. And I have to say some of them are better off. It's likely that many of these things involve a form of dissociation…"

"So, tell me about dissociation then?"

"Ah," replied Minnie, getting up from the kitchen table to explore her cupboards for biscuits and finding them bare, "Did you ever see the film 'Sybil'? With Sally Field and Joanne Woodward? It was sometime in the seventies…"

"Yes. I did, I think. It's about multiple personalities, isn't it?"

"It is. Well, mostly it's not really like that. The film's way over-cooked and dramatised. I forget how many personalities Sybil was supposed to have but… anyway, it doesn't always work in that way, even if someone does have the tendency to develop another personality to deal with a trauma which is unbearable to them."

"Ah."

"The idea of Dissociative Identity Disorder or Multiple Personality Disorder, as they called it then, is still going through a lot of denial, dispute, opposition, especially in the UK. The public idea of it is derived from Sybil and a few other rather baroque cases, where the person has many separate personalities who don't communicate with one another. It's also thought by ardent believers to be caused, almost exclusively, by sexual abuse of the child. I'm sure it is in some cases, but nothing is ever that clear, and I doubt that is. The theory is that the young child is so afraid of the parent but still so dependent on her or him, the child dissociates – so that these different aspects can be dealt with by what are, virtually, separate personalities. After all, the baby or young child can't flee or fight. It's too little, so the only thing it can do is freeze, the other important evolutionary adrenal function – and that just might lead to such a dissociative reaction. It's an interesting idea but I truly hope that most tiny patients aren't abused so catastrophically or have such a catastrophic reaction as to cause dissociation. They may end up with schizophrenia rather than DID or they may even end up with delusions and hallucinations in dementia, many years later. We, as a profession, don't know. Well, yet anyway! There have, of course, been grown-up people, still are grown-up people, who dissociate because of horrendous trauma that they are unable to cope with. If they have the innate ability to put the awful object right out of their mind…"

"So," asked Christie, "What about dementia sufferers, then? Older people often get senile, don't they?" She suddenly realised that she might be talking to one of them, although Dr Latimer was probably still only in late middle age. She added "Present company excepted, of course." She gave a short and rather humourless laugh.

"That *is* rather insulting, you know. And would be worse if it were true. Happily, it isn't. Certainly not every older person gets dementia: the percentage does go up with age, until around 90, then it drops like a stone. There seem to be very few people with dementia who are 100. Perhaps people who get there have been doing something right. We don't use the word 'senile' either. It only means 'ageing' and dementias don't only happen to older people. There are some who get it in their forties or fifties: anecdotally, the youngest was only 21!"

Christabel looked shocked at that.

"If I asked you why they could get it, would you tell me?"

"I really can't," answered Minnie, "There are probably many reasons. Most authorities say it's multi-factorial, that's a lot of things working together like a perfect storm. Some of them are genetic, poor diet, stress, head trauma, immune system problems, diabetes, maybe even an infection. Could be anything. Personally, I hope it's over-consumption of cottage cheese. Then I can give it up and have some actual cheese before I die."

They laughed, but soon centred back onto the serious matters under discussion. Christie asked about the prospect of a cure, and Minnie replied that there are treatments which slow some types of dementia down, for some people.

"It's obvious, though, when you think about it, that if there are 100 different types of dementia, and there probably are, it will probably require 100 different cures. It's a bit mind-boggling to tell the truth."

Christabel sat at Minnie's kitchen table and felt she knew less since she began to know more. None of this was of much help. She walked down North Street towards the hotel, stopping for traffic at Golf Place. There was much more traffic in the town now: it had increased hugely since the only other time she had been there, three years ago. Such an anachronism this place; ancient and modern, technological, and mediaeval, town and gown. She felt as if she was being led a merry Scottish dance.

"Time for a proper chat with MJ," she thought. "Time it was all sorted out."

*

The morning after Ben's late chat with Jake Ellwood he decided not to go into the department. He was too tired and feeling quite…he searched for a word. Trammelled, he thought, not a word in common use.

Maybe this was depression; he really couldn't be bothered with any of it. He ducked back underneath his downie, and pulled it tighter around his neck and shoulders, leaving his chin out so he could be sure to breathe properly.

He thought about the long session with Jake – which had been very interesting. He thought about Christabel and about dear old Minnie. After a while he could no longer head off thinking about the talk he'd had with Paul Grant. The idea of early retirement.

Because he wasn't as sharp as he used to be. Because he told stories in seminars. Hell fire, that was ridiculous, wasn't it? He was as good a teacher as he'd ever been! He had already written a great question for the end of term exams for the first years he'd taught in the seminar the other day. About lichen. No, antibiotics. That's right. The lichen one was for something else. He couldn't quite think what, so he put it out of his mind.

From his bedroom he could hear a key turning in the street door. Bloody hell, who was that at this time of the day? Whoever it was hadn't rung the bell. How rude was that? He struggled out from under the downie, and shrugged on his dressing gown, which had been draped over the rail at the bottom of his bed.

Ben appeared at the top of the stairs in time to catch a woman he didn't know, as she hung her coat on the hall rail and turned towards the kitchen.

"Who the hell are you?" he shouted at her, "And where did you get my door-key?"

She stopped in her tracks and turned back towards the source of the yell.

"Oh," she said, "Professor. It's me, Mavis!"

He jumped down the stairs two at a time and landed in the hall to discover her standing there with a shopping basket full of cleaning things and one or two items of grocery shopping. He reached into the basket and removed a pack of fish fingers.

"Did you steal these from my freezer?" he roared.

She jumped back, away from him, as if he were going to hit her.

She shouted 'no', that she'd never do that, she'd brought the fish for his lunch, and she'd noticed his supply of strawberry jam was low, so she'd brought two jars of that too.

This was not working out as Ben had expected. The unknown woman didn't seem to be embarrassed that she'd been caught in someone else's house, or that she'd been there to steal things. As his anger and fear began to recede, Ben began to crave a fish finger sandwich.

It had to be cod fish fingers, on buttered white bread, two slices, with plenty of salt and pepper and Heinz tomato ketchup. It was his greatest comfort food, the cook at home used to make it for him when he was young – for when he was feeling shaky or shocked. He looked up and recognised Mavis, his cleaner and general factotum. She looked very angry. Had he had an outburst?

*

Mary-Jane Fulton answered her cell promptly, as if she had been expecting a call. She said the cottage was entirely full, up to the roof, with dust and she was thinking of calling in a contractor.

"What kind of contractor?" asked her future wife, "Do people do just dust?"

"I don't care," said MJ in her laid-back Californian accent, "Someone who isn't me should be doing this!"

For a split second, Christie wasn't sure whether that was a dig at her, but she knew she was just imagining it: MJ never criticized, she said what she said, nothing between the lines. Anyway, Christie offered that she'd be there as soon as possible.

"And I need to talk to you about Uncle Ben, no, not the rice!"

That joke was ancient between them. Christabel was very bright, but she still relied on Mary-Jane's sharp lawyer's brain, disguised by the laconic attitude, when she needed extraordinary precision and super-incisive advice. She summed-up where she was and the several players in the St Andrean melodrama. MJ was silent for a few moments.

"What does James Sinclair think is going to happen?" MJ asked, cutting immediately to the chase.

"He's afraid that the spotlight will turn onto Uncle Ben and the US Department of Defense project at the university will be compromised. They can't afford anyone looking too closely."

"Iffy, then, is it?"

"Oh yes. And expensive."

"They always are. Any idea whether they're getting anywhere with the project?"

"No idea at all. I don't really think the project itself has anything to do with anything. The problem seems to be that Uncle Ben has seen something he shouldn't have. I wouldn't have thought it was all that dangerous – with his advancing age and vagueness – but you know how all Americans are paranoid. Except you."

"Of course. Especially where the national security is concerned." She hesitated, thinking about that, "How can you find out more about the project? There's no one better at hide and go seek."

"Thanks, as always. But I'm sure I'll turn up something I can't live with and have to do something about it. You know what I'm like."

"If you expect me to make it all right, you shouldn't. You know my reaction to bugs and gases; not to mention animal experiments. I can't, intellectually, get around the Geneva protocols. The words 'the use in war of asphyxiating, poisonous or other gases', 'justly condemned' and 'binding alike the conscience and practice of nations' do something weird to me. You know that, and I've infected you. No pun intended!"

"I'll probably lose my job," said Christabel.

"Doesn't matter now, does it?"

*

"Jake Ellwood."

"Jakey, it's Kate."

"Ah."

Kate rarely rang him these days, they had been divorced for a year, and separated for three. She only ever rang him about one subject.

"You aren't busy, are you?"

"No. Paperwork."

"I was just going to ask if you could let me have a bit more money this term," she said, "I have to do some travelling for my practical work...I need to go to Manila."

"Manila? What's at Manila?"

"A hospital full of people who need psychologists," she said, "And they're so desperate that even nearly-qualified ones like me will do."

He waited for a few moments to hear whether she had anything else to say. She didn't. He was thinking of how happy they had been once upon a time. A short time. He had recruited her to be his magical assistant straight from her A levels. He had picked her out of the audience to help with an effect – mainly because she was very beautiful and was wearing a sky-blue silk dress and had sparkles in her hair.

He had asked her name and, when she said, 'Katherine – known as 'Kate', he had fallen, immediately, for her Geordie accent. She did very well with everything he asked, and he sought her afterwards in the hotel bar. She was drinking lemonade.

They chatted and he ventured a compliment about her dress and her elegance; about her skill in helping him. It turned out that the dress belonged to a friend; the elegance and skill were all her own.

On their second date, he offered her the job of permanent assistant.

On their third, he asked her to marry him.

They had known each other for a year when she became Mrs Ellwood; had known each other for four when she became Ms Slater again.

Now she was on the 'phone asking for £2,000 for a research trip to Manila.

"Ow, Kate, love," said Jake, "I don't have it. I think I can manage about £500 but even that's stretching it a bit."

"Can't you get a bank loan?" asked Kate, who couldn't, being a student.

"Not really. Look, can't you go somewhere else, or apply for a grant, or something?"

"I've tried," she said, sniffling a bit, "I can't find anything and the project's strictly pay-your-own-way…"

"Somewhere closer?" he asked, "Europe?"

"Oh, Jakey, I want to go to the Philippines! It'll look good on my CV. And when I get a really good job next year, I won't need any more of your money!"

"Well, that'll be nice," said Jake, "Look, love, leave it with me and I'll see what I can do. I can't promise but I'll do my very best."

"I know you will, darling," she said, gently putting down the telephone.

"Oh, bugger!" said Jake.

It wasn't that Kate was a bad person; she was, really, quite a good person. She was a wee bit spoilt by over-indulgent parents, but she was trying to do something independent, for herself, wanting to be a clinical psychologist mainly to help people.

She was clever enough and determined enough. Good for her. The only thing wrong with her was that she had been too young for him, oh, and the fact that she didn't have anyone else to get money off. Be nice if she could get married again. To a millionaire.

Jake wasn't a big whisky drinker, but he wasn't an abstainer either. Thinking of his and Kate's money problem, he gave in and poured himself a glass of the good stuff. He sipped it slowly, completely out of ideas about what he could do.

*

Christabel and Raffaella walked so quickly down the West Sands that the little dog could hardly keep up. They were having a conversation about whether Christie's life in America was truly over.

Christabel was explaining to Raffi that there would be pressure on her to stay in her job, she didn't expect threats, they were British after all, but people would not be best pleased. By the time they reached the Eden estuary, Christie had persuaded the little dog that they would have a lovely life in Surrey, with Mary Jane and the ferrets.

*

He looked around the room and noted that it was about three-quarters full. Misty with smoke, which shouldn't be there, settling nicely into the plush forest green velvet draperies. He wondered how often they had the furnishings cleaned. There was a line of three sharp-looking academics front row stage left. He allowed himself an internal smile. They were there because they weren't easily fooled. Deal with them later. He picked out a young woman sitting halfway back. She clearly didn't want to be here. Her chunky boyfriend had left a possessive arm across her eau-de-nil silky lap.

"Perhaps the lady in green would like to help me with this effect?" Jake asked in a voice a few steps above a whisper: she looked scared and embarrassed; he could see through the smoke. She stood up suddenly, propelled by the boyfriend, against her will. She tried to sit down again but he wouldn't let her. Jake walked across the room, stopping a row in front of where she had been sitting and to the side. He spoke to her in a gentle voice, telling her not to worry. Simultaneously, he reached out and took the arm of the boyfriend.

"You know," he said, "A man might be better for this one!" He laughed with the audience. Surprise made the large young man easy to manipulate to the front of the room. He was sandy-fair and thick-necked, probably a team-man. Jake asked him what time it was, baring his own wrist where the boy's watch was currently situated, to the delight of the lady in green. After various small humiliations, including producing the victim's glasses, wallet and trouser belt, Jake let him return to his seat, half regretting not making his trousers fall down.

He found several items belonging to one academic in the clothing of another and performed the effect of the Suspended Man with the third – who was quite sure he had been awake throughout.

He did a couple of mentalist moves, using a pretty academic wife who was enchanted with the fact that he knew what she was thinking. They were well warmed-up now and he was ready to do one of his Maskelyne effects – the old razor-blade thing – to begin squeezing the awe and building the finish. He was only booked for fifteen minutes, a dinner-dance act. People would be going back to the dancing shortly. He asked for a volunteer and another academic, stood with alacrity. He wouldn't be fooled like his colleagues had been.

Jake got him to feel the sharp edges of the blades and assure himself that the twine was normal unbroken fishing line and was exactly six feet in length, with a fishing weight on one end. Even before he had resumed his seat, Jake had begun to feed the line into his own mouth - pausing occasionally to pop a blade in with relish, as if he were eating oysters.

When all the blades and separate line had disappeared, he wiped his mouth delicately with an ivory damask napkin procured from the nearest table. He walked around the area they had cleared for a stage, performing a few contortions so they could see his stomach was rebelling. A deep sigh when he reached centre stage and expelled the weight on the end of the line from his lips.

The audience, in unison, counted the blades as they came back, tied along the length of line. As he pulled the last one free, he bit down on the artificial blood capsule cemented to one of his back teeth - and the surprise of the people in the room jumped another notch with the trickle of fake blood running from the corner of his mouth.

"Oh my God!" shouted the second academic, rising from his chair, "He's hurt, get someone!" Jake raised his hand and caused the flash powder in a brass dish on the small table to ignite with a whoosh. There were panic noises in the audience: they didn't really expect anything more than a few sleights-of-hand card tricks at these lounge entertainments - but Jake had always bigged up his act for the purposes of surprise and awe.

He made himself disappear and reappeared from the back of the room with a large piece of gauze and crossed sticking plaster on his cheek. Plenty of satisfying oohs, he thought, as he walked back to the centre. He let them look at him for a second, then ripped the plaster off. That, he thought, hurt. Ouch. He bowed as they applauded and disappeared for the last time.

*

The doctor was a plump and sensible-seeming woman, middle fifties, with a lot of bright silver hair piled haphazardly on top of her head, fair, freckled, skin without make-up (he thought she'd probably been a natural redhead once upon a time) and a suggestion of a beginning double chin. Her navy skirt and sweater with a pale pink blouse underneath were neat and of good quality but not new. She sat back in her armchair and prepared to answer his questions over a nice cup of tea.

Jake had been embarrassed asking Ben Furness whether he had any pals in the town - someone who could talk about him. Ben, however, had taken it well. He'd said that he quite understood why Jake would need to talk to someone else; wasn't a bit offended. He'd suggested that Dr Latimer knew him well enough; been around forever anyway...

Jake had arrived at her house at the far end of North Street just before her stipulated 4.30, teatime, and was surprised and pleased to be conducted to a seat on a comfortable blue velvet sofa, in front of which was a coffee table laid with an embroidered white cloth and real afternoon tea. It was rare, these days, to be offered small sandwiches, scones, and cake, with a Georgian silver tea service and nice china. He could have been in his mother's house.

Dr Latimer's grey eyes sparkled at him across the tea table as she raised her cup and sipped. He took a deep breath and said that Professor Furness had given him permission to talk to her about him.

"I was a bit embarrassed, but I need someone who knows him and can probably be a bit more objective than, perhaps, his, er, niece".

"Fire away; I hope I can help. I know him..." she hesitated, "Pretty well. You know how this place is; one sees people, one says hello. And I'm known for my objectivity!"

Jake picked up one half of a buttered scone and bit into it. It was spread with actual butter and studded with plump sultanas. He got straight to the main question.

"Would you say he was devastated enough by his wife's death to have hallucinations?"

She looked considerably taken aback and put the cup down on the table.

"His wife's death?" she said, pausing, "I'd have put him down as one of the better copers with anything of that sort. He loves his work; possibly is obsessed by it, always helps. Obsessive people tend to substitute. He isn't hallucinating, is he?"

"Not in the usual sense, as far as I know. But he does seem to have been experiencing something rather weird and I was trying to find out what reasons there may have been. His niece, Christabel, came to see me. She is very worried."

"I thought you were an academic, Dr Ellwood. Why would she come to you?" She had spotted the oddity right away, sharp woman. He took another sip of Earl Grey. He'd introduced himself as a friend of Ben Furness, as a lecturer in the Medical School.

"'Cos of my book," he said, "I wrote this book, you see, about this sort of thing; about damage to the temporal lobes sometimes leading to experiences of great meaning and ideas about God…"

"Ah," she said, "You asked me about hallucinations of his wife. Or did I misunderstand?"

"No, well, I meant any kind of hallucinations. It happens, doesn't it? When someone dies? I was trying, I think, to work out if he was that way inclined before I got to the nitty-gritty".

"What are you talking about, then, Dr Ellwood? What kind of hallucinations do you mean exactly?"

Jake gazed briefly around the room, looking, if he was honest, for any signs of religion. There were no obvious crucifixes or holy pictures; no pictures of any description apart from what looked like a good oil painting of flowers hanging over an antique sideboard. A nice little black cat was waiting expectantly under the coffee table.

"Holy visions," he mumbled, "Maybe a saint or something."

Dr Latimer looked curious and asked him if he'd read Dr Dean Hamer's book about the God Gene?

"Yes," he said, "Part of my research for my own. And Matthew Alper's, 'The "God" Part of the Brain', which is interesting but a bit...er..."

"You didn't take to them, then? Sorry," she said, "I haven't read Alper's, or, actually, yours. I will do if you think it would help me understand where you are coming from?"

"You probably don't need to read them," he said, "I can give you a bit of a run-down. Unless you want to do the basic critical read yourself – and make up your own mind."

"Well, I would," she said, "But please give me the, what, 'run-down', if you can. It would be easier and quicker!"

"Um, well, oh, and there's Michael Persinger's God Helmet as well."

"Hell. Whatever is that?"

"You might have seen it on television," said Jake, "Richard

Dawkins went over to Canada to try it on. It's about electromagnetic stimulation of the temporal lobes, in pursuit of the idea that the feeling of salience, significance, spirituality, presence, is in the temporal lobes – or at least in the left temporal lobe, if you're right-hand dominant, and the stimulation can trigger it, allegedly. Dawkins, you might guess, didn't feel anything. Dr Persinger's answer was that Dawkins happens to be very un-suggestible. Surprise, eh?

"But it seems impossible to reproduce Persinger's original findings, and his measurement protocols were self-invented. And it wasn't a true double-blind experiment, because the psych students he used as subjects had a definite idea of what he was interested in.

"There was a Swedish psychologist, Pehr Grandqvist, who tried a properly blinded repeat in 2004. He couldn't achieve a similar result, and Persinger blamed the experimenters for not using the equipment properly!"

"You don't like Professor Dawkins either?"

"It's funny," said Jake, "You'd think most scientists would, wouldn't you? With him championing evolutionary science and rubbishing all the God-stuff? But a lot don't like him at all. Undergraduates study 'The Blind Watchmaker' in first year biology classes. They write an essay and everything. Some have problems because they haven't written an essay since they chose science subjects at school! I heard about one, granted she was a mature student, who wrote that, if Dawkins didn't exist, we'd have to invent him, giving him credit for his excellent writing but condemning him as a showman and a charlatan!"

"And her department liked it?" asked Minnie.

"Her department loved it!" replied Jake, "Especially when she said that following Richard Bach's 'Illusions – Memoirs of a Failed Messiah', she had written in her copy of 'The Blind Watchmaker', "everything in this book may be wrong!""

"So, what about Alper, then?" said Minnie, "I know a bit about Dean Hamer, I read his book. The idea of the VMAT2 gene coding for an adaptive trait of transcendence didn't seem particularly likely to me. I suppose having cytosine instead of adenine, in a single gene, *will* make a difference, but it seems more likely that it would be a group of genes rather than one single one. Most things are."

"True. There's a thing someone[1] wrote in a magazine that I specifically learned so I could quote it at any display of piffle. It says VMAT2 could well be titled:

"A Gene That Accounts for Less Than One Per Cent of the Variance Found in Scores on Psychological Questionnaires Designed to Measure a Factor Called Self-Transcendence, Which Can Signify Everything from Belonging to the Green Party to Believing in ESP, According to One Unpublished, Unreplicated Study."

"That's good," said Minnie, "But what about Alper?"

"Ah, yes. Matthew Alper, who is a science historian, reckons that the brain is hard-wired to believe in God – an inherited trait of our species. He argues that religion is so widespread that it must be an evolutionary inheritance, that fear of death naturally selected an instinct for religious belief, and specific parts of the brain trigger religious belief

---

1 Science writer Carl Zimmer

as a survival mechanism."

"So, really, just one argument, divided in three then?" said Minnie.

"Um. Atheistic and materialistic," said Jake, "No real science at all."

He buttered another scone and put some homemade jam on it. He wanted to ask Dr Latimer about temporal lobe epilepsy, just to touch all bases. He assumed that, had there been any question of that, she would already have told him.

"The other thing, just for completeness, is to ask if Ben has had any indication of temporal lobe epilepsy?"

"Ah, no, not that I know about, and I would. Know if there were."

"Would you? You know a lot seeing as how you aren't his doctor!"

"I know," she said, "It's just that I'm a very wise person and I listen to a lot of gossip!"

"So, you don't think that he's a 'temporal-lobe personality', then? Prone to religious feelings?"

"Don't be silly, he's so completely against anything like that. Are you, anyway, assuming that the 'temporal-lobe personality' exists at all? I wouldn't have expected you to..."

"No," said Jake, "I really don't. I did look up Saver and Rabin from 1997, though, and it didn't appeal to me anymore than it did then."

"That's a non-starter then," said Minnie.

*

When he got into the department the following morning, Jake popped into the lab to see Felicity. She was working at her computer, drinking tea over the keyboard.

"Wonder if you could do something for me Felicity?" he asked. She said that she would if she could.

"You live in North Street, don't you? I wonder if you could possibly drop off a book to Dr Latimer at number fifty. If you could do it when you're going home?"

"Of course," she said, "What is it?"

"A copy of my god book," he said, "She said she'd like to read it."

"All right," she said, "Can I pick it up at the end of the day? Will you be in your room?"

"Probably," he said, "If I must go out, unexpectedly, I'll leave it on the desk. You'll be able to find it, it's a ghastly shade of green."

Felicity was aware that he leaves his door open, one of the few lecturers who did; he always said he had nothing to hide.

*

It was fair enough, Jake thought, for the Prof to ask him for some information about himself. He gave him the CV and the short version of his unfortunate marriage. Ben, however, was interested in his childhood: where he came from, how he got to be where he was. It was the gentle interest of a mentor rather than a patient. They were at Ben's South Street house now, waiting for Minnie Latimer to join them for morning coffee.

Ben had pulled a small low table into the centre of the large Persian rug, all pale green and pink and cream. He'd thrown a small white embroidered tablecloth over it, saying that Free had embroidered it, "It's the sort of thing she liked to do." It was clean but rumpled; needed ironing. Ben went to the kitchen and carried in a tray with coffee mugs on it and a plate of biscuits.

"I can make scones," he said, with pride, "But I didn't have time today."

Jake was talking about his mother when the front door opened, and Minnie came in. He'd decided to leave his father until he had warmed up; reactions could be strange; people didn't always understand.

"She was Inverness, born and bred," he said. "A 'good family', I suppose you might say. I never knew them because her parents disowned her when she married my father. She never saw them again, I believe."

"Harsh," said Minnie, savouring the mug of coffee between her warming hands, "Although, people used to do it at one time".

"What was wrong with your father?" asked Ben, making a fair assumption that something was.

"Oh, he's a blockhead."

"That's not very nice," said Minnie. "Everybody has some redeeming features!"

Jake laughed. As usual.

"No," he said, with a sigh. "No, he really is. A blockhead. He's one of those people born without normal pain sensors, congenital analgesia; he could push hooks through his flesh without it hurting. He was what they call a 'carny' in America; worked in a freak show."

There was an immediate silence in the room and both older people put their mugs down on the table. They were a long way from the first not to know what to say.

"My mother was a Red Cross volunteer," Jake said. "She was on duty when the big show came to Inverness for a month and she was very upset about Payno the Geek, especially when he put a steel hook through his nose. She ran into the booth to help him.

"She thought, she told me years later, that he was an escaped lunatic exhibitionist, hurting himself in front of an audience. He had to tell her that he was, although not exactly a lunatic. She found later he had read everything and wrote luminous poetry. He was, otherwise, totally beyond her experience. They were married after the show moved on to Aberdeen. She adored him."

"Presumably," said Minnie, a little breathless, but recovering her speech before Ben, "The circus was the reason your grandparents disowned her?"

"Freak Show," corrected Jake, "But, yes, I suppose that was the reason. People are funny about freaks, and I only have what my parents said. I did know my father's parents a bit; I met them when the show went back to the US. Did I say they were Americans? No? Well, they were. All on the carnival circuit. My grandmother was a contortionist and my grandfather a magician. That's one reason why I do magic. I inherited the talent.

85

"They were all very proud of me when I got my PhD, though, and they came over for my graduation ceremony. The grandparents are dead now, of course, and my mother died of a heart attack some years ago. But I see my dad every couple of years. He's retired now, so either I go over there, or he comes here."

"Well," said Ben at last, "That's quite a background. It makes mine seem very boring."

"The whole thing is quite difficult to explain to people," said Jake. "Have you heard the Dire Straits song, *Devil Baby*? It talks about Freak Shows and Carnies in the States and equates the desire to stare at them with the trend towards 'tell all' television."

"And the 'Devil Baby'?" asked Minnie with a shudder.

"It's just one of the freaks listed in the song," replied Jake, "With the 'Monkey Girl', the 'Alligator Man' and the 'Big Fat Lady'. The question is which are the freaks; these or the audience which pays to see them."

"I remember going to see *The Elephant Man* at the New Picture House," said Minnie, "That made a similar point – John Merrick had neurofibromatosis and was very physically damaged, although he had a sensitive soul. The famous Sir Frederick Treves kind of rescued him from a carnival but, in the end, he was just in another, in drawing rooms with upper crust people staring at him. I doubt he was ever accepted as a real person, although he was one, of course!"

"Precisely," said Jake, "I came across a throwaway line in a novel I was reading the other night. It referred to 'freaks' and 'humans' as if they were exclusive categories. Anyway, my dad stayed with the show, doing the management latterly, until he retired to Florida. He lives in what he calls 'Freak Village', it's really Elm Court Village, but it *is* full of freaks, as well as other carnival people. He doesn't perform now but plays golf and writes poetry. He hosts a poetry corner show on local radio. He's a great guy!"

Minnie felt she should try to get back to the reason they were here. She asked Ben about how he'd been, not seeing Free anymore.

"Oh, it's unspeakable. I can't really describe it. I had no idea how it was going to feel. You know, doctor, that I knew she was going to die; she'd been given about 6 months - although in fact it was just a bit more. Somehow, knowing doesn't help. You'd think it would. Feels like just the other day…"

He paused, the tear, unremarked, already running down his cheek. "When she was ill, I was able to fuss around and take care of her. I'd get her up when she felt well enough, and we'd go out. I could push her for miles in the wheelchair and we'd some-times go out in the Morris, just to Crail or up to Montrose sometimes. I always thought the sea air would do her good. Once we even drove to Stonehaven.

"When we were at home, I could make her nice wee meals and we'd sit together and eat them. She liked to watch Coronation Street for some reason, and we'd do that together too. I was able to get a bit of time off from the department; I'd stood down as Chair by then. Of course, she loved St Andrews, she was born here."

Jake was touched by what the man had said: he could imagine him bending his academic frame into domestic life, carrying out his labour of love as precisely as he carried out his experiments. Minnie was fascinated, for her own reasons, at the level of detail in what Ben had said.

"When it was over, I came back here and realised how quiet it was. I put the television set on and the kitchen radio and then went and got the wee radio Free used to listen to in the garden and put that on too. It still wasn't enough, so I just turned them all off and went to bed. I stayed in bed for a week. But then I got up and went to work."

"I'm so sorry," said Jake. Minnie just nodded a couple of times.

"How long," she asked quietly, "Had you been married when this happened?"

"Oh," he said, "I'm not sure, a long time. I've always thought working that out would mean that I'd really lost her! Silly, I know."

Minnie and Jake exchanged a covert look

"How has it been since you've been working less?" asked Jake, trying to get a handle on his more recent mental state.

"Oh, not too bad. It's still a bit quiet but I go out quite a lot. I pretend I'm getting on with my book a fair bit! I do a bit of teaching; I see a few friends. Some old farts I know have family coming to visit them and I wonder what that would be like. Since Wisp left... I take the dogs out..."

He stopped and looked around the room vaguely. Then he said, "Ah, no. No, we don't have dogs anymore. Slipped my mind. When the last one went, we didn't think we could cope with losing another. They don't live as long as we do. It's too sad." He looked down into his coffee mug still full on the tray.

"Well," Ben said, getting up from the chair, "Think I'd better be running along. I've got to have a sandwich and then go and see this chap at Montgomerie Hall. It's something to do with a book. Maybe he wants a collaborator?" He picked up a disreputable briefcase which had been leaning against the skirting board by the door. "See you later," he called cheerfully. And left.

*

They hadn't stayed long in Ben's flat after he left: that would have been too weird. They returned to Minnie's in North Street because it was just around the corner and Jake, anyway, was unsure whether turning up at his own flat at Montgomerie Hall was a good idea. He was very taken aback by Ben's behaviour, although Minnie didn't appear at all uncomfortable.

"You might think dementia, probably," she said with a sigh, as she put yet another kettle on and they both leaned against her kitchen cupboards. "I saw no signs the other day when I talked to him. He seemed almost exactly as he used to be. A bit older, of course, but nothing I hadn't seen before. Although that does happen when you see someone very regularly; you don't always notice changes."

"It's not particularly unusual, though, is it?" said Jake. "A lot of older people get it."

"Yes, of course, but not all and it is said that keeping your brain going helps. I've never been sure of that though. I've known too many university people who got it to believe in use it or lose it." She poured boiling water into the pot and waited for it to brew.

"Oh, good grief," said Jake, perching on the edge of the kitchen table, "It had to be that didn't it? I suppose that explains it all?"

"You sound disappointed, Jake," she said, calling him by his first name for the first time. "You really shouldn't assume that a dementia-type diagnosis would explain everything, you know how hugely complicated the human brain is. There is a whole range of functional brain states which can account for altered consciousness. And I often wonder whether everything we think we know about mental illness as a whole is wrong!"

"Yeah, but a lot of that is psychology – beyond my ken. Don't know why I wanted it to be something else."

"I think, sometimes," said Minnie, "That all the magic is going out of life. The current generation seems the least imaginative ever: students come to university just to qualify for making money rather than to be educated. People seem to get greedier by the day. It would be nice to have someone who has visions, wouldn't it? Just to show us that there's something else; something we can't measure or quantify.

"Oh, by the way, thanks for sending your research assistant around with the Book. I read part of the first chapter last night. It sounds interesting. The only thing I was worried about was whether you could be objective about Ben's vision thing if you are a committed scientific materialist."

"I don't think I am," said Jake, "I'm not at all sure about any of it. It occurs to me sometimes that objectivity might not be all it's cracked-up to be."

*

"No, I've been avoiding him," said Christabel, picking up her gold fountain pen from the desk. "I thought it best. I stick out like a sore thumb here. It's a wee grey city in more ways than one." Sinclair's smile could be heard over the telephone line: he was well aware of Christabel's high opinion of herself.

"I think you're right to do that," he said, "But I would be a lot happier if you just got him out of there. This Ellwood man, you thought, might be able to help with that…"

"Yes. He's very committed to his own way of thinking and quite defensive about his book. That's why I chose him. I wondered, though, if one of the divinity people might be better. Professor Reilly, the Dean, is extremely sceptical about this sort of thing, and can be very… *effective*, when he feels like it," she broke off, picturing Martin Reilly in her mind. He had been stunned by her and she had a feeling she could manipulate him. She had felt that there was more to Jake Ellwood than met the eye; maybe her original selection had been in error. Christabel did not like making errors. There was food for thought in considering why she had done so, whether it was a mistake at all.

Sinclair swore and then asked her if she was going to change her plan.

"Yes, I am. Martin Reilly is a better bet: he can put down all this nonsense and won't even be bothered to sniff around. And he's well known in church circles. My uncle won't get any further when Reilly's finished with him."

"Good. I don't want any big crowds gathering hoping to see things. You remember what happened in Ireland? They really made a mess of what we were doing there. It's serendipity that this should be one of your relatives."

"My only relative", said Christabel, "The only one I have."

"Notwithstanding," said Sinclair, "He's a bloody nuisance. Get back in there and make him feel you only want the best for him, get him to co-operate. Talk to his doctor and get him to examine him for being senile. You must establish that immediately – before the whole story gets out and people start to wonder. And cut off this Ellwood character." It went quiet, although she could hear him breathing at his usual low rate.

"Oh, and Furness?"

"Yes?"

"I've always trusted your judgement. Don't let me down."

*

"I was wondering why I'd been sacked," said Jake. He was on his office telephone to Minnie Latimer, between lectures. "She was very curt and said she thought it best that I didn't involve myself further *in any way*. Her italics there."

"How odd," said Minnie. "She seemed very nice when we spoke to her the other day in Brittles. It was obvious she was concerned about Ben. How was she with you when she asked you to help?"

"Nice," he replied, "Although, now that I think about it, she was very insistent on doing it her way; finding out exactly what was going on, getting me to agree to interrogate Prof Furness. Not especially caringly, I suppose. Then she banned me!"

"Still, it's most peculiar. Do you feel banned, then?"

"I do. There was a threat under it. You know, as if she'd said,

'Don't go near him or else'. Not what I expected at all. I only met her last Monday, haven't really had time to do anything much. I asked her what I'd done wrong, and she said there was nothing. She just wanted me to stop 'bothering' her uncle. She said: 'We'll leave him alone for the moment; no good can be done by upsetting him just now."

"Have you upset him?" asked Minnie.

"Not that you'd notice," he said. "The only funny thing was when we went to his house, and he left us and went to visit me."

"That was when we decided what might be wrong, though, wasn't it?"

"Yes, but we didn't tell anybody, did we? And what is special about 'just now'?"

✦

Margery Niles, a GP

Dr Niles had asked Ben to come and see her before he remembered he wanted to book an appointment. This was unusual. He was healthy, generally, just a bit of wear and tear making walking harder than it used to be. She'd known him during a lot of his time in St Andrews, although she hadn't been there when he'd arrived 20 years ago. She indicated the patient chair in her surgery, smiling in welcome. She told him that his niece had telephoned her; mentioned that his memory wasn't so good. How did he think it was?

"Fine," said Ben. "I've always had a really good memory. Not quite as good nowadays, but that's just age, isn't it? When I realised I was getting a bit absent-minded about appointments and such, I developed a reminder system. I write them down. It works fine."

"What about other things?" asked Margery Niles. "For instance, do you know what day and date it is and where we are now?" Ben looked at her in amazement. What was she getting at? Was she trying to catch him out?

"Of course," he said. "We're in the Health Centre in St Andrews and it's Monday, twenty-third October. He added the correct year and spontaneously told her who the Prime Minister was and asked if she needed him to confirm his date of birth, although the receptionist had already done it. Dr Niles, a solid middle-aged woman in a wine-coloured suit with a fancy scarf draped around her shoulders, wrote all that down and told him how well he'd done in an irritatingly encouraging manner.

"You'll have to try harder than that," he said, "You have both a clock and a calendar on that wall and we must be in St Andrews Health Centre because you're my doctor and I've lived in St Andrews for yonks. What else do you want to know?"

She leaned over and referred to a note on the desk. She asked him about his family and, hearing that there was only Christabel, asked how well he got on with her.

"Dear Christie. She's a lovely girl in many ways: beautiful and intelligent and personable. But she's got half of my brother's genes, and Charlie and I never got along. Her mother was what the Americans call flaky too. Nice enough but wouldn't trust her as far as I could throw… er… you."

She asked about his general health and reasonably satisfied, let him go.

Ben Furness had been the last appointment of the day and Margery made a brief note in his file, closed it, and put it back on the trolley. She was walking towards the door when she suddenly stopped, suddenly thought, what? He's a biologist but he said Christabel has half her father's genes! He means half of her genes were inherited from her father of course... But then, I wouldn't have expected him to imply that I was fat either.

She picked up the 'phone message from Dr Ellwood and emailed Nuclear Medicine for an MRI appointment for Professor Furness. Soonest.

*

Christabel was worried. Uncle Ben's GP had just rung the hotel to tell her, within the restraints of patient confidentiality, of course, that he was mostly fine. She'd said that he was bright as a button and there was no need to worry – just a little bit of vagueness, nothing to be concerned about. It could be the beginnings of Alzheimer's Disease, but it probably wasn't and, even if it was, it certainly wasn't very advanced yet. She'd commended Christabel for her concern for her uncle and told her she was referring him for a brain scan 'just in case'.

Christabel gazed through the window for a while, having a think and chatting to the little brown dog. She hadn't expected it; she thought the GP would see Ben's strangeness straight away. It was no good, she'd have to stay in St Andrews a bit longer. Shit, that was a nuisance. She rang MJ and explained that she couldn't come down to help redecorate their brand-new old country cottage this weekend.

When she rang him, Martin Reilly wasn't in his office: the St. Mary's operator told her he was teaching until 4pm and then she'd probably be able to catch him in the Senior Common Room. Although Christabel hated hanging around, even on the telephone, she ordered a cup of coffee from room service and waited until 4.01 before trying again.

"Good afternoon, Miss Furness," he said, stressing the second syllable in the American fashion, "And what may I do for you on this cold afternoon?"

"Professor," she said, "I wonder if I could come and see you as soon as possible? I greatly need to talk to someone about my Uncle Ben and all these hallucinations he's been having. I wouldn't normally bother you, but he insists that they're of a religious nature and I need a real expert on such things to explain to him that that's ridiculous."

"He has spoken to me previously, you knew that – and of course I am something of an expert..." said Reilly. "I'd be happy to talk to you".

"He told me he'd talked to you, yes. But I thought if we both gave it a good go this time maybe we could convince him. I think some of his friends are taking it a bit too seriously... But I'm convinced he's confused and going a bit gaga. He needs to be somewhere where he can be taken care of, at his age. I know he's not old but, apparently, one doesn't have to be!

"I know that he's at least wandering off - the last time he had what he calls one of his visions, he was out in the countryside on his own. He could get lost or hurt. It would look bad for the university – to be in the news like that. As well as being bad for him, naturally."

"I *have* seen a change in him," said Reilly. "I don't know him well of course but he clearly isn't the man he was. Perhaps you could pop in and see me? I'm free at ten-thirty on Tuesday; we could have morning coffee in the Senior Common Room."

"I know you agree with me that we only want the best for my uncle," said Christabel, "I think we should have a proper talk. Yes, I could make Tuesday morning. I'll see you then. And thank you."

"Now what am I going to do with you?" Christabel asked the dog, whose tail was wagging sixteen to the dozen as it saw her pick up the lead with which she had replaced the stocking she had used to adopt it from Waverley Station Car Park, where she had been commandeering a taxi. It was clearly lost, dirty, smelly and in need of a loving home. She could offer it one. She loved dogs. For now, the little brown short-haired bitch could travel with her. She abandoned trains and drove herself.

She was cross that she couldn't just extricate herself from this St Andrews lark and go straight home to MJ. Comes of working right up to your resignation taking effect, she thought. A matter of personal honour.

✦

Ben's Diary entry 4

Christie arrived with a wee brown dog in tow. She wanted to use my bath to clean her up. I suggested she try showering her with warm water and some of that baby shampoo I use because it doesn't smart if you get it in your eyes – and I always do. Free and I used to do that with ours; except with Paddy, he didn't like it. The others were all fine though. Free showered them and I scrubbed Paddy in the bath. He was awful for going in mud; Springers always are. He'd just jump in the mud hole and turn around laughing at me. God, I miss him. All of them.

Christie said she's calling her new wee bitch Raff. It's short for Raffaella apparently. Italian. Her last holiday.

✦

Meredith Williams, a Hot Researcher

Meredith Williams was making himself a cup of coffee in the kitchen on the first floor of the Genetic Engineering Building, near his private office. There was no one else of consequence there; it being Sunday afternoon. The department had no under-graduates, but even the postgrads and postdocs were away about their own business. Florrie was in the laboratory though, pacing up and down waiting for his results. Never mind; he'd have to wait. Yankee git.

Florrie, despite his peculiar name, was not at all feminine. He was well over six feet in height and solidly built. His pepper and salt hair was cut into the semblance of a US army buzz cut, he wore a dark suit with a white shirt and conservative tie. He would have been suspected, in the States, of being a member of the secret service. Anyone so classifying him would have been correct.

Florrie was conscious of the fact that Williams didn't like him and that he was taking more time than he needed to produce the week's data on Blue Bag. Florrie's own superior expected the figures to be sent to him in Washington by 5pm Greenwich Mean Time, lunchtime in the Eastern United States. He would not be a pussy cat if they weren't.

Florrie cursed roundly: he'd already been pissed off when Meredith Williams had told him earlier that he was giving a talk about the work of the department on St Andrew's Day. What the hell would he say? Florrie had to report this to his boss and then all fuck would let loose. Meredith Williams had said it was too late to cancel the thing; it was already in the printed programme. As if that mattered.

Not going to happen, thought Florrie, wishing there was a way of getting stable people to run these projects. It would be a lot less trouble if they weren't so weird.

Still, it was a weird project. Florrie had no understanding of any of it. The General wanted Meredith Williams and he was very clear, to anyone who would listen, that he had paid through the nose for him. Brilliance at this stuff didn't come cheap.

Security was paramount, though. No one could know about Blue Bag. There would be interest. There would be upset. There would be questions in Congress. Even the pathetic Brits would cause trouble. That was why the staff was so rigorously selected and controlled. Not one of them could ever divulge what was happening here. Not one of them would ever dare. He growled to himself to make sure.

Professor Meredith Williams looked out through the first-floor window, down towards the car park. His beautiful sports car, PMW250, stood there in his special reserved space. His eyes danced over its exquisite periwinkle blue lines, its whitewall tyres, its white leather trim, its elegant dashboard slightly visible through the windscreen. It was his one concession to luxury, his extravagance, his reward to himself for his genius.

His brow furrowed as he remembered that he'd have to drop it off at the garage tomorrow morning unless, of course, he didn't quite make it home tonight. Once again, there was a peculiar noise coming from somewhere underneath the driving seat. He had no idea what it could be but then, he knew nothing about cars, had only learned to drive a year ago. Never mind, the garage would put him right.

They were the experts.

Martin Reilly, a Dean of Divinity

On Tuesday at precisely 10.30, Christabel entered the Senior Common Room in St Mary's College. It was a large, airy room with rather dour oil paintings of eminent deceased Divines on the walls. A few, somewhat less eminent Divines were seated on easy chairs thinly distributed throughout the room. There was a grand piano in the corner, under a rust-coloured, fringed, chenille cloth. Practically everything else was dark green; old-fashioned but elegant. Her sharp eyes picked up Martin Reilly's navy-blue hair sitting behind a coffee table, cup and saucer in hand, and a Bounty bar on a small plate in front of him. He rose as he saw her.

"Come in, come along in," he said, in his fake Morningside accent, "A terrible day, I fear." His old-fashioned charm, Christabel thought, not for the first time, was deeply artificial. She could admire that in him: she was accustomed to it not working quite so well in others. She said good morning and replied to his question about what she wanted to drink. He brought her the black coffee promptly, as soon as she had settled herself in a chair in the same group and was smoothing her maize-coloured pencil skirt in place.

"About your dear Uncle Ben", he opened, sitting back in his chair, and crossing one leg high, over his opposite thigh. "I think there must have been some deterioration?"

She told him there had been, that Ben was thinking he was seeing some strange stuff these days.

"Why," she asked, "Should an atheist scientist, no matter how normally dotty, start having visions unless he's gone off his rocker?"

"That's just what I said to what's-his-name, you know, the neurologist from the Bute. It seems odd your uncle consulted him, to say the least. I can think of a hundred more suitable people who would be better qualified, not to mention devout. Stuff like that just doesn't happen; I doubt if it ever did."

Christabel looked at him with some surprise. He was sitting there, sipping his coffee in a delicate manner, his dark trousers showing a shank of pale leg above grey socks. He was wearing a grey jersey under his jacket, and she noticed the gold bangle on his right wrist balancing the gold watch on his left. The grey moustache was a poor match for the navy-blue hair.

"Are you an atheist too?" she asked him.

"Good heavens, I'm the Dean of Divinity," he said with an irritated look. "I'm just sceptical about these things after my many years of scholarship... I believe in God, of course I do, I just think He manifests Himself in more modern ways these days: in compassion and charity and being kind to the least of His children, made in His image and likeness. Miracles and visions and other superstitions were very much of their time.

"In biblical times people were unsophisticated and needed to be helped with understanding. Similar with mediaeval times and the nineteenth and early twentieth centuries. Nowadays, we understand much more about the world; how things come into being, science…" He trailed off.

Christabel was surprised, but then again, surprised that she was surprised. Still Reilly could help her, she felt sure of that, Jake Ellwood probably had too much curiosity to be safe.

"Would you be prepared to say that my uncle was imagining things, if you were asked?" she said. "I'm just thinking of what might happen if it gets to the press: you know how enthusiastic they can be about a scandal."

Reilly leaned forward in his chair, untucking his legs from their ancient male dominant pose.

"Yes, of course," he said, "In fact it might be a good idea if you and I initiated that - so that they don't get a garbled story in the first place. If you think that would be a good idea, I can telephone a friend on *The Scotsman*… might be as well."

He looked down at his Bounty bar and then picked it up and tucked it in his pocket.

"After all, we don't want the sort of people who tend to flock around such things, in St Andrews: one only has to look what happens in Ireland. Some schoolgirl sees the Virgin and then all hell, figuratively speaking, breaks loose!" He smiled, showing his small yellowish teeth, and sucking unpleasantly. "I'll go and ring Joanne Critchley now," he said. "Come with me to my office; we'll see if she's in…"

*

Raisin Monday is a St Andrews tradition which goes back into pre-history, or to around 1974, depending on who you talk to. Originally, it is said, it was mid-way through Michaelmas Term and an opportunity for students to go back to the country farms whence they came to get their meal-poke refilled to last until Christmas.

Because of the system of "academic parents" – senior students who were supposed to show bejants (it means "fledgelings") the ropes in their first few weeks, it was also a time to thank them for their care. This was done with a pound of raisins (hence the name) but had morphed into the more modern bottle of wine; and academic parents gave their children the traditional "raisin receipt". Whatever they could think of.

Minnie had invited Ben to come with her to the lecture theatre in the corner of the Quad, up one floor, next to Upper College Hall. They'd have a good view from there, with one or two other old stagers and a long-retired groundskeeper, who retained a worrying concern for the Quad lawn, upon which he had spent his gardening life, and which had to undergo an unspeakable ordeal at Raisin-tide.

Eggs and flour had been banned in the Quad for years and shaving foam encouraged instead – the local supermarkets stocked up. The first set of bejants in the Quad was a big group of girls, selected for their height and blondness, in a cardboard Viking ship, their horned helmets clearly homemade by some of the "senior women" in University

Hall. Following bejeants were wearing all kinds of fancy dress, and were guaranteed to be as humiliated as their academic parents had been when they were 'raisined'.

The tradition was for more senior students to stop fledgelings and demand a forfeit, usually that they recite the first verse of the "Gaudy" – 'Gaudeamus igitur...'

"Bit bothered," said Mr Flannigan, the retired groundskeeper, who was pacing and fussing. "I think that cloud over by the chapel railings is flour!" Minnie scanned the students as far away as they could get from the window through which she was observing proceedings.

"Good grief," said Ben, "People are passing things through the railings from the street!" He asked Mr Flannigan whether they should do anything to stop it.

"No," said the old man, with a deep sigh. "Nothing we can do. Kids these days. Nothing anyone can do."

*

Christabel, reclining on her hotel bed, with Raffi's furry head on her stomach rang James Sinclair in London. If he swore at her, or yelled in any way, she had resolved to bawl him out and scream her resignation from the hotel battlements. For the couple of months since she and MJ had completed on the cottage, it had only been a matter of time and opportunity.

She was connected to him immediately, told him that she'd initiated Martin Reilly and sand-bagged Jake Ellwood. He didn't say anything for a little while – the slow breathing again.

"I've changed my mind," he said, "I've decided to take care of

Ellwood myself. I doubt that you have the balls to do it."

Christabel, who was used to his referring to anatomy she didn't have, no longer found this kind of talk offensive due to repetition. She did, however, find his sentiment upsetting.

"What do you mean?" she said, although she knew quite well, "How long have I worked for you?"

"Years," said Sinclair, "But this is your uncle. I think your feelings for him are going to get in the way. Your last personal assessment said you might be mellowing somewhat. I can't, I won't, risk this. It's too important."

"Okay then," she said, "You'll get my resignation before the weekend."

"It's not as easy as that," he said.

"Bloody is!"

Joanne Critchley, a Serious Journalist

Ms Critchley, being an old friend (who had "done very well"), came to visit Martin in his home in pursuit of the story. He lived a little way from St Andrews in the East Neuk village of Crail. Mrs Reilly was temporarily away, at a computing conference in England, so the household consisted of Martin, his teenage daughter, and their two enormous, shaggy ginger cats. He had arranged for Arabella to go to a friend's for supper so he could talk openly to Joanne.

They had talked mainly about Joanne, her job at *The Scotsman*, her book about the Holy Land. But now, over a not-too-awful blended whisky (journalists will drink anything), Martin explained about Prof Furness and the Holy Visions. A vast ginger cat leaped at Joanne, stamping on her, and trying to curl up on her lap, disrupting her hold on her iPad.

"Sorry!" said Martin, making no attempt to dislodge it, "He likes company."

"What's his name?" asked Joanne, stroking the cat's huge head whilst shifting her knees to get more comfortable.

"Tom," said Reilly, creamily. "The other one is Dick. Full names St Thomas Aquinas and Professor Richard Dawkins. They spend a remarkable amount of time arguing about the existence of God." Joanne couldn't help giving him a funny look.

"This is clearly some kind of senile hallucination," Joanne risked, moving the conversation away from the subject of cat theology. "Has he seen a doctor?"

"I'm sure he has but you know how they are. They try to paper over it – after all, it's their fault that all these people are living so long!" He sighed in exasperation, opening his arms to receive the Feline Professor for the Public Understanding of Science who was jealous of his brother's comfortable seat. "I just thought that maybe you could, sort of, interview him or something; you know, it might interest your readers?"

"You mean hold him up to ridicule?" Joanne was a wee bit curter than she needed to be. Reilly smiled the unctuous sincerity he kept for occasions like this.

"No, no, not at all! I was just... I felt that getting the proper information from the proper source might help you, rather than the sensationalism. And I thought seeing it in your sort of respectable paper might persuade him it's just a bit of silliness. He's apparently started going back to work in Biochemistry too, obviously he's not in his right mind...he's been on sabbatical, to write a book for a couple of years. Not surprising really, what with his wife dying and, I believe, his daughter ran away from home... It's a sad case."

Joanne was quiet for a minute, making a notation on the iPad rescued from under St Thomas Aquinas. Eventually, she looked up and across at the Dean of Divinity, her old acquaintance (never, ever, a friend) from university – so long ago – she took a calming breath and choked down her revulsion.

"No. It's not for us," she said, "Not the sort of thing which would interest my readers at all. Certainly wouldn't get past my editor. It could be very nasty. And the poor man..."

"Didn't think you journos bothered about that sort of thing," commented Martin, "All kinds of hacking and poking into people's private lives... Not really very nice."

"Well, if you think that," said Joanne, "That is what you think." She rose from her chair, sliding the cat off her knees onto the floor, where he shook himself and gave her a baleful look, "I'm leaving now. Don't bother ringing me again."

She stalked out to her car, marvelling at the hypocrisy of clergymen and academics (and academic clergymen), leaving Martin Reilly stunned at having discovered integrity where he least expected it.

*

Martin's next port of call was a rather different sort of newspaper, and a rather different sort of spin. He had once spoken to the journalist in question; he'd telephoned for comment on the previous Pope's unheard-of abdication. He wasn't, if Martin recalled, a religious specialist; he was some kind of gossip-column person. Well, maybe that would be better.

*

On Friday afternoon, the university was winding down for the weekend. Jake had paperwork to finish off, which he didn't want to take back to Montgomerie Hall. It was quiet outside his office door, and he felt that this probably made it safe for him to put some music on. He had a MP3 player and dock in the office, but rarely used it because his door was constantly banged open by undergraduate advisees, postgraduates, and postdocs, not to mention refugees from Montgomerie Hall pursuing him, and the old codger from the next room moaning about the music.

Dr Wisearse had already left for a weekend conference at Newcastle University and was in no position to criticise his choice of 'Bat Out of Hell'. Just as he was gearing up to sing along with 'I would do anything for Love (but I won't do that)', the phone rang. He paused the Loaf and answered it. He looked at his watch and wondered who could be calling at 5.45 on a Friday night.

"Ah, Hello. Is that Dr Ellwood?" said a male voice he didn't immediately recognise.

"Yes, Jake Ellwood here."

"Oh, Jake, I don't know if you remember me. It's been a long time."

The voice was American, probably Pacific North-West. Jake tried to think who he might know in Washington State or Oregon, even Northern California. He could only think of one person, a fellow doctoral student at UCLA, where he'd done his PhD.

"Kermit?" he said, "Is that you?"

Kermit (whose face he couldn't remember unless he was the frog of the same name) Whittaker was a graduate who had crossed over from biochemistry and, in those days, was running a project something to do with neurotransmitters. Jake couldn't recall exactly what.

Kermit said that it was, indeed, he, and he was ringing to ask Jake whether he wanted to apply for a job in America. The excellent company Kermit worked for was seeking good people, brilliant people, for its new diversification. Kermit had thought of Jake. The salary would be three times what he was currently earning. Kermit would be in Edinburgh until next Thursday; could Jake come and meet their CEO? He would only have to indicate he wanted the job, and it would be his. Jake, who could hardly manage to insert a word into the sizzling stream of conversation, agreed to meet Kermit at 2pm on Wednesday.

*

St Andrew's Day dawned cold and sere, much as it always did. There was a myth in the Town, and in the University, that thirtieth November was a day of celebration. It never, ever, felt like that. Minnie didn't know why they bothered.

She had got out of bed groaning as usual, let Polly out, had a bowl of porridge and read the Citizen. She was going to a public discussion in the evening but hadn't quite decided whether to do anything during the day. It always seemed incumbent on residents to do *something*. She pulled the listings from her kitchen notice board, where they had been partly covered by shopping vouchers and the latest letter from Xavier, the child she sponsored in Mozambique.

There was a tour of the zoology department's Natural History Museum billed, but she had done that several times. In fact, she remembered going in for the first time when she was about twelve and being really upset about the stuffed animals. They were interesting but sad and she had spent much of her time looking at an Indian tapir. She had secretly named him Raji and had gone to visit him on a regular basis - every time the doors were open, that is; not that often. She wondered if Raji was still there or had succumbed to moth.

No, not the Natural History. She could go to Chemistry. The wee ginger-bearded man was doing good stuff, she'd heard but then, she was going to the Chaplaincy Centre this evening to hear a Scientist (big S) discuss genetic research with a Quaker from the Economics Department. That would take care of science. She decided to plump for an exhibition of illuminated manuscripts in the library - and get her brain rested for later.

*

It was almost 7.15 when Minnie came out of the house for the second time that day and walked along North Street, through Greyfriars Gardens to the Chaplaincy at the west end of Market Street. They had been doing some modernisation recently and it looked better than it had for dilapidated years. Signs of modernity, she thought; that and employing the Chaplain part-time. The room was full when she got there, and she found a seat near the front – as usual the room filled up from the back.

Professor Meredith Williams, from the Department of Genetic Engineering, was already seated at the front of the room facing the audience. The professor was rather a short man with a closet baldy hairstyle. Minnie was interested in how he kept it all shipshape in the wind. The sparse bronze hairs were currently draped over the glowing baldness, but she estimated that they'd trail out at least a foot from his head in a St Andrews gale. She wondered if he affected a hat outdoors. A balaclava would be more efficient. The Quaker economist hadn't arrived yet.

Mary Ellis, the (part-time) University Chaplain, wandered in with an anxious look on her pretty oval face. She was dressed conservatively in black but no dog collar: she hardly ever wore one, that, too, being the modern way. It was 7.35 and they were going to start late again. Mary gazed around the room and spotted a few men she didn't know distributed through the audience. Obviously, they had different faces, but looked strangely alike anyway. She decided that they were Americans; a lot of those around at the moment.

The Quaker arrived, with a tail wind of falling leaves. She was tall and skinny and elderly, with her hair in a messy grey bun and a no-nonsense skirt and jumper. A grey raincoat was over her arm. She flustered in, apologising for her lateness, and placed the coat over the back of her chair before sitting down. Mary Ellis took her place at the front and the audience went quiet. She introduced the participants and gave a mild warning about people getting overheated on subjects like these.

"We hope that we can have an informative discussion without resorting to name-calling and common abuse," she said. She had a nice voice. "I understand that feelings run high on such things but let's remember that we are members of an ancient and eminent university; and that cutting-edge work is what we are about."

She surrendered the floor to Professor Meredith Williams who, in his Welsh accent and with his Welsh twinkle, gave them genetics for the under-fives. Minnie listened to him with a smile on her face. There was nothing new here yet, but she was enjoying Meredith Williams: he was a picture of the pathology of several functional mental illnesses, including the narcissistic abominable hair.

He was curing diseases now, Alzheimer's and Parkinson's, the ones the big hitters doing research with a high yuk factor always mention - assuming, correctly, that they are the main diseases that the public dread most. Any frightful strand of research could be justified if it was going to help cure such awful things. He spoke for a little while about the technical (incomprehensible) details of genetic engineering and then sat down.

Marlene Devenish did not have a twinkle in her eye, although the rich glint of eccentricity was available in abundance. Her thesis was that, although a great deal of money was being spent on genetic engineering research, not much benefit was coming out of it. She talked about government funding and about benefits accruing to defence (and defense) departments.

She stated that most really expensive research had to be thrown down the laboratory sink and that any benefit to humankind was in short supply. She said that it was only defence departments which could afford to junk the work which didn't pan out, in the hope of finding something they could use to destroy something else. Her opinion being that universities should re-order their priorities and not be slaves to governments of any country or colour.

When she sat down, there was a generous round of applause. Mary noted that the Americans were not clapping. Minnie applauded, although she was well conscious of the propaganda content of Dr Devenish's speech. As a species of scientist, herself, Minnie knew that many alleged advances and treatments were useless in reality. She largely accepted the idea that only antibiotics and transplantation techniques had carried medicine forward much over the last hundred years. Most other things were flashes in the pan: they promised everything and delivered not very much.

A graduate student was on his feet. Minnie thought she had seen him in chapel. She thought he was a PhD student in Practical Theology; Mike something-or-other. He was asking Professor Williams whether his research was paid for by the Ministry of Defence. Williams was geniality itself. He said of course it was.

"Dr Devenish is quite right," he said, "It's only the British Defence Ministry, and the US Department of Defense, which have money to spend in the hope of getting some-thing useful these days. Other funders look for guarantees… which no honest scientist can give." He beamed around the room, the very picture of an honest scientist. Mike was trying to ask another question but had to surrender the floor to a pushy female from the back who was quite as insistent.

Minnie, turning in her chair, recognised her as Jake's research student, Felicity, who had brought her a copy of his book in the shocking green dustcover.

"Professor," Felicity said, "Can you tell us what research, precisely, is paid for by the UK Ministry of Defence and the Americans?"

"Well, no, you can't really expect me to tell you that," Meredith Williams raised half out of his chair to reassure her. "I can't tell you what percentage of our expenditure is paid for by anyone. There are such things, Miss, as confidentiality agreements… but it's just because of the possibility of commercial advantage…" His voice tailed off, clearly expecting her to understand the enormous difficulty of his position.

"But," said the young woman, "we should be able to know what research our own university is doing and where it gets its money!" There was a lot of noise, as the audience debated this among itself. Meredith Williams was fully on his feet now.

"Yes, of course," he said, holding onto the silkiness of his voice, "And you can come out and have a tour of my department any time. Why don't you come tomorrow? We aren't doing anything which would offend you, you know. University departments are open to strict scrutinization; anyone can walk in off the street and see what we are doing any time."

He returned to his seat with a beam of his headlights at the girl at the back. Marlene Devenish and the Chaplain both spoke briefly and there were a few more easy questions, but the discussion was essentially over. Minnie walked from the Chaplaincy Centre with one thought in her mind. Did he say, she asked herself, that there is no secret research going on in any university department in the country? The only answer she could think of was yes.

*

Felicity was sure she was being followed. She'd read Rupert Sheldrake's *The Sense of Being Stared At* and was sceptical about it, as well as most of his other stuff. Nevertheless, she felt, now, that she was being stared at; being followed.

She had left the Chaplaincy discussion as it broke up, trying to avoid anyone she knew so that she could process what had been said, she had waved to a few people including Dr Latimer, to whom she had delivered Jake's book. She was especially annoyed that Meredith Williams had used her own subject, the genetics in Parkinson's Disease, to justify the unpleasant research he wasn't talking about.

It was as she opened the street door with her key that she felt someone behind her and turned to find no one there. She wasn't going to be intimidated, she thought. She'd take up Williams's invitation and have a look round his department as soon as she got some time. She wondered if anyone ever had.

*

On Tuesday evening, just before Jake was expecting to leave the department, Kermit Whittaker telephoned to say that his Chief Executive Officer had had to leave Edinburgh because of another urgent matter and would not be able to meet with him the following day.

"But I have another, better, idea," said Kermit, "How about coming over to Paris for the weekend? You can see the CEO sometime on Friday and then we can have some fun over the weekend!"

Jake's spirits rose at the mention of Paris, it was a city he liked a lot. The back of his brain thudded a touch at the idea of fun with Kermit

Whittaker and his boss, but, really, why not? He hadn't had any fun for ages.

"I'll send a car to pick you up on Friday morning – tell me your address – and we'll deliver you back first thing Monday morning. Pack a good suit, we'll be going somewhere high-class."

"Okay," said Jake, pondering whether the only suit he had would do.

✦

Felicity Malcolm, a Research Scientist

Felicity met Dr Latimer in North Street as the doctor was hobbling down the street to go shopping. They stopped, for a moment, exchanging greetings, saying how cold it was, again.

"Saw you at the Chaplaincy on St Andrews Day," said Minnie, "Thought you asked a good question…"

"Didn't get much of an answer, though, did I?" said Felicity, pulling her inadequate jacket around her, "I thought it was a fair enough question to ask – although I didn't really expect he was going to answer it to my satisfaction. I think he's a particularly slimy specimen."

"Yes, he is, isn't he?" said Minnie, "Did you go to visit him and have a look at what he's doing?"

"Not yet," she said, "But I will as soon as I have time. I'm in the middle of writing up for my PhD, and I'm pressed for time. I am going to push on though. I wouldn't trust that man with… well… anything. I have a feeling that his project is highly suspect. If it wasn't, why would they be doing it down there?

"My own work is in genetic influences on parkinsonism, why would I not know what they're doing? I'm a member of the university for goodness' sake!"

*

Ben was walking again when he began to feel odd. This time he managed to sit down before everything started to whirl around him. He was out on the West Sands and there happened to be a bench. He settled, hoping that it wouldn't be too dizzying tonight.

The man, as usual, appeared. Not really hovering above the ground, he was standing there; it just happened that his feet were in mid-air. The picture, if one could call it that, was becoming sharper. Ben could see the man, the background, smell the bacon and the fresh air smell.

The man was moving his lips, trying to speak, but Ben couldn't hear him. He noticed, though, that the wounds, which he now saw in both his hands, were actively bleeding, and the side of his brown homespun robe was wet with a dark stain. The feet, on a level with Ben's knees, could be well seen now. They were bleeding too. A lot of blood – but it was disappearing, not clotting but not staining anything around him. Except the palms of his hands which were dripping into the space between them and the ground, but not reaching the grass.

Then everything mingled together and started whirling like before and the music turned into a scream and he found himself on the bench, on the West Sands. With no other human being around.

*

The gene-sequencer was running, and Meredith Williams was checking the latest batch of results. He was certain that they would get it right soon: six years of intensive work surely had to have the desired result. Had he not believed that he would have given up long ago. They had had important results, though; good, successful results. The application of rigorous principles had been added to visionary thought. They must be near a breakthrough.

He'd always been intrigued by how things came to be - and by how they might be altered: his work in the States had been on the cutting edge then. Now, his work in Scotland was in the forefront of all that was being done in the world.

Unfortunately, he still felt like he was in the States, what with Florrie and Bettany and all their clones looking over his shoulder all the time. That was why he'd done the lecture on St Andrew's Day - just to feel part of the university rather than the US Department of Defense.

They said they lived in hope of something they could use - and weren't bothered if nothing came of it. This was not true. Not with Blue Bag anyway. Florrie was watching every step of the way. General Challoner wanted a penny-by-penny break-down of costs. Meredith Williams secretly bridled at this; how can you put a price on the creation of life?

Vic Gateside had been an important asset, though: a first in zoology and a doctorate concerned with the strange world of amphibian genetics, he was a great manipulator of DNA. He was good at the numbers too. Williams, himself, was a neurosurgeon, who disliked patients, and that was still where most of his personal workload lay – not with patients.

Williams didn't particularly want to go into the Animal House. He didn't like the smells and especially didn't want to talk to the technicians, who had a revolting tendency to anthropomorphise the experimental animals. Animals are animals, he always thought, and they are inferior to human beings. How many breakthroughs in science would have failed had not they been tried on animals first?

And there would be many more, although few would be like his. The Nobel Prize in Physiology or Medicine, or he missed his guess. He was the only one in the entire world doing work this advanced. One had to be decent to one's animals, treat them kindly and reduce any suffering to an absolute minimum. They were animals, though and animals were not people. He went in to have a look at them.

*

They had talked about all kinds of things, about hallucinations and vision quests, and Minnie had contributed from her own store of knowledge about patients she had known in the past. Don had seen two women having tea under a non-existent tree out-side his second-floor flat, Maisie had warned everyone that there were ghosts in that cupboard – she wasn't afraid, but she thought other people might be.

Jake had talked about his god-book research: Saints Bernadette and Thérèse of Lisieux had both been consumptive; Teresa of Avila had been, in his opinion, an erotomaniac and completely aff her heid. There had been lots of examples of the face of Christ in pizza dough, even the name of Allah in half an aubergine; the phenomenon not being restricted to Christianity. He felt that there was a good case to be made for hysteria being at the root of a lot of this. Although what that was, he didn't really know, although he had read Charcot, Janet, and Freud.

Jake's own research in the area, though, was about brain trauma, and the location of damage to the brain resulting in an increased sense of the spiritual. God, if you like.

"Damage to the temporal lobes tends to produce a deeper feeling of meaning," he said, "And there are famous cases where people who had been damaged had reported visions – certainly some who seriously thought they were called by God, to a special mission."

Ben had never, as far as he knew, had any brain trauma.

Jake mentioned, just for completeness, the opposite syndrome, Capgras', where familiar people are felt to be imposters, probably because of the lack of the feelings one normally has for them, "A lesion or damage to the pathway between face recognition and the amygdala, it's called prosopagnosia." Other people disagree.

Minnie had had patients with schizophrenia who had many auditory hallucinations, voices telling them they were evil, that they should hurt or kill someone or themselves, as well as people with dementia, who had been reported as having very strong delusions as well as vivid hallucinations.

"Some people with Alzheimer's Disease have benign hallucinations," she said. "They just see people who aren't there, but some other types of dementia can cause nasty ones. There's often a sense of persecution with those – or the delusions, which can be worse, that something is true when it can't possibly be." She stopped and then followed up with, "Don't remember hearing anything much about holy visions though!"

Ben, sitting alone on the sofa and feeling a bit like an

experimental animal, contributed some of his own professional thoughts about alternate consciousnesses; vision quests and the hallucinations which could be caused by a variety of fungi.

"Of course, a lot of Native Americans, especially medicine-men (who don't have to be men, by the way) used to seek visions by way of magic mushrooms. Psilocybin was an important substance. Some of them still do – I seem to recall that there is at least one church which uses hallucinogenic substances in its worship... I did a bit of research into that once because I'm interested in mycological products, although I'm not an anthropologist. It's absolutely fascinating."

Jake cleared his throat and exchanged a look with Minnie. She raised her eyebrows slightly and, taking the initiative, said in a low voice,

"Did you ever actually take anything in those days, Ben? After all, we're probably talking about when everyone was taking 'mind-expanding' drugs, aren't we?"

The professor said that he had, indeed, tried to induce a vision in the late sixties or early seventies.

"I was in Berkeley, on an exchange, when they had some riots and I found myself next to a group of Lakota people on campus. They invited me to visit the reservation on my way home. I did the whole new age, sweat lodge, vision quest thing..."

"You took something, then?" asked Jake, just to be sure.

"I did, wouldn't you?"

"Do you think," said Minnie, "That some of this could be a flashback?"

Ben, who was looking down at his feet, found his voice and asked whether it might help if they could decide who he was seeing, or what he wanted, or something… He had borrowed books about saints from the public library. He had already decided the drops of blood on the man's hands might have been stigmata in the 'holy' sense, that is, signs acquired resembling the wounds in Christ's hands. Jake and Minnie simultaneously decided to go along with him, and they talked about what they knew of saints (not much).

"I think it might be Francis of Assisi," said Ben. "He was a monk, so the rough robe is right, and he was supposed to have the stigmata, hence the wounds. But what could Francis of Assisi possibly want from me?" He sighed deeply and looked at his visitors with bewilderment in his brown eyes. As Minnie got up, saying she really had to get her shopping done, and Jake, realizing that Ben was losing concentration for today, said he should go too. Ben escorted them to the front door, saying,

"It *was* the holy thing you were interested in, wasn't it? Not the child? With the nose?"

*

Ben settled down, when they had gone, on the sofa with the cushions under his head. He was amazingly tired; couldn't understand why just talking tired him so much these days. After all he was still a good walker; his expeditions into the countryside testified to that. He didn't notice that he had dropped off to sleep.

It was warm in his drawing-room, the winter sun shining through the window.

Four-year-old Wisp was sitting on the window seat with a drawing book and crayons. She was concentrating hard on drawing and colouring a picture of Paddy, the liver and white Springer Spaniel. Her lips were pursed and her eyes screwed-up, searching a good likeness.

Such a beautiful dog thought her father, such a beautiful child.

He took in the scene, though slightly concerned that he should probably be somewhere else, doing something else. Wisp was wearing a funny, shift-like sort of dress that he'd never seen before. It was an odd sort of no-colour, not what she would have chosen, not at all what Free would have suggested. She wasn't colourless, though, not with her pink cheeks and her auburn hair.

She turned to Ben, as if to ask a question and, as she turned, her face began to look strange... as if...

He immediately woke-up.

*

Jake was waiting in the glassed-in porch of Montgomerie Hall at 8.15 on Friday morning. He had arranged for Felicity to run the seminar for first-year biologists – it was well within her capacity, and she should be doing more teaching now anyway.

A car drove up the Guardbridge Road, past the North Haugh Science Park and turned in to the semi-circular driveway. The car was a large navy-blue Range Rover, with all the fixings. A man in a dark suit (do all Americans have dark suits, white shirts, conservative ties? – he wished he had the franchise, that would pay for Kate's trip) climbed out of the driver's seat, asked him if he was Dr Ellwood, and invited him to get in.

"Do you want to travel in back, or ride upfront with me?"

Jake decided on up-front and was surprised at how high the vehicle was, how much he could see from his seat. He had to occupy himself with looking out of the window as the driver did not speak.

It did not take long to get to Ingliston airport and, after checking-in with the babysitting help of his driver, checking his carry-on, and reporting air side, it took even less time to fly to Paris Charles De Gaulle.

He was met by a clone of the driver and whisked to a very nice hotel, not the Georges V, but something good. The driver said that he should change and be ready to be taken to meet Mr Zonanisky in half an hour.

Jake checked in and went up to his suite(!), wondering how he was going to change into a suit he was already wearing. It was a standard navy-blue sort of a suit. Elegant enough when it was new. He got married in it.

*

Jake, who was pretending he'd forgotten his one and only tie (which he couldn't find), bought a new one at the hotel gift shop, trying his schoolboy French on the sales- girl who spoke perfectly serviceable English. It was a bottom-of-the-range, polyester job, dark blue and black stripes. He hoped it would do.

He was picked-up in yet another navy-blue Range Rover and taken to another hotel, an even nicer one, decanted onto the pavement and sent up to the *Suite Romanesque*, where both Kermit Whittaker and Burton Zonanisky were seeing someone else.

Kermit welcomed him and bade him take a seat, serving him coffee and offering a plate of Danish pastries; Mr Zonanisky would be available in about five minutes.

The other interviewee left and Zonanisky patted the seat of the sofa next to him to encourage Jake to sit there. Jake, who wasn't accustomed to this sort of thing, complied uncomfortably.

"Now then, Doctor Ellwood," the youngish-looking American, who had clearly had work done to his face, said, "I've looked at your résumé and talked with Kermit here, so I don't want you to talk about any of that shit. What I want to talk about is about how ambitious you are; about how hungry you are. The one I have in mind for you is a great opportunity and you seem just the right man!

"It'll mean coming over to Spokane, to our headquarters, of course and setting-up and running the new division. First, tell me where you see yourself in two years."

Jake, who had expected, and prepared, an answer to the related question of where he wanted to be in five years, was taken aback but, thinking on his feet, well bottom, sharply truncated the timeline and said:

"I have been seeing myself as Chair of Neuroscience at the University of St Andrews but now that other possibilities have shown themselves, I want to be the Head of a Division of Baker and Dobinsky Medical Services Inc."

Jake tried to control the blushes attached to that piece of smarmy dialogue. He had very little idea what Baker and Dobinsky did, and there was no such post as Chair of Neuroscience at St Andrews. He had no notion of whether B & D had Heads of Divisions either, but Mr Zonanisky was smiling broadly and moving his visibly elderly hands in encouragement.

"Correct answer!" he said delightedly, "Now, tell me, did you, personally, set-up the co-operation agreement you have with the British Home Office to do their forensics for them? I understand it's very remunerative. A brilliant financial deal?"

"It is, apparently," said Jake, "But I only advised on procedures and things, and found some space so we could do the practical work. The university hired people and made all the financial arrangements…"

Kermit was twitching on the periphery of Jake's vision, wanting to have him say something else. What could it be? Probably to embroider his rôle in the Forensics agreement. Um. He turned on the sofa cushion to favour Kermit.

"I was thinking, Jake," Kermit said, "That you were the one who persuaded the university to dream it up in the first place – you know, when the Home Office was cutting back services because of money. You said, didn't you, that the university could find a way to carry-out the work more cheaply, because they already had huge expertise…"

"Oh, er, yes," said Jake, not sure why Kermit was talking all this rubbish. His financial skills allowed him to balance his cheque book, when he needed to, but that was about it. Oh, and some project-related statistics.

It was time for Kermit Whittaker to take over and explain the vision of what B & D had in mind for him.

"You will start as Vice-President for Scientific Services," said the

American, "First, to work on the structure of the program. It will probably take about two years to set-up as you want it, before it starts work. We'll get you all the best people, because it's going to operate at a very high level of quality, the best forensic services the world has ever seen!"

Jake thought that sounded ludicrous but decided against saying anything, thinking of his phone call with Kate.

"At first, there'll be a lot of travelling," said Kermit, "Around the States. You'll have to take meetings with many forensic pathologists, until you get the right, more junior people, to undertake all that, while you talk to State Governors and other politicians. You'll have to help us lobby Washington too – DC, I mean, not the State! They won't need much persuasion as long as we're saving them money!"

"The project is no less than taking over all forensic services from all local people and centralizing them in our own organization. It's huge!" said Zonanisky.

"But we know you are the right person to do it," said Kermit, "Perhaps the only person in the world, who can!"

"Jolly good!" said Zonanisky, trying for an English accent, "You are exactly what we want. Kermit has told you the salary?" he named a salary about ten percent higher than Kermit had said and added that there would be generous expenses, bonuses, and stock options too. He asked whether the stunned scientist would do them the honour of joining them?

Jake, too bewildered to refuse, said that he would be pleased to.

*

In the Range Rover, going back to the hotel, Kermit (who had elected to accompany him for some reason) invited Jake to join 'some of the guys' who were in Paris for a conference, for a night out. They would be doing the usual Moulin Rouge, Folie Bergères things and then go to one or two private clubs. Jake, still feeling drunk from meeting the CEO of Baker & Dobinsky Scientifics Services Inc., found himself agreeing, against his better judgement.

They picked him up, in a navy-blue Range Rover, at ten o'clock, and began a pub-crawl around the City of Light.

*

And then it was Christmas and the Wee Grey City shrugged off most of its young, and gained several Christmas shoppers, who thought it would be cute to do their festive searching in such a quaint place. The air was glassy with cold; clear, freezing, translucent.

There was a Carol Concert, just for the town, in Holy Trinity Church. It was the sort of thing to which everyone went, believer or not. Minnie encountered Ben in the rudimentary garden in front of the church. She was lingering because she had been into the church after the heating had broken down - at a thing for One World Week in October. Ben was not aware that, after standing singing for a few minutes, the damp started to creep up one's legs, not stopping until it exited through the top of one's head.

"Got your woollies on?" asked Minnie, pulling the extra layer of wrap around her, over her royal blue winter coat.

"We'll be inside," said Ben, as if that mattered.

"Oh, it's way worse than being outside," said Minnie. "The

heating's broken and they don't know when they'll have the money to fix it. It's appalling. I don't know why they didn't change the concert to one of the other churches. Hope Park has heating, so does Martyrs. And the University Chapel might hold enough people if the Council of Churches would humble itself to the university!"

"I'm beginning to wonder why I wanted to come," said Ben, with a laugh. He folded his arm into Minnie's, and they went into the church. Sitting near the front (where no one wants to sit), they had a chat about the weather forecast until the body of the kirk filled up and "Hark the Herald Angels" began.

✦

Ben's Diary entry 5

I always enjoy singing carols; even though I'm not very good at it. Always seems to make Christmas, though. Without carols, I don't get into the mood for it. Dr Latimer was at the service; she likes carols too, and she has a good voice. Like Free's – a round contralto. She invited me round to hers for Christmas dinner; said she always does the whole thing, turkey, roasties, nice veg but no sprouts. I could have hugged her. I HATE sprouts. No Christmas pud, though, she doesn't like it. Who was it who didn't like it before? Can't think. Never mind. She's going to make a spectacular ice cream pudding, she said. That sounds great, doesn't it? I am looking forward to it. I LOVE ice cream.

*

On Christmas Eve, someone from the Ministry of Defence telephoned Joanne Critchley at *The Scotsman* and told her that it was not in her interests to engage with "that mad old professor" who'd been seeing visions in St Andrews. The someone didn't give his name. His voice, loaded with threat, made her blood run cold – and her journalistic super-sense prick up its dangerous ears. She did not tell him she had no intention of 'engaging with that mad old professor'. As of five seconds ago, it would no longer have been true anyway.

PART TWO

CANDLEMAS TERM

✦

James Kemp, a Tabloid Journalist

It was a couple of days before the new term started that the balloon went up. Ben answered the door at 10 o'clock in the morning to a tabloid journalist called James Kemp who had heard that he had been having visions. The journalist was quite charming, and Ben let him in. He said Professor Reilly had spoken to him on the 'phone.

Over coffee, they chatted about the awful weather and the way the meteorologists were losing the plot. Kemp, setting his coffee down on the table, took a moment and then got straight to the point.

"Can you tell me exactly what you see?" he asked. "I've been studying some stuff we have in our archives, but I haven't been able to find anything terribly convincing. Most of this type of thing, glimpses of the ineffable and that – they seem to mostly be just a kind of feeling. A feeling of spiritual significance; do you see? There aren't many reports of people actually seeing anything... Just kind of colours and stuff. Someone said she'd seen cilia – is that the word? – coming out of the walls..."

"I see a man," said Ben, "But it isn't just that. The whole experience is much more. I smell things, I hear things, I even taste things. The picture, as it were, is only a small part of it." He looked slightly bewildered, as he did when describing this to someone for the first time.

"Yes, well, maybe we can take it a bit at a time. Just tell, me, for now, what you see."

Ben sipped the last of his coffee. He smiled gently, remembering, now, how the visions made him feel.

"It starts with light, and colours," he said, "And, during the winter there was snow whirling round: the whole thing was beautiful to look at - like a paperweight. You know, the sort of thing they call a snow globe in the States; very, very pretty; the sort of thing which looks as if it should have significance, even though it doesn't. And then the man appears in the middle of it all."

"You don't *see* a kind of paperweight, though? It's real?"

"Of course, the paperweight's only my way of describing what it might look like."

"What does *he* look like, the man? Can you describe him to

me?" The journalist was making squiggles of shorthand on his pad, "Start with the face and then we can go onto the rest."

"He's very tanned, like from working outside in the sun," said Ben, "But there's something that tells me he's kind of pale underneath it; tired too, maybe worried. A pleasant enough face but wrinkled, and the beard's a wee bit overgrown. The beard is greying, although the hair on his head is quite a young-looking brown. I can't see much of it but I'm aware he has that bald patch - I forget what you call it - monkish, you know. He's got dark eyes, a bit sunken."

He stopped, thinking. "It's pain," he said, "That's what I'm seeing in his eyes, on his face. He's in a lot of pain. It's like when Free was very ill. Free was my wife, you know. She looked like that. Bearing pain bravely; pain beyond anything any of us can imagine. But refusing to let it stop her doing anything."

He took a deep breath, almost crumbling into the chair. He hadn't made any connection between the man in the vision and his wife before. The journalist carried on squiggling and then said, "What type of thing is he wearing, then?" The professor looked at his visitor's own outfit; dark trousers, nicely creased down the front, a pale blue shirt, dark blue tie. His shoes were black lace-ups, well-polished.

"It's a robe thingy, a habit, is it? Brown, rough. It doesn't quite touch the floor: I can see his feet. They're not very clean. They don't actually touch the ground, oddly."

"You said that he had the stigmata," said Kemp.

"No," said Ben, "I said he had blood on his hands and feet - I only heard the word from the Dean of Divinity later. And I only saw the feet the last time I saw him, it was dripping on to the ground. I have no way of knowing that that is what it is. He could have been injured or something."

"Probably that, though," said the journo. "Hands and feet - and I imagine his side too. The wounds of Christ on the Cross. Apparently, there's also an expectation of blood dripping down his face; the Crown of Thorns…and scourge marks on the back?"

"Definitely didn't see any of that," said Ben, coming out in favour of the evidence of his senses, "No other blood. And I'm not entirely sure he was bleeding from his hands and feet much; maybe his injuries were healing?"

"If it's the stigmata, it doesn't heal," said Kemp, "The holy person carries it with him to the grave. Apparently."

"Well, I don't know." Ben was beginning to feel a little snappy now, "I can only say what I perceive through my senses, I can't be expected to make stuff up to order." The journalist looked a bit affronted.

"Have you ever seen or felt anything like it before?" he asked.

"How d'ye mean?"

"Well, any kind of visions or hallucinations, that kind of thing? In the past, you know…"

"Not like this," said Ben. His gaze shifted up and to the left. A kind of vague expression came over his features. He'd certainly experimented. It had been fascinating to think that ingestion of those mushrooms, the subject of his legitimate research, should have such strange effects, lead to the experience of an alternate consciousness. He'd known, when he first heard about them, that he had to have that experience. It would have been a betrayal of his intellect to refuse.

"I did some work when I was in America, you know, years back," brushing an imaginary bit of fluff off his knee, "I was working with the fungi, and there were a few with some interesting effects… All legitimate you understand. Obviously, I had to try - it was in America."

"So, you tried magic mushrooms, then?" The journalist stopped writing and put his notebook in his pocket. He had enough.

"Yes," Ben confirmed, "4-phosphoryloxl N,N dimethylethamine. It's called psilocybin, the active ingredient that is. There are nearly 200 different species that contain the chemical. The hallucinogenic effect happens when the compound is dephosphorylated in the body. The hallucinations were just swirling colours and sounds; although I have to say that there were feelings of deep significance too, although I wouldn't say they were necessarily spiritual in my case… But it's a very long time ago."

The journalist got up from the chair and began to move towards the door. Ben, still sitting down and feeling in rather a pleading sort of position, went on, feeling he could somehow dilute his account by adding to it.

"It's not too different from the effects of ayahuasca - although that tends to be in the southern-western States and Central America - and there's peyote, of course, that's a plant, a succulent. There are Native American churches which are allowed to use it in their services even though it's banned amongst the general population."

"Bit of a fantasist, then, are we, Prof?" asked Kemp, turning and smiling in a self-satisfied sort of way. "Are you one of those people who think aliens have landed and the government is hiding it from us, by any chance?"

"What, little green men? Absolutely not," replied Ben. "I do think that there are other intelligent lifeforms in the universe, of course, it would be ridiculous, not to say incredibly arrogant, to imagine we are alone amongst all those millions of planets. But I've never thought that they visit us; communication and travel will probably be too difficult for the next several hundred years. I understand that about twenty-five percent of Americans not only think aliens are already here but that they themselves have been abducted by them and probed. Good grief!"

He quoted the famous lines from Lewis Carroll, *Alice Through the Looking Glass*: the White Queen answers, when Alice says she cannot believe impossible things:

'I daresay you haven't had much practice. When I was your age I always did it for half-an-hour a day. Why, sometimes I've believed as many as six impossible things before breakfast.'

*

The one with the child, thought Ben, that must have been an hallucination too. The police were only humouring me. I couldn't possibly have seen what I thought I'd seen... and yet... He remembered the child extremely clearly; the strange-looking face, the deformed legs. He rather thought there was something a little peculiar about the arms too.

It rang a vague bell somewhere at the back of his brain. He'd seen something a bit like that before; no, he'd read about it. He paused for a moment and then decided that he hadn't at all. Whatever it had reminded him of, it had faded. It couldn't have been anything important. It hadn't been a multisensory experience either: he'd only seen and heard her. No, that wasn't right. He'd touched her too – and she'd touched him, she'd punched him in the stomach. It *was* different. He had the odd feeling that he should have photographed the bruise.

Tomorrow, the undergraduates would be back from their Christmas break - he'd begun making wall-charts so he could see the pattern of the weeks better. He was finding understanding an ordinary diary quite tricky these days - the idea of having everything laid out on an easy-to-see wall chart was much better. He had tried a commercially available one but had found that completely impossible. In the end he'd made his own; he was quite proud of it. The shape of time was completely clear on the wall of his kitchen.

Outside, the street was quiet and dark, except for the streetlights on the other side. It was cold, too: St Andrews was always colder in the days leading away from Christmas than it was leading up to the holiday. February would be the worst month.

"What was I thinking about before I side-tracked onto the weather?" Ben asked. He had noticed this years ago; a tendency to distract himself into other lines of thought - no problem, though, it was part of being a creative thinker he told himself. What had he been thinking about? Something of no importance he felt. Never mind.

*

At 8.15 on the Monday of the first week of Candlemas Term,

Jake Ellwood was in his room in the Medical School, cogitating about hallucinations, distracting himself from not having heard from America. He had been researching hallucinations during the holiday, instead of doing his own work, and had become fascinated by it. Apart from his interest because of Ben Furness, he thought there might well be a further publication in it; a follow-up to his god-book. Of course, he might not have time to write it, or do any more research, with Ben, on it. There was the new job to take into consideration.

He had telephoned Kate as soon as his hangover from the Paris junket had finally quieted down. It had been the most pernicious hangover he'd ever had, even counting his student days. She had sounded miserable when she answered the 'phone.

"Hello, Kate," he said, "I have really good news!"

"Oh. Really?" she said, disinterested, not believing him.

"Yes. I've got a new job. In America. Loads of money. You can go to Manila to do your research. No problem!"

"You're kidding!"

"Of course, I'm not kidding! Would I?"

"I never know with you," she said, "You have a weird sense of humour!"

Jake, who clearly remembered her telling him he had no sense of humour at all, said that he wasn't kidding, he really had a fabulous new job and could afford to double what he usually gave her, as well as the £2,000 for the Philippines. She asked when he would have the money and he had to say he didn't quite know. But he would go to the bank and get a temporary overdraft. That would do, wouldn't it?"

"Of course," she said, "Thank you, Jakey."

He only realised she hadn't asked him anything about the new job when she'd hung-up.

*

The pathological mechanism of hallucination was fairly clear; a brain damaged in whatever way, organically or chemically, could perceive things which weren't there, things which the person's eyes might insist upon, in conjunction with the sensory circuitry, but which the higher centres were no longer equipped, for whatever reason, to deny. So far, so good.

There was also an idea about the person hallucinating something because he or she needed it in some way – the idea that many widowed people see their dead partner fits neatly into this category. Still, there was a lot more to it than that. Jake had read a piece about a patient with Alzheimer's Disease who hallucinated an apprentice, in the Day Centre – which he saw as his workplace – and seemed to be able to act out his anger upon the unfortunate lad. He had shouted and screamed at the apprentice for being late, for being useless, for being idle, but never appeared to have any doubt that he existed.

Then there was what Ben had mentioned, at the very end of their latest talk, "the child." Jake had not followed it up at that point because Ben had shown signs of extreme tiredness and he'd thought, along with Minnie, that their very intensive session needed to be ended.

Ben had, however, emailed Jake to say that he'd been to Ninewells Hospital in Dundee and had an MRI scan. He wondered if Ben would share the results with him.

*

"My God," said Jake, sighing deeply, "I *wish* you hadn't tried hallucinogenics, it does complicate things."

"Are you saying *you* wouldn't have?" Ben asked, staring at the younger scientist.

"Oh, good God, of course I would have. But I'm not the one having visions now!"

"Sorry."

"Don't worry, we can work around it, I daresay." Jake turned to Minnie, who had just come in the door of Ben's flat, again, without knocking. Saying "Hi!" before turning back to Ben, he said, "Well, you emailed me that you'd been for a brain scan. How was that?"

"OK," said Ben, "The doughnut thingy was a bit intimidating and claustrophobic. And you have to keep still."

Jake had been referring to the results and he made a mental note to try to communicate more precisely.

"Did you get the results?" he asked. Ben added that he had.

"My GP isn't too worried," he said. "There's a wee bit of shrinkage of the right temporal lobe – I could have told them that, it's the bit where I used to keep my memory for numbers and that isn't so great anymore. A wee bit of loss of very high-level function... Nothing to worry about. So they say."

Minnie said that that was good news as she went into the kitchen to brew up. Jake said:

"Last time we talked, you mentioned, at the very end, what you described as 'the child'. I didn't ask about that at the time as I thought you were too tired. I have, though, been wondering what you were talking about."

Ben pulled a face and sighed a sigh.

"Yes," he said, "It was at the end of the summer, and I saw something else I was a bit confused about. Not just the vision."

*

"He still hasn't told me anything about the subject from Blue Bag," said Christabel, holding the telephone between her ear and shoulder while the leather buffer in her right hand buffed the pale pink nails of her left. Sinclair was on the line again; he was bothering her a lot, wanting to know details. She assured him that everything had been contained, no need to worry. Sinclair wasn't so easily put off.

"It's the Cousins," he said. "They say they need us to be absolutely sure; everything rides on this."

Christabel sighed in exasperation.

"We *are* sure," she said, "Why won't they believe us?" It was Sinclair's turn to sigh now. When he answered, his voice was colder than she'd ever heard it.

"We need to give them something," he said. "Otherwise, your dear uncle may not have a happy future."

The line went dead, and the heart Christabel didn't have lurched at the threat.

Ben's Diary entry 6

I was "door-stepped" this morning; I think that's what they call it. On the way to the department and there were eight or nine people jostling one another on the steps of my house. They were shouting and photographing me with those wee telephone cameras. I closed the door; I don't like that sort of thing. Didn't go away, though, and going through the back is a much longer way around. Eventually, they seemed to have gone and I opened the door again. They'd only gone quiet though. They were still there. Cameras were flashing too, and I wondered what on earth they wanted. They must have had the wrong house. I held my briefcase in front of me and charged through. They were so surprised they let me. Ha!

*

Minnie didn't have to open the newspaper to know that all hell had suddenly broken loose. The headline on the tabloid in the newsagent's had told her most of what she needed to know. It was of a very large size and screamed across the width of the page above a 'candid' picture of Ben, scarf flying, clutching his overcoat inadequately around himself, staggering along the West Sands in a gale.

"Nutty Professor sees the SAINT in ANDREWS!!"

"'He has the stigmata' says atheist academic"

"Of course I believe in aliens, it would be ridiculous and arrogant to think we are all alone in the universe"

"I've been abducted by little green men and probed – says biochemist!"

It was partly derived from a much smaller and quite sober item in the gossip column of one of the broadsheets, on page 7 and with no picture. A local stringer presumably. Other pictures in the tabloid, though: Ben looking bemused coming out of the street door of the house, his briefcase held in front of him like a shield. Minnie bought a broadsheet and a tabloid and looked around to see if anyone else was running the story. Discovering that all of them were, she left the shop, rushing down to Montgomerie Hall in the hope that Jake would be in.

Happily, he was in and had already read all the newspapers. He was a bit stunned that Jim Kemp could have made so much out of what Ben had said, last night, that he'd told him. Possibly, the Prof hadn't quite remembered. It was, of course, quite possible that Kemp had manufactured a lot of it from whole cloth. That tended to be the function of the scandal sheets.

*

Meredith Williams was in the lab this fine morning, slipping on a white coat over the grey trousers and the purple woolly jumper, waiting for his first strong black coffee to brew in the machine he had got for Christmas from his aunt. The background climate was never quite warm enough in the mornings since the university had begun economising on the heating.

The building was somewhat isolated, away from the central

system, but at the very limit of modern design. Because of his defence work, he was able to pay his way: it was only the bits the university still controlled, like his supply of graduate assistants, equipment, and heating oil, which he couldn't keep close to his chest. He'd even come up with a solution to the problem of securely cleaning the highly classified building.

He filled his coffee mug, the one with the legend "BOSS" on it and sipped; he'd have preferred "PROFESSOR BOSS".

Meredith had a good feeling about today. Florrie had gone back to the States over Christmas and not come back; he would enjoy not having him gazing over his shoulder. As long as it wasn't out of the frying pan into the fire... He knew that this project was so important that the best people would be assigned to it. In the case of those who controlled the project from on high, that meant the most ruthless. Maybe he would begin to miss old Florrie.

He stood contentedly at the window, looking, for only the second time that day, down to the car park. His beautiful, shiny, periwinkle blue convertible stood there again, its white upholstery winking in the pale sunlight through the windows. Oh, how he loved that car. He had bought it as a present to himself for passing his test at the fifth attempt. It was a pity he would have to go home, again, on the bus. The car would have to be collected by the garage, again. He was not sure what the trouble was this time – it smelled funny when he turned on the ignition.

He heard the door buzzer sound twice and imagined that one of the Yanks had answered it. The building security didn't allow anyone to come in or out without a great fuss. That was the only other difficulty, besides the presence of the Yanks. Even if he wanted to work through the night, he had to cover all their weird security angles. He knew the project was highly secret, of course he did. But this was St Andrews, after all. One could leave one's car, unlocked, in South Street for five days. One had done.

Meredith Williams heard the lab door mechanism engage, as the retinal and hand scans were completed, allowing Bettany and a man he didn't know into the room. Bettany had been on the project since the beginning, even longer than Florrie. Head of Security. The other man was rather short and stocky, dark black and shaven headed. He wore one of their usual dark suits with white shirt and conservative tie, covering a well-muscled upper body. No sweater. He would find it cold in here.

Bettany was introducing him. Williams missed his name the first time round and had to ask for a repeat. Apparently, the new man was replacing James Florrie; his name was Maxim Denfrell. The professor asked for it to be spelled. He'd never heard the name before. What names the Yanks had. Denfrell firmly shook Williams's hand and said something banal about looking forward to working with him. He asked for a tour of the laboratories.

"I'm not sure I have time just now," the Professor told him, "And there are no post grads in yet. It's the day after the holidays," he explained. "We don't worry too much about them being in yet..." The new man actually went "Humph!" to Williams's surprise.

The expression on Bettany's face spoke volumes. Such things as that it didn't matter whether there was anyone else to do it, Williams had better do it himself; things like limitations on Williams's time being of infinite indifference to both. Williams found himself feeling slightly intimidated – not a feeling he remembered too well from his early career. He'd been a high-flyer for a long time.

He made them walk up the stairs to the second floor, as punishment and, going through the double doors, spread his arms to take in the lab, saying:

"This is the Secure Genetics Lab. This is where all the important stuff goes on. That is why it is highly secret." He indicated the sequencers and other equipment for manipulating the contents of embryonic cells, all sitting on their own benches, along with computer terminals, and the doors to the electron microscope room and the radioactive samples and biocontainment rooms. He said that there were other labs in the building, as well as the growth tank facility which took up a lot of space.

"I'd be especially interested to see that," said the new man, speaking rather melodically in what Meredith Williams imagined was a southern accent. "That's the heart of this research, is it not?" Williams let out an exasperated breath.

"No," he said, "THIS is the heart of the work, the Genetics Lab. Without this there would be no need for anything else because we wouldn't be doing anything."

Denfrell didn't look as if he'd been slapped down, and Williams felt his eyes locking with a fellow high-flyer.

The two Americans followed him around the bench and stood behind him as he opened a blue door in the left-hand wall. The corridor leading from it wound around the side of the curved building and was interrupted by the door of a lift. Meredith Williams said:

"Here's the elevator, gentlemen," not quite sure whether to put the emphasis on 'elevator' or 'gentlemen'. Williams having used a plastic key card on a chain around his neck to unlock it, they travelled smoothly to the third floor. Even the lift was the very best for America's star scientific pet.

The Growth-Tank room occupied almost the whole of the third floor, with just two small rooms leading off it: the Frozen Sample Laboratory and the Radiation Laboratory. There were no windows. The large room accommodated a narrow staircase at the far end, leading right down to the 'nursery' of the animal house in the basement. The chemical smell from the growth tanks mercifully concealed the smell arising from the staircase.

"This," said Meredith Williams, "Is where the genetically manipulated cells are grown on. It's a very delicate process to get them to divide correctly and to differentiate into the tissues we want. But we've had considerable success. Oh, yes."

Denfrell had walked towards the first tank and was leaning over it. It was about two feet long and one foot wide, with a depth of another two feet. Inside he could see virtually nothing except murky liquid being pumped in at one end and out at the other.

"Is the growth medium continuously re-circulated?" he asked, looking up at the Professor.

"No," said Williams, deliberately keeping the pride out of his voice, "The cells are continually washed in new fluid, with carefully modulated growth factors, so there is never any contamination. We had a little problem with that, oh, about five years ago. Now we use the nutrient fluid only once. When the sixth manipulation has been completed, the tissues are re-settled in the large tanks over here." He walked over to where four much larger, reinforced glass tanks occupied a section of the floor separated from the many small tanks by an industrial-type hoist mechanism.

Picking up Denfrell's enthusiastic expression, he told him that there were no Stage Sevens in the tanks at present, as they were starting a new generation this week.

"A lot of preparation to do, gentlemen," he said, leading them through the door back to front of the lift. "I'd be happy to let you see more another day, when I've more to show you…"

Denfrell, spotting the spiral staircase at the far side of the tank room, asked where it went.

"Ah, that?" said Meredith, "That's an extra laboratory that was planned to continue a related kind of work. When I moved the labs here from the old building, I meant to continue it. But this," he waved his arm around to indicate the tanks, "Took off more quickly, because of the extra funding. I made the decision to discontinue the virus work – we just use the lab as a cupboard now. Suppose we might use it in the future."

He watched them enter the lift and press the buttons for the ground floor before turning and hurrying back through the growth-tank room and down the long nursery staircase.

*

"These are awful," said Minnie when she and Jake had laid out the papers on his coffee table, which was more accustomed to carry-outs and honours assignments. "I am quite surprised that so many newspapers are interested!"

"I'm not," said Jake, "They seem to get more and more vulture-like as time goes on. And St. Andrews always seems such a respectable place, doesn't it? The Scottish University with the most English folk? It's an easy target. Lots of people among our neighbours to the south still think we're the next layer below Oxbridge, so if their children can't manage the Common Entrance, they apply to St Andrews…"

"S'pose so," said Minnie, "That's why the university has tripled its undergraduates in the last twenty years."

"Are you an alumna?" asked Jake, who didn't know.

"Yes," she said, "I did my preclinical here and my clinical at Dundee – as students used to in those days. I came back here because I'm so fond of the place."

"It does that to you," said Jake, "With all its oddities and its 'traditions' – it ties students to it forever."

"Some break away," said Minnie, with a sigh, "But some of us become St Andrean fossils, like me."

She looked a little sheepish about this and made him wonder what tied her to the place. She didn't strike him as being one of the whimsical types who can't leave.

Minnie was looking at the worst of the tabloids, with the James Kemp by-line. It was clear that he had talked to Ben directly, whereas most of the others had cut and pasted it and added a little waffle of their own.

"Nutty Professor sees the SAINT in ANDREWS!!" she said, "That's horrible. With the usual standard of pretend cleverness. He has a legitimate quote lower down, though. "Of course, I believe in aliens, it would be ridiculous and arrogant to think we are all alone in the universe". He told me he'd said that. The reporting just appeals to the lowest possible level."

"Why don't you read it to me?" asked Jake "Then we can, maybe, discuss anything we find as we go along?"

"Yes, why not?

'Your reporter was asked to go to St Andrews yesterday to bust open a new scandal which has exploded in the town, which thinks so much of itself that it never responds to any of our reporting.

The university was founded in 1410, the first one in Scotland and the third oldest in the English-speaking world. It is one of the old-fashioned academic institutions which still prides itself on educating students from the best public schools in Scotland and England, as well as the best brains of the many young people who want to come over from English-speaking countries like America, Canada, and Australia.

St Andrews University boasts one of the most important Divinity Colleges in the world and trains a good many ministers of religion and other theologians. It also features departments of science and other subjects.

Dr Benjamin Furness, a fungus-expert, who says he is an atheist, has told your reporter that he has been seeing visions recently, all around St Andrews. He thinks they may be of a saint or holy person, or of some kind of space-alien. He confirmed, yesterday, that he has been abducted by aliens on several occasions and has been experimented on. He does not know why.'

"Holy persons AND aliens?" said Jake when Minnie had stopped reading and flung the paper to lie in a lump on the carpet.

"Wouldn't have thought they would be compatible," she said, "But I daresay he asked for it, with introducing the wee green jobs!"

She was both troubled and dismissive of all this but leaned over to pick-up another paper and re-settled her gold-rimmed glasses back on her nose.

"I've been abducted by little green men and probed – says biochemist! They can't even get that right!"

"What about the stigmata?" asked Jake.

"Oh, that's in one of the more moderate ones. I guess that the low-aiming ones don't expect their readers to understand the word. "He has the stigmata' says atheist academic.' They say that he's had 'unusual' experiences, several times, but they seem to confine themselves to the holy vision thing – no sign of aliens. They give the definite impression that he's off his head, though. They mention he's 57 and that Alzheimer's can affect people who are under 65. They don't say how young, of course, just a big fat hint."

"What will they do next?" wondered Jake, "How long would you reckon it will run?"

"As long as they want it to," said Minnie.

*

James Sinclair, on the telephone to Christabel Furness, at the Surrey cottage for Christmas, made his degree-level fury clear to his agent, although she was, in truth, no longer his agent. He was yelling at her about her 'mistake'. She had no idea what he was talking about.

"Your crazy uncle," he spat, "What the fuck did you think you were doing, calling the scandal-sheets? The cat's really out of the bag now!"

"I didn't," said Christabel, lying smoothly as she realized that he was talking about what Reilly had done. She had known. She hadn't cared. But hadn't Reilly said he would talk to his friend on 'The Scotsman'? Hardly your scandal-sheet…she waited for Sinclair to say something else, something more intelligible.

"You mean he did it without consulting you?" he continued, not lowering his voice much, "You said you could control him!"

"I did," said Christabel, "I could. But I don't work for you any longer. I resigned. I think, maybe, you should go and fuck yourself." She put the telephone receiver back on its old-fashioned cradle and went to join MJ, Raffi, and the cats, who were sitting performing their daily homage to the very beautiful Christmas tree in the sitting-room.

✦

Max Denfrell, a Navy SEAL

Max Denfrell stood in the middle of the mean little kitchen in the mean little house in mean little Saynt Andrews. He guessed he'd have to start using the word "wee" in future. Everybody else did. He'd served in London, in the US Embassy for a while. The word "wee", to him, meant "urinate". It was beyond his comprehension why the limeys couldn't speak their own language. They invented it.

Paul Bettany, the Station Chief, had driven him round to the wee house in a street in what he'd called the New Town. Neither the town nor the house looked very new, with the grimy walls, diseased paint, and the kitchen units from the year before yesterday.

It was all ugly but, by a huge margin, the ugliest thing he'd ever seen was what Bettany had referred to as a three-piece suite, in the parlour. It had to be seen, in all its molasses brown and tan cut velvet magnificence, to be believed. It had cookie crumbs ground into the pile. Everything was a nightmare. Nothing would ever be all right again. In the kitchen, there wasn't even a coffee maker. He'd walk into the town and buy one. At least the salary was generous.

Denfrell had come to St Andrews to serve as Night Security Superintendent on a scientific project called "Blue Bag" and no one had thought to tell the ex-Navy SEAL what it was all about.

He just knew it was indescribably important to the Department of Defense. He had been assigned at a special request from a General Peter Challoner at the Pentagon: apparently, they'd recently removed another operative from the project. There had been no need to brief Denfrell in detail, as he had a gift for quick reactions and smart decisions. His scientific background consisted of a bachelor's degree in Social Anthropology. That, his commanding officer had commented, was quite adequate. His more relevant qualifications were in something quite different.

He put his thick, quilted jacket back on over his suit, this was a freezing cold place, tucked the key to the nasty wee house, on its tatty bit of string, with a brown cardboard label, into his pocket and, making his way through the nasty wee bit of garden, took the uphill route to the centre of Saynt Andrews. Such as it was. They had some nice coffeemakers in James Pirie's in Greyfriars Gardens. He bought one.

✦

Ben's diary entry 7

I haven't been writing in my diary lately. I think because I was so shocked about what that journalist wrote about me. He made out that I was a nutty old professor who sees things – and he wasn't particularly complimentary about St Andrews either. I love the place, always have; this is where I was happy with my dear Free. The mark on the page is a tear. I still weep, even now. But only in private. People would think it ridiculous. They don't know how I feel though. They can't.

I'd never have spoken to him if I'd known. I should have known. I didn't think I was so feeble I needed protection, although, all the time he was here, I was thinking who I could have had with me, young Jake or Christie or Minnie or Free. God help me, I wanted Free.

*

Jake's first magic performance of the year was on 8th January. He had been offered work over the Christmas and New Year period but hadn't been minded to take it; there had been various difficulties. Now, there was work to be done, and money to be earned. His salary at the university was adequate for his simple needs but he really had to give

Kate something extra while she was doing her master's in psychology, not to mention the Manila thing. Anyway, he had his magical heritage to consider.

The lights had gone down in the Glasgow Dinner Theatre and his personal take on Pepper's Ghost had begun. For this, of course, he needed an assistant, as well as a whole night and day to prepare the set. It was a straightforward, though celebrated, illusion and he'd brought one of his undergraduate students, a nice wee girl called Naomi, who was also in need of the money. She performed awfully well, and he was sure he'd use her again. He had to have absolute confidentiality – but he knew Naomi understood that.

When the illusion was complete, the round of applause was encouraging. Jake was aware, of course, that many people knew how it was done these days; but it could still be arresting if done properly. He made sure it was done properly. He looked forward, anyway, to no one knowing how he did his finale.

✦

Vic (Tubby) Gateside, a Geneticist

Felicity Malcolm arrived at the Genetic Engineering Laboratory just after 3pm. She had been busy all morning setting up the rest of her chapter headings in the Medical School and had taken a late sandwich lunch in the flat in North Street she shared with a postgrad from Evolutionary Biology. Although it now seemed a long time since she had stood to question Prof Meredith Williams on St Andrew's Night, she remained determined to get to the bottom of him. Before the lecture, she had been prepared to like him and appreciate his expertise but had found that he revolted her, and that she did not believe a word he said.

Her PhD project was concerned with genetic implications in Parkinson's Disease and Dementia with Lewy Bodies, the dopamine transporters and receptors and their disruption. There might be a specific connection between medicating to improve the mobility disorders in Parkinson's Disease and the development of a related dementia.

The literature had been pointing more and more towards the idea that the dementia which some people with Parkinson's Disease got, and the disease named with some form of the words 'Dementia with Lewy Bodies', "Lewy Body Disease' and 'Diffuse Lewy Body Disease' were the same entity, although this had not yet been agreed.

Felicity was interested, especially, in the DAT1 dopamine transporter gene and the DRD alleles, which code for various types of dopamine receptor. She wondered why other projects concerned with the same sort of subject were under the control of a different department. Which was keeping them secret.

She'd read the relevant information sheets on the university website and had become more puzzled rather than less. The website talked about genetic engineering as cure for various illnesses; Meredith Williams had talked about his funding from Defence Ministries. Felicity could not make that equation balance.

She rang the bell at the door of the department. There was no obvious public entrance, but she hadn't really expected one. She waited in the freezing wind. Although she'd realised it would be cold, it was one of those St Andrews days when the sun was bright and tended to fool even old hands: she had decided to walk down from town instead of riding her bike.

During the last bit of the walk from the Guardbridge Road to the new building, she hadn't seen anyone go in or out of the department. It took about five minutes and three rings on the bell before anyone answered the door and Felicity was rather surprised that it proved to be, not the uniformed university janitor she was accustomed to in other buildings, but a large, broad man in a dark suit. He said good afternoon in an American accent and asked how he could help her.

"I've come for a look around," she said, when she had returned his greeting. "Professor Meredith Williams invited me to at his talk on St Andrew's Day. I haven't had time before, but I'd really love to have a look around now!"

The American looked at her as if she were out of her mind and muttered something indecipherable before retreating and closing the door.

Felicity stood outside reflecting on whether he'd told her to piss off or whether he was going to ask someone else if it was all right. A couple of minutes later he returned and opened the door again, looking at her with the faintest of smiles.

"I am told that you can come in," he said. "If you wait here, I'll get someone to show you around." He ushered her into a large, deserted foyer, painted in quiet shades of grey and blue and indicated a matching sofa and chairs, around a blond-wood coffee table.

She took a place on the sofa as the man disappeared through a door. It was about ten minutes later that a different door opened and a young man, with long fair hair in a ponytail, appeared. He was quite tall and very slightly built, wearing an open lab coat over jeans and a green sweater. He pushed his wire-rimmed glasses up to look around the foyer, coming towards her with a friendly hand outstretched to take hers.

"Hi," he said, not in American. "I'm Tubby – Tubby Gateside. 'Cos I'm skinny, you understand!" He laughed and she joined him; she liked him on sight.

"The Prof asked me to give you the tour," he said, "Although I think he was a bit surprised that you'd turned up. He didn't think anyone was that interested."

"Oh, I am," Felicity replied. "I really am interested in what you are doing here. I'm a neuroscientist by trade, and I'm working on genetics and dopamine disruption. I hadn't heard about your work over here. So, I thought, perhaps, we could compare notes?"

Tubby was escorting her through the door he'd entered by, into a curved corridor.

"Yes," he said, "I think you'll find a lot of what we do very interesting. We're working on cures for some genetic diseases – some real nasties. We're getting results too. The Prof's very gifted, you know. And we're very well-funded. He's really good at that side too!"

He walked along the inside wall, letting Felicity take the window side. She noticed, as she walked, that the building was indeed very isolated; nothing but open fields between here and the North Haugh Science Park about a mile away. They arrived at a white-painted door with the name Dr A.V.R. Gateside on a silvered sign.

159

"So, you're a postdoc," said Felicity, "What's your speciality?" Opening his office door and indicating that she should enter, Tubby told her that he had originally been an amphibian geneticist but had become interested in "all the exciting things" which were being thrown up by genetic engineering.

His room was as much of a mess as Felicity's shared one in the Medical School: there were the usual shelves crammed with books and piles of them, along with a lot of magazine articles and other paper, on the floor. His desk had long disappeared under an avalanche, and he would have been hard pressed to access his computer if it hadn't been on a separate computer station.

"Sit," he said. "Let me get you coffee or something. What would you like?"

"I'd prefer *something*," she said, smiling. "I'm not good with coffee, it gives me migraine."

He found a kettle under one of the piles and went about making tea in beakers with the university crest. They sat, looking at one another, across the messy desk.

"I was wondering," said Felicity, "What your main project is over here. Your professor said that it was nothing secret but I'm a bit baffled because of the Department of Defense funding…"

"Oh, that," he made a gesture, pushing the query away. "That's just an example of how clever the Prof is. See, he's got them eating out of his hand but he's sure they don't realise that what we're doing has absolutely no military use. Because they're all thick as a whale omelette, they don't follow. He's a great talker!"

"What are you doing, then?"

"Take a look at these photos," he said, producing a large, crimson leather album from somewhere on the desk and opening it at the first page. Some things fell to the floor. "This'll give you the best intro. Then I'll show you some of the labs. I'm sure you'll be interested; it's cutting-edge stuff!"

Felicity took the big book from him and looked at the five pictures on the first page. They had all been taken in a hot country, showing two or three children in each. It was obvious that there was something badly wrong with the children. Their stature was small, and they were very thin, although it was obvious that they were more disabled than starving. They appeared to have very small heads and huge noses.

"Have you ever heard of microcephalics?" Tubby asked. "Those ones are in Pakistan, near Lahore? They always used to serve the temple, the one on the left in the first photo looks after worshippers' shoes for example. The temple is where barren women pray for a child and if the child is born with microcephaly, she gives it to the temple in the hope that she will have other, normal, children. Some do.

"But it's a clearly related series of genetic faults, obviously, and some families have several children with it. It's often taken to be a judgement of the god – all the mother's children will be microcephalic until she does give one to the temple."

"The cortex doesn't grow, then?" said Felicity, "And they never develop higher cognitive skills?"

"Precisely," said Tubby. "There are supposed to be some of

normal intelligence, although I've never seen one – I tend towards thinking it's wrong. They live a reasonable length of life considering the level of brain damage; a few have even had children of their own. Their IQ is exceptionally low – about thirty on Stanford-Binet. We don't yet fully understand how it is inherited, only that there is a series of six genetic faults which code for it." He was getting into his passion for the work now and had forgotten to drink his tea.

"There used to be a tale about microcephaly being induced rather than inherited. Of course, that was when no one knew too much about genetics. People used to say that some poor people bound children's heads so that their skulls couldn't grow properly and so the condition developed. I've asked myself why parents would do this, but I decided that it's just an example of religious mania… and maybe a way of disposing of excess children! But, of course, it isn't true anyway. If heads were bound tightly enough to stop the skull growing, brain matter would exit through the foramen magnum – and they'd die, obviously."

He was well into his theme now. "No one had ever seemed actually to have known anyone who had their head bound anyway; it was always a friend of a friend of a friend. Anyway… It's genetic, definitely. Overall, it's a neurodevelopmental disorder, characterised by a marked reduction in brain size caused by impaired cell proliferation and death of cortical progenitor cells and their neuronal progeny."

Felicity was turning pages in the album, seeing other children; then realising that many of them were adults of small stature. Some of the later pictures clearly weren't taken in Pakistan.

"You're trying to cure it by genetic manipulation, then?" asked Felicity.

"Of course. And we have had quite some success. It's interesting that we don't have to go to Pakistan to find microcephalics, though. There's a fair representation of the required genetic material in the population which emigrated to Leeds and Bradford in the sixties and seventies.

"Clinicians connected with us see one most months – and they refer them to us. I'm just starting to assess them myself now. I administer a battery of tests and talk to their families. If they fit our criteria, the group carries out the treatment in one of the big general hospitals in Yorkshire."

"And you've managed to make some of them better?"

"Improvement, certainly," he said. "A few have had stem cell therapy and, as their body cells are replaced, the new ones don't have the faulty code. Early days yet – but great potential! We're bound to get it eventually." Felicity was amazed, she had been certain that genetic engineering was some way away from actual cures for the more serious genetic ills. Now, faced with all this, she could hardly process it.

"What's going to happen, though," she asked. "Is the brain going to grow? What will happen when the growing brain reaches the restricted skull? Do you have some way of increasing the volume? Because the bone will have ceased growing years ago…"

"No, hold on a bit! We aren't there yet," said Tubby. "That's just one of the things we're working on. And of course, it doesn't apply if we get hold of the child early enough. We can make the skull grow too. It's very exciting. The Prof's working with mechanical engineering in the States and all sorts of possible solutions are coming up. Look, let me show you some of our equipment."

He rose from the desk and opened the door, standing back to let Felicity out. They walked along the corridor to a lift and went up two storeys. The second floor appeared to be like the ground floor, except that instead of the door to Tubby's room, there was a large internal window and glass door into a sizeable laboratory.

People in white coats were busily working at microscopes and at computer terminals, as well as standing in small groups drinking coffee. Just like any other laboratory Felicity had ever been in. As they entered, several people yelled "Hi!" to Tubby and an older man with thinning grey hair came over to them.

"What ho, Jacky!" said Tubby in a cheerful voice. "How's it hanging, buddy?"

The older man grimaced at the Americanism; Felicity suspected a widespread contempt of the Americans. He reached for a laboratory notebook, the cover having the university crest.

"Going fairly well," he said, in Aberdonian. "I've sequenced the genes for Subject B7.23. Clearly defective in all six." He held out the book for Tubby to initial the last completed page. Tubby produced a gel pen to do it in purple ink.

"I've been telling Miss...?" Felicity provided her name and he added "Felicity Malcolm" before telling the man what she had already been told and asking if he would kindly show her the sequencing.

"John Henry Redman," he said, holding out his hand to shake hers. "I'm Tubby's assistant. Humiliating, isn't it?" They walked towards the genetic sequencer sitting, along with its own computer set-up, on the first bench. Jack waved her onto a traditional lab stool and

164

began demonstrating his baby.

*

"Well, what about magic mushrooms?" asked Minnie. She and Jake were sitting having a nice afternoon tea again, in her cosy sitting-room. "It does put rather a different complexion on it," she said, buttering her third half-scone and reaching for home-made raspberry jam. "Who knows what kind of long-term effects that might have."

"I don't know, though", commented Jake. "It could be a red herring. Just because he took psilocybin, it doesn't necessarily mean he *isn't* having holy visions. We know so little about alternate consciousnesses. I was reading something which wondered about the idea that, if the brain makes selves, it might well make more than one each. And mentioning that dreams are times when we can BE things rather than just pretending. It's really intriguing!"

"I suppose the more-than-one-self idea would account for some things, wouldn't it?

It might be a way of explaining how dissociative identity disorder works." She looked vague for a moment, "But what about the child? That seems to have been different, entirely separate. I was wondering if he was seeing it because he was searching for his own child..." She looked sad about this; appropriately, Jake thought.

"Yes," he replied, "I think that *is* a different thing. He saw something odd at the end of the summer. I think it just happened in proximity to this vision thing – so we tend to consider them together. I don't think the child was a hallucination, though, do you?"

*

165

Reilly was reclining comfortably on the small sofa in his room at St Mary's. Ben Furness sat on a chair opposite. His expression had soon changed from being vaguely pleased to see Reilly to being concerned about why he had been asked to come.

"Well, old friend," said Reilly, "I was wondering if you've had any of those troublesome vision things recently…"

Ben glared at him. He was by no means Ben's "old friend" and he wasn't at all sure that he liked the description of his visions as "troublesome."

"How d'you mean?" he asked, head on one side, like a marriage counsellor.

"Oh, you know," answered Reilly, "You came to me a while ago. Said you'd had a couple of funny experiences. You thought you'd seen a saint or something."

"Yes," said Ben, "And you weren't very interested, thought saints should only appear to excessively holy people, didn't you? Thought Sister Honoria would be more appropriate than me?"

Martin Reilly saw the change in expression on Ben's face and began to feel alarmed. The guy was looking put out, a bit angry, maybe. Reilly hated confrontations, would walk ten miles to avoid one.

"Don't be upset," he said, shuffling in his seat. "I didn't mean to offend you. I just wondered, because you haven't been round recently to see me, whether you'd had any more or… anything".

*

Ben didn't tell Martin Reilly anything he didn't know and was quite pleased about that. He reflected on how much he didn't like Reilly; how much he wished he had never spoken to him about the visions. He chided himself for that but wondered how he could have known better. He was in Tesco, in Market Street, doing some shopping when it happened again.

A checkout operator, a young man, asked him if he was all right: did he want to sit down? A young woman shopper assisted him to a bench with its back to the shop window. She asked a passing supervisor if he could have a glass of water.

Ben is now somewhere else; a park he knew in Liverpool, as a child. It is beauty-fully green, and he can hear a medley of Beatles' songs and traffic horns on Lime Street. The monkish man appears, as before, and gazes at Ben in what the professor feels is a pleading way.

There is no super-cello music now, only John, Paul, George, and Ringo, singing 'She's leaving home', most plaintive of their songs. The man is clearer now, the glass-like barrier looks as if it has been polished. The blood from his right hand is still leaking and dropping to the ground. Now, it has already touched, flowers are growing, exquisite white lilies, surrounded by leaves of the brightest, glowing-est green.

"What?" asks Ben, "How can I help?"

Another voice cuts in as the gleaming green of the leaves expands and takes over, so he can hardly bear it, the vision disappears.

"How can you help with what?" asks the young woman, standing over him with a glass of water.

*

"What do you *really* think about all this?" Ben asked Minnie as they sat in his flat. She had called round to see how his cold was doing. She'd rung the bell as a test of whether he was at least answering the door.

"I really don't know, Ben," she said. "The magic mushrooms do muddy the water a bit."

"I suppose so," he said, snuffling a bit. "There seems no reason why I shouldn't have a flashback, I imagine. Just that they don't seem like I think they would seem if I did. If you follow me."

"Let's have coffee," said Minnie, getting up. "I can do it; I know how the kitchen works. Unless you'd prefer hot lemon or something."

"You know what I'd really like?" said Ben. "A glass of warm milk with some cinnamon in it. My mother used to give us that when we had colds and Free took it up after we got together. It's... very pleasant." Minnie went to the kitchen, getting sugar and cinnamon out of the cupboard.

She had found an elderly box of cinnamon with an opened sachet in it. She sniffed it and thought it was less fragrant than it should be. She opened another sachet and put a couple of spoonsful in Ben's mug, just as his mother would have done. He was savouring his drink in the drawing room when she, putting her tea on the side table, told him she had come across an old reference to peyote in a library manuscript about the proceedings of the Spanish Inquisition.

"Yet another hallucinogen," she said, "Lots of them, aren't there? This said: *'The use of the Herb or Root called Peyote... is a superstitious action and reproved as opposed to the purity and sincerity of our Holy Catholic Faith, being so that this said herb, nor any other cannot possess the virtue and natural efficacy attributed to it for said effects, nor to cause the images, phantasms and representations on which are founded said divinations, and that in these one sees notoriously the suggestion and assistance of the devil, author of this abuse.'* She read from the note she'd made at the collection in the library, 'It's dated 1620, Spanish Inquisitors against heresy, depravity and apostasy in Mexico City."

"Enough to make you want to take it, I should have thought," said Ben with a humph. "It's interesting that all these things relate to religion, isn't it? Do you think all the manifestations of the Virgin and saints were chemically induced; even if they were naturally derived chemicals?"

*

Tubby popped round to Felicity's flat the day after she had visited him in the department. She arrived at the door in her old towelling dressing gown, with her hair up in a towel, straight from the shower.

"If I say you look nice," said a shyly smiling Tubby, "Will you go all tough and feminist on me?"

"I might," she said, laughing. "What can I do for you?" He put his hands behind his back and bowed his head, looking up through his light blonde fringe to say that he wanted to ask her to do him a very special favour.

"Could you possibly come with me to a dance on Thursday?" he asked, "Not a date or anything. Well, unless you want it to be... It's just that I must go, the department has booked a table and my name has come out of the hat; "Gateside and partner" and I don't have one. You don't actually dance, do you?"

Felicity who had danced at every possible opportunity, even pre-ballet class when she was three, said that she did. In fact, she was rather good.

"Well, I'm, er, not," said Tubby, "But I can probably manage to shuffle a bit and there will be loads of men who *can* do it properly. I've been to these things before. I always feel really inadequate!"

Felicity looked at him, standing on her landing, dressed in jeans and a blue sweater, with no coat, despite the cool day, and told him she didn't mind if it was a date.

*

"Do you believe in ghosts?" asked Jake from the depths of his thinking sofa.

"Why, are you thinking it might be an apparition?" replied Ben.

"Something we need to consider. I don't suppose you do?"

"You think I'm so arrogant that I think I know everything about everything?"

"No, of course not. But I thought it was worth asking. Most scientists don't." They were, once again, in the Warden's flat at Montgomerie Hall, where Ben had turned up unannounced and Jake had laid aside his marking to chat. He had begun to feel that he got a lot more from the professor when he chatted rather than when he tried to interrogate.

"I'm not absolutely sure there is nothing," said Ben, "Though it might be a recording… There's something, isn't there, about walls retaining imprints… I've never seen anything like that though." Jake, staring up at the dark blue ceiling of the sitting room, had a sudden thought.

"We could do an experiment," he said.

"Parapsychology?" asked Ben. "Do you know someone?"

"No. I wasn't thinking about that precisely. I was thinking about an illusion I can do. 'Pepper's Ghost', have you heard of it?"

"I haven't. What do you do?"

✦

Ben's Diary entry 8

Talking to lots of people; Jake, Minnie, even sanctimonious old Martin. He was obviously trying to find out what had been going on. I didn't tell him anything; I really don't like him. Minnie is incredible, though. She keeps up with loads of things. I do remember her being quite outspoken when we went to that Art History thing ages ago. She didn't let the lecturer get away with anything! He really wasn't expecting confrontation from the oldies. Serve him right. Conversation with Jake was very interesting, he was proposing an experiment to do with his magic. He didn't tell me much about it as he wants it to be as blind as possible. He wouldn't even tell me what his proposition is – that secret! Och weel… I really must get around to reading that Green Book…

*

The phone rang just as Felicity was finishing her eye make-up with a sprinkle of shimmery silver sparkles. She made a mental note not to forget to give herself a spray of the good perfume she didn't wear for work. She suppressed a groan as she heard Tubby's voice say sorry.

"It's really awful having to say this," he went on hurriedly, "Could you pick me up instead of the other way around? I can't get the old Green Dragon to start. She's had it really. I think I'm going to have to scrape up for a new one." Felicity let out her breath in relief.

"Yes, of course, Dinah's in and she'll always let me borrow her Mini. It's no trouble. You said you live in Hepburn Gardens, didn't you?"

"Forty-eight," he said, "Top flat. You'd better come up because I'm going to have to change – got oil on my shirt. And hands, naturally!"

She arrived at the early Victorian house just shy of the time he was supposed to collect her from North Street. He buzzed her in, and she climbed the stairs feeling a little nervous and excited, appropriate for their first date. Felicity would probably have gone, even if she hadn't been so taken with Tubby, because she loved to dance.

He was at the door of his flat when she reached the first floor, taking her into his arms and kissing her on the mouth – with more pressure than she'd expected. She felt herself returning the kiss with parted lips. He was a great kisser.

As they went into the sitting room, she found herself admiring the dinner jacket which made his shoulders look almost broad, the very nicely starched white dress shirt and the tie, loose around his neck. Against her better judgement, she was quite impressed that he tied his bow tie himself. He offered her a sherry.

"It's rather a nice dry one," he said, "I think sherry is quite sophisticated!" He smiled, a little coyly, in recognition that he was impressed with that thought. She accepted, taking a seat on the sofa, although she didn't like sherry.

He poured and excused himself to put his cuff-links in. Felicity looked around the comfortable flat. It was certainly bigger than her own but not over-furnished. There was something minimalist about it, with white woodwork and magnolia walls. She got up to examine the oil painting over the fireplace and discovered it was an original, an abstract in blues and greens. She had no idea what it was supposed to represent but discovered, on resuming her seat, that she liked it very much. It made her feel quite happy.

Tubby's two three-seater sofas, no chairs, were a sort of sea green leather, with squashy cushions. The whole room was very calming and peaceful. What wasn't peaceful was the noise suddenly coming from another room – a loud bang as if someone had fallen over, crashing into something. She started up and covered the distance to Tubby's bedroom at speed. Opening the door, she saw him standing by a chest of drawers, holding his wrist, the remains of a table-lamp smashed on the floor around him.

"Sorry," he gasped, "Stupid thing fell over and caught me on the arm!"

"Let's look", she said, taking the wrist in both hands. There seemed to be a cut on the back of his hand which was probably bleeding out of all proportion, and the heavy base of the lamp had raised a swelling the size of an egg on the back of his wrist. "Hold it over your head. That'll stop the bleeding then we can have a proper look." She let him go, unwound her silver cobweb shawl, and threw it on the double bed.

Tubby let out an amazed wolf-whistle as he took in her bare shoulders above the crimson silk of the dress with a strongly boned bodice and the shining waterfall of her long hazelnut hair. She wore no jewellery except the pair of silver and diamond drop earrings her parents had bought for her twenty-first birthday. She was taller, courtesy of the four-inch killer heels. She asked him where the bathroom was.

Felicity collected antiseptic, cotton wool and band-aids and, when she returned to dress his hand, he was sitting on the bed, arm still above his head.

"This is throbbing a bit; getting a bit sore," he said. "Can I put my arm down now?" She went to sit beside him, avoiding the broken glass on the carpet. They stayed like that for a while and Felicity became acutely conscious of the warmth of the man next to her, cuddling up for comfort.

He put his near hand, the injured one, on her knee, stroking the crimson silk. It was her very best dancing dress, the one she had bought with the £500 her grandmother had left her, with the insistence she spend it on something absolutely non-practical. It nearly was, a silk dress not being deeply usable, but to Felicity, a wisp to pack into a suitcase and to dance in.

She felt a jolt of electricity as he began to nuzzle her neck and caress her bare shoulder with the other hand. She gasped, her mind flying loose from the thought of how exquisite his touch was.

*

Lower College Hall was all dressed up, not for a Graduation Ball, despite the marquee on the Croquet Lawn, but for grown-ups. The occasion was ostensibly a charitable one, but it had a strong flavour of university politics as well. It was, essentially, a dinner dance. Jake, who had been booked to do a set for actual money, was watching from the contrived wings as the twelve-place tables filled up with men in DJs and ladies in fancy gowns.

The long top table, where the Principal would sit with her guests, was as far away as possible from the stage-block platform, at the other end of the room. In between were several other tables. He recognised a few of the people arriving from science: Organic Chemistry had a whole table, with the three people over spilling onto the next one, where French had set up camp. He recognised one of the lectrices, in black, looking very French: she had once come over to ask for a part-time job in the lab. He hadn't had one to give her.

Suddenly, he spotted someone who looked slightly familiar, on the arm of a man he didn't know. They made a great looking couple; he tall, with a blond ponytail, and smart in his dinner jacket, she smaller, with wonderful shiny clean hair and a triumph of a red dress. He was still trying to place her as they took their seats amongst the microbiologists and geneticists. The young man held her chair for her to sit before settling himself across from her and ordering their drinks from the passing waitress.

It was at least half an hour later, when the tables had filled, that Jake recognised Felicity. Her hair, usually scraped back on her head and often under a laboratory cap to reduce the chances of contaminating samples, was loose and flowed down her back.

She seemed somehow taller. He couldn't see her legs because

the dress was long, almost to the floor - although there appeared to be a split up one side, the edges braided with fine silver lines. The dress itself was a fabulous colour in contrast to her brown hair. Her shoulders were bare, when she had removed the finest of silver shawls, the skin creamy and succulent. She looked elegant and, instead of the usual scrubbed look, she was beautifully made-up, with something sparkly on her face and hair. Jake took a deep breath. The only word he could think of was "Wow!"

He looked around the room as the starter was being served. His own, truncated, meal was already on a tray behind the makeshift curtains - a miniscule portion of smoked salmon with salady things and spelt bread, crowned with a larger dollop of horseradish cream; more salad arranged around an individual Beef Wellington (salad because the vegetables would have been cold); a complicated, moulded pudding, consisting of a version of crème caramel and chocolate mousse, prettily decorated with whipped cream rosettes. As usual, before a show, the condition of his stomach precluded his eating any of it.

At the table, among the microbiologists and geneticists, Felicity was not especially enjoying herself. As rather a good cook, she considered the meal negligible; she had come to dance and just wanted the feeding part to be over, the speeches done, and the dance floor cleared.

She had talked to Tubby in the car, and he had warily agreed to attempt the waltz. She was keen to persuade the band to play for an Argentine Tango – her favourite dance – but she would really have to find a partner who knew what he was doing. Tubby declared a definite amateur status on this. No chance, he'd have a beer instead. She looked across the table at him and, not for the first time, admired his shoulders under the dinner jacket. Their time in the bedroom had been brilliant and she saw him blush slightly as he saw her gazing at him.

"Do you know Professor Furness, Felicity?" he asked, indicating the grey-haired academic next to him, "He's in Microbiology".

Felicity hadn't met him, but she quickly found out that he liked her dress and, fantastically, knew how to do the Argentine Tango.

"Used to cut quite a dash at one time," he said. "My late wife made me go to lessons because she could dance, and I couldn't. Surprisingly, I liked it – especially the Latin. I can manage a pretty good Cha-Cha too!"

"So, write me down for both of those," said Felicity, laughing. "I didn't think I had a chance of finding a partner – and my boyfriend..." she looked at Tubby under lowered lashes as she said the word, "Insists that he can hardly dance."

The professor laughed and commented on the younger generation not knowing how to sweep a girl off her feet. Felicity, who knew that Tubby was extremely good at that, returned his laughter.

*

The Principal and her entourage arrived and took their places at the long table. Felicity gazed at her in disbelief. The few times she had caught a glimpse of Principal Fleming, on her occasional passes through the department, or in the street, she had been wearing elegant black, with discreet gold earrings and modestly heeled black court shoes. Tonight? Well, tonight was certainly different.

Professor Fleming had assumed a full-skirted, antique gold satin frock, with an unfortunate large, floppy bow on one shoulder. It was a huge error. Her fair hair was pinned up but was rather too short, bits were constantly escaping, and the effect was wind-tunnel already.

Felicity wondered where she had managed to find those high-heeled sandals in the exact, ghastly, shade of dirty gold. The only good thing about the Principal's outfit was a husband, draped over her arm. Mark Fleming was wearing a traditional dinner jacket with black cummerbund, wing collar and black tie; his short, very curly, dark hair, close to his head, his dark eyes twinkling with interest.

Most of the rest of the Principal's party were academics from Brazil and Argentina, with whom the university was negotiating a doctoral student exchange. That was the subject of the short speech, given by Principal Fleming; welcoming Professors Gutierrez and DaSilva and their parties to St Andrews and apologising for the weather. She went straight from wishing everyone a lovely time to a one-to-one serious conversation with a South American in a powder blue tuxedo, while Mark sloped off to the bar.

When Jake's set was over and he had reappeared from the back of the room, he returned to the wings and watched Felicity and her partner, as well as Ben Furness, dance. Her own partner, whoever he was, was clearly not a very good dancer. He managed a shuffling waltz and a rather peculiar foxtrot, in both of which he stood on Felicity's toes a lot – Jake could see her wince.

Felicity was a beautiful dancer. Jake, no dancer himself, didn't really know what he was looking at, but he could see she had real grace of movement and was stunned when he spotted that she was wearing incredibly high heels. That, of course, was why she was taller. What a fool I am, he thought.

When she took to the floor hand in hand with Professor Furness, it was a whole different thing. The band had been persuaded to play *Jealousy*, a Frankie Laine song that Jake remembered from the old pile of 78 rpm records that his mother had had at home. As their legs intertwined in the complex moves of the dance, he began to feel the emotion; and when it had finished, he realised that he had forgotten to breathe. Well, there you have it, he thought. Felicity after all.

*

Felicity met Ben again, after they had danced half the night at the Principal's event, when they both turned up in the Ready Meals section of Tesco in Market Street on the following Saturday morning. She had really taken to the Professor: he was a pleasant companion as well as a good dancer. Felicity was feeling strange because she still thought someone was following her. She wondered if Prof Furness would walk her home and help decide if she was paranoid.

"I'm not really that keen on these things," said Ben, putting a chicken curry and a beef casserole in his wire basket, "But they are easier than making everything from scratch, just for one, when you're busy."

Felicity, who thought all ready-meals were reprehensible and was buying sausages and mash on her flatmate's instructions, tentatively agreed, and asked if he had a lot of shopping to do.

"No," said the professor, "Just these and some milk. Then home and get some work done."

"Do you mind if I walk with you?" asked Felicity. "We had such a nice time on Thursday night... I wondered if we might have a wee chat."

They walked along Market Street, talking about how much they had enjoyed the dinner dance, and when might there be another? As they approached the top of Church Street, where Ben could have been expected to cut through towards his own flat, Felicity, flushing pink, asked him if he could walk her home. Ben looked at her in astonishment for a moment before his upbringing said that of course he would.

Felicity had the feeling that he wouldn't even ask for an explanation, but she gave him one anyway, as they continued along Market Street and cut through into North Street.

"I just get the feeling that someone is following me," she said, achieving a deeper shade of pink. "I know it's paranoid, but I could swear there's someone. But when I turn around, even if I do it super-quickly, there's never anyone there!"

"Do you feel in danger?" he asked in a low voice, "That they want to do you harm?" Felicity looked thoughtful.

"I'm not sure. I think they're just watching me for now. But I have no idea why." They arrived at Felicity's front door, and she invited him for coffee. Their conversation turned serious very quickly, with Ben delivering himself of the opinion that something very fishy was going on in the town.

"There seem to have been a lot of very large Americans ever since last summer, and they seem to be all over the place. We've always had a fair number here, the university encourages them – because they pay high fees – but they're usually quite young, seasoned with the occasional older postgraduate. These are different; they aren't students at all. I have been wondering what they're all about for some time…"

Felicity looked down at the surface of the small dining table at which they were sitting, tracing a scratch in the wood with her index finger.

"I think I know where they're coming from," she said. "They're security staff from the Genetic Engineering Laboratory out past the North Haugh, by the Guardbridge Road."

Ben looked at her in surprise, saying that he wasn't aware that there *was* a Genetic Engineering Laboratory in St Andrews.

"Oh, yes," she said. "Professor Meredith Williams and his team, they're doing some remarkable experiments in researching cures for Parkinson's and Alzheimer's and MS, and that microcephaly thing they have in Pakistan. My boyfriend, Tubby Gateside, is doing some really interesting work." She reverted to a previous version of pale pink as she said, 'my boyfriend'.

"Microcephaly?" said Ben. "Small brain? What does that look like, do you know?"

As he said this, he appeared to become a bit anxious; his hands wringing, until he noticed it and carefully placed both, unmoving, on the tabletop.

"Yes," she replied, "Very small head, looks like a very large nose. Their intelligence is very low, obviously. But Tubby's trying to cure them by manipulating the six genes which control it. They've had some great results too; I don't think any cures yet but getting there. They do the treatments in Bradford and Leeds. Apparently, there are subjects there because of Pakistani immigration." Ben was looking a little distracted as he listened to her. He said:

"I wonder if that's what I saw last autumn? I thought she was a child at the time but perhaps she wasn't. These subjects sound rather like the person I saw… I was very concerned at her being out all on her own. She wasn't properly dressed, and she was injured and very frightened. She hit me and ran off… Could it be that she had somehow got out of whatever accommodation they have over there on her own? I was very upset: she wasn't well cared for."

"I suppose one of the microcephalics could have got out by mistake," she said,   "But I'm sure that Tubby would have made sure she was properly looked after. He's very kind. I know defence research has a pretty bad history, I don't exactly trust that Professor Williams, but there are ethics committees. University research must be reasonably ethical, legal, and above board… Mustn't it?"

"Do you really think so?"

*

The newspapers were having another go at Ben and the St Andrews scandal. Jake had asked Felicity to meet him at Minnie Latimer's house; he would bring the newspapers with him. Minnie had told him about what had happened on St Andrews Day, and that Felicity was concerned about the Genetic Engineering Laboratory.

Felicity confirmed that she was, and that she had now been down to have a look at what was happening. She asked if it would be all right if she brought her boyfriend, who worked there.

"Oh, er, perhaps not this time," said Jake, "I'd like to keep it to just a few people at present. We don't necessarily want to spread it around the whole university!"

"I'm sure he wouldn't," said Felicity, taken aback by Jake's unexpected denial, "I was thinking he could give us the word, kind of from the horse's mouth…"

"Maybe later," said Jake, "Although I really want to discuss it properly with you. Dr Latimer said that you dumfounded Professor Williams when you asked an awkward question?"

"I think I did rather," said Felicity, "But I didn't get anything like a proper answer!"

"You didn't think you would, did you?"

*

Max Denfrell was wandering around the laboratories alone in the middle of the night. He was switching the low lighting on and off selectively as he walked through the various rooms. He had decided he should have a proper look round on his own, without any florid academic explaining getting in his way.

He had started on Dormitory Corridor A, in the sub-basement, where there were only nine occupants. He was required, anyway, to have one of his staff make sure each subject was its allocated room, before the building was locked down for the night. Tonight, he had said he would do it himself. No one thought there was anything odd about this because Denfrell had quickly become known as a manager who could undertake any job his staff had to do and willing, when necessary, to do it himself.

As he looked through the reinforced glass in the first door, he saw the subject was not in bed but sitting on the floor with its back to the wall. It was incredibly still. He watched it for a minute, and it didn't move. The next subject, adjoining, was in bed and had thrown the covers off; it was very restless.

The one after that seemed to be asleep, wrapped in blankets, as did the following two. Two subjects shared the next room, and one was standing up against the far wall, whilst the other was sitting on the bed crying. Denfrell could not hear its cries through the soundproofing, but the sight of it was obvious.

The last two rooms contained one more each. One was sitting at the child-sized desk, in the dark, but the other was immediately behind the glass when Denfrell opened the blind. Its flaming eyes and grimacing mouth, thrust as flat as possible against the window, induced Denfrell to take a step backwards. It appeared very aggressive.

The large room in the rest of the sub-basement was called the "Animal House" but, officially, it was "The Nursery": the place where the subjects lived until they were sufficiently grown to occupy a place in the upper Dormitory Corridor, referred to as "B". It was under the supervision of veterinary nurse, Margaret Thomas, who was a Nurse Ratched sort of character, with large muscles and a confrontational manner. Of course, she did not work nights, so the nursery was under the supervision of an Australian nursing postgraduate student with First Aid qualifications – in case the younger subjects injured themselves during the night.

The first thing Denfrell noticed was the smell of urine and he noted that it was reasonably fresh rather than stale; he was aware of the difference, and that it meant a certain degree of cleanliness was maintained. The room was quite dark; just a soft glow from a desk lamp illuminating the far end of the room where Lauren Brooks was studying.

Snores and the assorted low cries of sleeping children could be heard from the half dozen cots and small camp beds, but the atmosphere was generally quiet and calm.

Lauren looked up from her books and said "hello" quietly. Denfrell motioned to her to come outside. When she arrived, the door sliding closed softly behind her, she looked questioningly at Denfrell.

"Is this all right, do you think?" he asked her, moderating his tone confidentially. "What they're doing here? What do you think?" She regarded him in surprise.

"I just do what I'm told," she said.

*

"Good grief!" said Minnie in an exasperated manner, when she had cast her eyes over the newspapers Jake had brought.

They were spread out on her coffee table and were making Felicity's eyes bug out with amazement.

Alien Abductee Professor Admits

Taking Magic Mushrooms!

St Andrews Scientist is Hopeless Druggie!

I was too Stoned to tell if Vision was real –

says St Andrews Professor!

"This is appalling," said Jake, "Although I don't suppose you can blame them, in a way..."

"Yes, I can," said Minnie, too offended to pour the tea, "I do blame them. How come they always turn it around and blame the victim? Poor Ben! He must be feeling horrible if he's seen these. And he always used to go for his paper early."

"He must have told a journalist about taking drugs, though, mustn't he?" said Felicity, "Or did they just make it up?"

Minnie and Jake looked at one another and both started to answer at once.

"Sorry," said Jake, "You tell her, Minnie, you've known him the longest."

"Thanks. Yes, he did tell the reporter who came to his house – about his visions and about the mushrooms – because of being a mycologist, you know. He was quite innocent when he took them; as well as when he told the journalist. And you know how good teachers tend to give you more information than you wanted...and Ben's always been a superlative teacher."

"I really have no idea how to handle this," said Jake, "Although I hope it's a bit of a nine-day wonder. If no one feeds it, it'll die of its own accord."

"Someone has to be feeding it, now, though," said Minnie, "Martin Reilly, d'you think?"

"What? Trying to get the right story in before the newspapers find out naturally?" said Jake, "With what motive?"

"What Martin thinks is the right story," corrects Minnie, "He could be protecting his own position – as the Dean of Divinity, who, perhaps, needs to separate 'respectable' religion from the craziness of a strange academic, protecting the University's reputation? Or maybe doing something else. Doing as he's told? The folks down at G.E. perhaps want him to weigh-in, because they know what he's likely to think and say – that there's nothing at all interesting to anyone who isn't into Conspiracy Theory; Ben's just a bit daft..."

"Can we connect it with what's going on in Genetic Engineering?" asked Felicity, "It's quite a coincidence that they are happening at the same time, don't you think?"

All three of them became silent, as they thought about that. It did require jumping to a conclusion, but they were aware that science frequently proceeds by jumps of intuition as well as dogged experimental work.

"Yes," said Minnie, "I think it just might be. Tell us about your trip down to GE, Felicity. It might give us some ideas."

*

Pepper's Ghost is an illusion which needs a lot of preparation and Jake was pleased to have Naomi along to help. She was quite wee and didn't look very strong, but she was. She could lift and move things which many men couldn't. This was Jake's appearance in Kirkcaldy, not too far from St Andrews. The illusion was complex enough and hard enough to set up that he hadn't especially wanted to do it just for Ben Furness. The best idea was to bring Ben in to see his act. Not, though, to see the preparation.

Jake had told Ben that it was a well-known illusion and asked him not to research it. When Ben had given his word, Jake was convinced he would keep it.

Although he wasn't convinced that Ben's vision was an optical illusion or a cynical attempt to fool him, he thought it was worth ruling both out.

✦

Ben's Diary entry 9

Well. Last night was great fun! Wee Naomi drove me to Kirkcaldy; I wasn't allowed to go in Jake's van because of the trick. He called it an "effect". He's very good. I've never taken to magic, but what he does is quite different from anything I've seen before. Not a playing card in sight. And the Ghost thing was marvellous. He told me how it works when we got back to mine. It's to do with reflections and mirrors of course, although it didn't look like it. The lights were very low of course and that helped. I could see that, if you really wanted it to be a proof of life after death or the existence of spirits or some such nonsense, you might believe in it. In its heyday anyway; back in Victorian times. I suppose I knew it was a trick, an effect, because ruling out the possibility of an illusion was the purpose of showing me the experiment, but I don't see how anyone without a pronounced bias could think it was real. I didn't anyway.

*

"Yes," said Joanne Critchley, standing at Ben Furness' front door, "I am a journalist, but I really haven't come to torment you about all that stuff that was in the papers. You have, very sensibly, not commented, and it will die down shortly. Don't forget that newspaper is ephemeral. Fish and chips tomorrow!"

Ben, who had opened the flat door hoping to see a friend, hopefully Minnie, was both disappointed and fascinated. The young woman was smartly dressed in a wine-coloured suit, with a lavender and navy striped shirt and a shoulder bag. Her hair was short and white, rather older than her years, he thought. She had superior cheekbones.

"What do you want, then?" he asked, moving the door slightly more towards closed.

"Just to talk a bit," she said. She lowered her voice dramatically, "Someone has been trying to make me drop it. I'd like to know why."

Ben opened the door, intrigued. The journalist entered the flat and took a seat on the light green sofa. She began by apologising on behalf of the press. She said some of them were a disgrace. She said she wanted to talk about why anyone would want to shut her up. Ben had no idea and said so.

"Not that I'd mind it all going away," he said. "It's just getting silly. I have no idea what's going on. Except I know it's not an illusion now; I know it's not a dream; I don't think it's an hallucination... Although it might be, I daresay – something to do with mild dementia."

"Have you been diagnosed with dementia, Professor?" she asked in a sympathetic voice. Ben explained that he wasn't sure. That his doctor had said that, if it was Alzheimer's Disease, it was only in the very early stages. Would he be hallucinating like this if it was that early? And his memory wasn't, really, all that bad. And a brain tumour had been ruled out by an MRI scan.

When she asked, he described the vision and said that it was always the same, although it had the funny feeling, when it was happening, that it was always new – he never perceived anything in it as being the same again. It was never boring. He stopped talking for a moment.

"You know," he said, "I think it does change. A wee bit anyway. The last time I had it, there were flowers and things which hadn't been there before. And each time, it's been clearer. I thought of that when Jake showed me an illusion last night."

"Have you wondered, Professor," she asked, "Why you should have been selected to have a 'holy vision' if, indeed, that is what it is?"

"Yes, all the time," said Ben. "I talked about that with the Dean of Divinity. He thought it unlikely. He thought there were actual holy people who would have been better suited…I don't even think that talking about being 'selected' is relevant!" Joanne looked thoughtful.

"Who said that about holy people?" she asked, "Martin Reilly? Yes, I imagine he would say something like that." Ben asked if she knew him, and she said she did.

"I'm the Religious Affairs editor," she said. "I know them all." She asked him if he thought there was anything about his experience that anyone could possibly want to keep secret. She asked rather diffidently, as if she couldn't think of anything and didn't expect him to either.

"Don't think so," replied Ben. "There are some funny things going on – but nothing to do with this."

"Funny things?"

"That child I saw. At the end of the summer. That's not a holy vision, just a peculiar thing."

"Child?"

Ben picked up his coffee and had a big drink.

"Um. Yes. It was at the end of the summer vacation. I was out walking, during the night. Couldn't sleep. Been insomniac since my daughter... and my wife... I saw her, she was sleeping under a hedge; she looked strange.

"She punched me in the stomach. I went to the Police Station to see if anyone had reported her missing. The sergeant seemed to think I'd made her up. But I'm pretty sure I hadn't. Haven't seen her since, though, even though I've wandered fairly far and wide."

When Joanne asked, he described the look of the child and she made notes. Then she asked him about his daughter and his wife. He had started to look a little upset; angry almost.

"Oh, well, my wife, Frederica, I called her Free, she died a while ago. Cancer I think; it always is, isn't it, when people die young? She was a local GP, although she sometimes thought she would have liked to be a psychiatrist. She decided to work part-time so she could take care of Wisp. She was two months premature and very small. We had her just about a year after we were married."

All this was recited very quickly as if he wanted to get it over.

"Where is – what did you call her? – Wisp, now?"

"Oh, sorry," said Ben, the upset evaporating, "Her real name is Lucy Elizabeth, but I said she was just a wee wisp when she was born.

And it stuck. Like these things do."

He hesitated and stared at his empty coffee cup. Joanne realised both cups were empty and offered to make more drinks. The professor just nodded mutely, gesturing, vaguely, towards the kitchen door. Over their second pot of coffee, Joanne reminded Ben that he was telling her about his daughter.

"Of course," he said, a little reluctantly. "I don't know where she is. No one does. She disappeared when she was quite young, I think. The police thought she'd gone away because she might have been unhappy at home. She wasn't, though. Free and I loved her very much: I don't know what we'd have done without her.

"I wrote to one of those charities again the other day; you know, the ones that find runaways – even though I don't think she was one – maybe I'll hear something good soon. I've made a nuisance of myself with the Salvation Army too. Especially since Free went. It seemed even more important. You know. There's never been a sign of her.

"The police gave me some figures, so did the Sally Ann, so many kids run away, they don't have a chance of finding more than a few of them... Someone said that we should consider what they are running away from rather than what they are running towards. I said Wisp couldn't have been running from us. We were so happy..."

"I'm wondering about the child you saw," said Joanne. "What do you think that was all about?"

"I haven't the least idea," he replied, "But I am a bit bothered about it. It made me feel... well... a wee bit unsettled. No one else seems to have seen her; and she's disappeared. I suppose it concerns me because of Wisp disappearing into thin air: I think of her, naturally."

"You don't think this wee girl is Wisp, though, do you?"

Ben looked at her as if she were round the bend.

"Of course not. Don't be silly, young woman. I just meant that there is a similarity because of all signs of each of them being lost. They aren't connected at all. The proximity of the visions to my sighting of the wee girl is just a coincidence: we shouldn't mix them up."

As Joanne walked down the stairs from Ben's flat, she reflected on what he had said. He had spoken the truth, she felt, we shouldn't mix up visions and physical sightings; we shouldn't automatically discount someone telling the truth because he might have early Alzheimer's Disease.

✦

Ben's diary entry 10

That new journalist was very nice. I didn't know if I should let her in – the other one, the man, he was quite nice too, but he was treacherous. The things he wrote! He not only made me look like a senile old codger, but he also made me look like a loony. And the others were worse, writing in the papers! This woman, though, she just asked me what I knew, without expecting me to make some great pronouncement about it. Then we had a nice chat. She asked me about Wisp, though, and about Free. Not many people do these days, although they used to. Time's supposed to heal, isn't it? Doesn't.

*

Back at her Edinburgh Religious Affairs desk, Joanne Critchley went online with the National Registry of Births, Marriages and Deaths, to obtain the birthdate of Lucy Elizabeth Furness. She had asked Ben, but he had fudged his answer, just telling her the child had been born at the Liverpool School of Tropical Medicine. Joanne thought this unlikely. There was clearly a limit to how much he would talk about his runaway daughter.

It was not that Joanne thought she could locate Wisp when the police and the Salvation Army had failed (and there didn't appear to be any sign of foul play, as the grieving father seemed to accept); she doubted that anyone could now, but she did smell a strong human-interest story involving faith and hope as well as charity. And she was just the girl to write it. Maybe it could even be a book. Um.

She found Lucy Elizabeth Furness' date of birth almost immediately. And her date of death, two days later, at the Liverpool Maternity Hospital.

*

Felicity submitted her PhD thesis halfway through Candlemas Term. Her viva would be scheduled for the beginning of Whitsunday Term. She would graduate, all being as expected, in June. As the term ground to an end, she had very little to do apart from the minimal amount of work Jake could give her in the department. She decided to go home to Yorkshire for a couple of days.

Tubby had told her that the treatment for the microcephalics from families in Leeds and Bradford took place in one of the big hospitals and she had decided to go and visit, see the brilliant new treatment for herself. It would be good to see the other end of the project

– perhaps talk to clinicians there. She'd thought, at first, that Tubby might go with her, but he was so busy that they hadn't been on a date for a month. Although some of that could be his disinclination to get in the way of her finishing her thesis; he was very appreciative of the work she was doing.

On Monday morning, Felicity took the King's Cross train from Leuchars Station, changed at York for Bradford, and walked to the hospital. They had never heard of the microcephalic project, she wasn't entirely sure they'd heard of St Andrews.

*

"They didn't know anything about it," said Felicity when she was seated in Minnie Latimer's sitting room. Minnie had made tea and there were scones newly baked. If she hadn't been so upset, Felicity would have been thinking what a wonder-woman Minnie was.

"You're sure?" asked Minnie, although she knew Felicity would be unlikely to have gone to the wrong place or asked the wrong people.

"Yes," the younger woman said, "And I telephoned all the other big hospitals, and the universities, and no one had heard of it. It simply isn't true!" She burst into tears and Minnie went to get a box of tissues.

"Oh, love," said Minnie, "I know it must be dreadful to have found out something like that. Just cry as long as you want."

She sat down on the sofa by Felicity's side and put a comforting arm around her. Eventually, Felicity's tears subsided, and she started to express her upset.

"I can only think of one reason why he lied to me," she said, "Because it's all a big con trick and they aren't doing anything to help anybody. They're doing it for some other reason." She stopped for a moment and then started to think of what, exactly, that reason could be.

*

Jake hadn't heard from Kermit or Zonanisky or Baker or Dobinsky for three weeks and he was beginning to feel a bit weird. He had looked the firm up on the Internet and it all looked fine. They were a large medical services company, with an apparently thriving insurance division, and a huge, newly built headquarters in Spokane, Washington State.

The Board of Directors consisted of several people Jake hadn't heard of, although that wasn't surprising. Zonanisky was listed at President and Kermit as Vice-President, Resources. They were a private company, did not seem to be quoted on the stock exchange. This rang a bell in his head because it tended to make nonsense out of the idea of stock options. Maybe they were going to go public and expected a big demand?

Jake took the time to use the cell-phone number he had to contact Kermit Whittaker and Kermit answered on the first ring, assuring him that everything was fine, and he would be hearing from them shortly.

Jake, not terribly comforted, said that was OK.

*

When Easter comes in term-time, there are several events in the Wee Grey City, mostly happening, like May Morning, at around the crack of dawn. There is an Ecumenical Service in the grounds of the ruined cathedral on Easter Sunday, there is a Maundy Thursday feet-washing service ahead of it. The whole thing feels a bit odd, but Ben goes because he is still trying to pursue a religious solution. It still does not to want to be caught. He is left, once again, not knowing what he should be doing. Then, in the chapel, he has a vision.

*

Ben hung about after the rest of the chapel goers have left because, although the Chaplain had made it clear that, on this occasion, it is traditional for everyone to leave St. Leonard's Chapel without the usual blessing.

It feels odd to leave without anyone telling him to do so and he is slightly bewildered. Although the candle-lights are still lit and the organist is still banging about up in the organ loft, Ben is essentially alone as he walks towards the ancient wooden door. What he thinks of as the anteroom to the chapel is just as cold as the chapel itself, but he begins to feel warm immediately the colours appear and start to whirl around.

There is a feeling of solemn age about this building, parts of which are probably from the Twelfth Century. Ben does not feel heavy, he feels light as the music begins – it is nothing like what the organist had been playing.

He is still inside the ancient building but is also outside in the country. He doesn't look up to see the sky but knows it is there. He is in a forest glade with beautiful trees all around. The trees are delicate, pale-leaved, and silvery. He recognises them as *Sorbus aria*, whitebeam, in spring because he has one in his garden.

The monk appears in the centre of his field of vision, but he is closer to Ben this time, only a few feet away. Ben realises, for the first time, that they have been moving closer to one another, as well as the scene becoming clearer, each time he has seen the vision. He had not noticed the robin sitting on the shoulder of the rough brown habit previously – but it looks like it has been there all the time.

Somehow, he hears birdsong above the music, and there are birds around the figure; he sees chaffinches and sparrows and a single Sparrow Hawk, watching, on a tree branch.

The saint is feeding birds from his hand, which continues to bleed and drop on the flowers in the grass. He looks towards Ben, his tormented face pleading for the scientist to hear him – even though he is saying nothing.

Then it's over and Ben, who has dropped onto a wooden chair in the anteroom, knows he is where he was before, and nothing solved.

*

Ben lives quite close to St Leonard's Chapel, which is behind the private girls' school in South Street, but after the vision, he has walked the other way, through the East Port, down to the harbour and the East Sands. It's still a bit chilly for people to bathe here and the pleasant beach is deserted.

The West Sands consists of a very long and relatively narrow space of pale sand, with dunes at the back, towards the Old Course of the Royal and Ancient. It catches the wind blowing up the Eden Estuary and can be very wild. The East Sands is as different as could be, a beach-shaped beach, with golden sand and a headland, featuring caravans for holidaymakers, marking its far edge. The sea seems calmer here.

Ben looks down at the good brogues he put on for church and decides to broach the sand anyway. He'll walk over to the rocky cliff at the far end of the beach and back, then take the path back up through the minimal ruins of St Mary's Abbey, past the Castle where Cardinal Beaton and his mistress watched the populace burn the protestant martyr George Wishart, and so back home. He decides he'll leave his sandy shoes downstairs in the hall until they are dry.

He's almost halfway across the sands when he feels the need to sit down and rest. He's a bit breathless, his mildly arthritic legs are aching because of the instability of the surface on which he's walking. He looks around, unsuccessfully, for something to rest his bottom on. He starts walking faster, more breathlessly, towards the cliff face and sees a rock in the sand upon which he can sit. He perches on it thankfully, wondering what the birds in the vision, are all about. He thinks of Disney films, momentarily, but it was nothing like that.

He realises straightaway that this vision is different; not only in happening so soon after the last one but is different in content. He never felt he was watching these, like a film or television programme; he's in them, fully engaged.

The golden light seems to illuminate the whole beach, replacing the darkening beachscape with a beautiful clarity. The smell of bacon has changed to reflect the gorgeous smell of being cooked on a picnic stove in the hunger-inducing open air. The music is sonorous but uplifting; nothing like he's ever heard before.

The monkish man appears in the middle but, this time, it is different. This time, he is holding the hand of a small woman, with a large nose and a very small head. She holds up one of her hands and it is actively bleeding bright red blood. Ben has only time to realise what he is seeing when it all dissolves into rainbows and movement: then it is gone. Ben screams in anguish.

*

"I went to the General Hospital in Bradford," said Felicity, confronting Tubby in his lair, "But they said they didn't know anything about the microcephaly project!"

Tubby looked as if he had been slapped.

"Oh, bugger!" he said, "I wish you'd told me you were going. I would have rung to prepare them. I could have given you the passwords and things. Then they would have let you in to the Centre."

"You mean it was there really, it was just secure – secret?"

"Of course," he said, "Despite what Prof Williams says about everything being open and above board, it's actually a very sensitive project. It's the Americans who insist on that but, even so, we'd have to keep under the radar because of all the do-gooders!"

"Do-gooders?" she asked, "Like me?"

Tubby breathed a deep sigh of frustration and said no, not like her.

"You've seen the publicity about some of the animal labs at Oxford – and other places for that matter – where activists target scientists in their homes, as well as labs, and terrify their kids. Some of them go even further and let experimental animals go. They don't care that they could infect people with some horrendous disease, and the animals will probably die in the countryside because they're lab-bred and can't possibly survive on their own in the wild. There have even been bombs set in laboratories, some have even gone off!

"You're a sensible scientist," he said, "You know that we all have to do some things we don't care for. You must sacrifice mice and lab rats in your work, don't you? You know that we need to find out and we usually can't experiment on humans!"

Felicity looked subdued and found something to interest her in looking at her feet.

"I accept," she said, "That it's pretty stupid to use mouse models just because society says it's not permissible to use apes – they're too intelligent – and I don't particularly want to use apes either. But I do know that mouse models are analogous to humans in very few ways; they don't even have a big enough brain for most neuro-work!"

"Exactly!" said Tubby, "Anyway, that's why we have to be careful about security. Oh, I do wish you'd said you were going. Never mind. Next time."

Felicity, not usually the type, was feeling meek standing in front of Tubby.

"The other thing," he said, putting his arm around her shoulders, "Is that some of our patients can be quite unpredictable. They don't have the cerebral equipment to provide conscience or moral limitations. They can be quite violent." He stopped and then decided to say something else, "And I'd never forgive myself if anything happened to you. I just couldn't bear it!"

He turned her around, took her in his arms and kissed her. This made her feel a lot better.

PART THREE

WHITSUNDAY TERM

It was very quiet in the drawing-room; the windows were closed against the traffic noise and there was no sound of other people or music or life. The only smell was the light one of the lavender furniture polish Mavis used on her two weekly visits to keep the house reasonably tidy.

Outside the windows, looking over the street, the evening was cooling after a day hot for the time of year. There was a pleasant cosmopolitan feel about the town – a few of the coffee shops had even put out chairs and tables on the pavement. There were still a few people sitting drinking coffee or eating ice cream.

He was there, in the room, feeling the spaciousness of it, the clean but not too sparse style of it. He sat in his favourite chair, with his feet on the matching pale green footstool and a part-filled whisky glass on the table beside him. He was very warm and sleepy; he'd had a hard day. He was always rather sorry that the spring warmth precluded the lighting of a fire: Free used to say, often, that an open fire was the soul of a room. He drifted off.

She was standing there; he could see her in the reflection in the long glass doors dividing the drawing-room from the hall. Not very tall, her auburn hair was usually considered her best feature. He'd always loved her translucent skin adorned, he felt, with many freckles. He remembered her at twenty-one; the most beautiful girl he'd ever seen. She was bright, too, a medical student, later a doctor.

She walked across the room; not like a ghost, like the woman she was, her rather short legs stretching to cover the distance. She smiled down at him where he sat in his chair.

"Benedict," she breathed. She was the only person other than his late mother who had ever called him that: most people assumed Ben was short for Benjamin.

In the way of dreams, they were suddenly outside, walking arm in arm through the countryside. It was high summer, and they were on holiday - nothing to do, just being at leisure and together. She said something which he didn't catch; he turned towards her, puzzlement on his face. And then she wasn't there any longer.

He wanted to scream, Don't Go! But he couldn't speak, couldn't think of the words. Not a trace of her. And he was back in his green chair in their drawing room, and he was alone. No, he thought in the dream, she isn't there. She died. A cold, hard pain took hold of his stomach and twisted it. Free was dead. She wasn't standing by the drawing-room door. Truly, the scene did have the feeling of a dream.

Ben's Diary entry 11

OK. That was a dream, the visions were hallucinations, maybe, but the child I saw that time, in the autumn, the one in the shift with its peculiar face and legs... that was real. It didn't feel any more real than the visions, although more real than the dream. I know that was a dream; I've had it many times. I realized that the wee girl was real during my chat with that young female journalist, what was her name? – I can't doubt it at all now. But where did she come from and, most of all, where did she go?

*

Felicity Malcolm, as well as being a neuroscientist and ballroom dancer, was a born-again baker of cakes. She hadn't learned from her scatty mother. Violet Malcolm was a children's social worker as well as a farmer's wife, busy enough to almost neglect her own three children. Although the siblings had often cooked for themselves, in danger from the stove, they had never indulged in baking things.

It was only when Felicity, the eldest, had swanned off to Manchester University that she had happened to see a television baking show and become an avid convert. She was the only person not on television who made her own Danish pastries from scratch. Those and her Lancashire grandmother's genuine Eccles Cakes were her party pieces.

Today, however, she had got hold of what looked like an excellent recipe for American Chocolate Four Nut Brownies from the Internet. She was baking them for Tubby, a declared chocoholic, and the other scientists in the Genetic Engineering lab. She was sure they would enjoy them. It was a nice, comfortingly domestic thing to do. She had developed important personal feelings for Tubby over the last few months.

He frequently worked late, and skeleton night shift was always on at 7 o'clock.

Going at that time meant she could avoid seeing the abysmal Meredith Williams. The eight brownies would just go around. She had meant to mention to Tubby that she had probably gone to the wrong hospital on her trip to Bradford, but something stopped her from doing it.

*

"Tubby says that there's another laboratory in Genetic Engineering," said Felicity, meeting Minnie in Brittles' Coffee Shop and speaking from behind a huge wedge of Banoffee Pie, "And it was originally planned to be a virology lab where they would do things with human neuro-progenitor cells and the effect of certain viruses on them in the foetal brain. It was never used because the project was closed down, and it never moved out of its old building."

Minnie looked a little pale, Felicity noticed, even her usual pink-cheeks seemed faded.

"How interesting," Minnie said, "I wonder why they don't use the room? I never knew a lab that had enough space to waste…"

"Me neither," said Felicity, "They use it for storage. Maybe it's too small to push a virologist into? I was thinking, though, that the virologists work in the biochemistry and microbiology building, don't they? I'll ask Ben about it when I see him. I'm sure he'll know."

"I don't know," says Minnie, "I think that quite a lot of things which started out in biochem crossed over to genetics – and genetics always used to be done at the Bute Building– in the Medical School or in Botany, if it was plants."

Felicity, conscious that Minnie seemed a bit anxious, wondered why talking about this should have bothered her so much. She decided to take a leap of intuition.

"Ben didn't once work there, did he?" she asked.

Minnie's head was bowed, she was regarding the floor, saying nothing.

"Yes, he did!" Felicity concluded.

"Yes, he did," repeated Minnie, "In the old building. As did Free."

Felicity pondered, ploughing her way through the pie, as to why neither Minnie nor Ben had said anything about this before. Were they embarrassed to have had anything to do with something so yukky?

"Do you know all the details? Will you tell me about it?" she asked.

Minnie said that she would, but could they please go home, back to her own house, she'd make a big pot of tea.

Which you can hide behind, thought Felicity, uncharitably. The psychiatrist was totally upset. Felicity had decided, though, that she was going to get to the bottom of this.

*

Jake was still concerned about his brilliant new job in America, thinking not only about the money, although that was important for Kate's needs, but about increased opportunities to see something of his father. It was a long way from Spokane to Fort Lauderdale, but air services were good – and Jake would be able to afford them with all that money.

Lee Ellwood was healthy and active but there was no getting around the fact that he was now in his late sixties and could be expected to develop at least some of the problems of getting older. He had never remarried; had no special companion for his declining years. Jake, at his desk in the Bute and finishing a corned beef sandwich, brushed crumbs off his sweater and resolved to telephone his dad later, when Ft Lauderdale had woken-up.

For the moment, he would telephone Kermit Whittaker and mention the job. It was already early tomorrow in Spokane. Unhappily, Kermit was out of the office.

*

"Ben and Free met there, for the first time," said Minnie, "In the Virology Laboratory. They were both doing an M.MedSci in Virology; hers was intercalated in her medical degree, he was following an interest prior to his PhD. She was twenty-one, he was twenty-three."

"What were they actually working on?" asked Felicity.

"Flaviviruses, I seem to recall," said Minnie, "And their vectors: ticks and mosquitoes. They are known in more than seventy countries, various types."

"Flavi-," said Felicity, "Yellow. Yellow fever?"

"Yes, among others. Dengue Fever, Chicungunya, meningo-encephalitis etc.,"

"Not malaria?"

"No. Malaria's well characterised. It's not a virus; it's a parasite – Apicomplexa: Plasmodium falciparum, malariae, ovale, vivax and knowlesi. Plasmodium falciparum being the most common."

"Aren't the others pretty well understood too?" asked Felicity.

"Understood-ish," replied Minnie, "But mechanisms aren't – or weren't – this was quite a time ago. There are genetic implications and immune system implications. All the possible work hasn't been done even now."

"I see. But what caused the laboratory to close down? There must have still been lots of work to do…"

"Oh, there was," said Minnie, with a shrug, "A huge amount. It only got to the end of year two of a three-year project. They both abandoned their theses and left St Andrews. Few people know what happened, although a few know it was something dreadful!"

Minnie was looking upset again, causing Felicity to wish she hadn't asked. This was obviously nothing to do with her. She should bite her tongue more often. Minnie picked-up a chocolate biscuit and then promptly forgot about it. Felicity could see the chocolate melting on her hand.

"There's another virus, the vector is the *aedes* mosquito, unlike the malaria mosquito which is *anopheles*. It's become known in the twenty-first century because of the outbreaks in Polynesia and the Pacific Islands, then in Brazil, although it's been known since 1947. You'll have read about it. It's ZIKV, the Zika virus."

*

"Okay," said Naomi, "I understand about illusion and sleight of hand, deceiving the brain and all that but what about the finale? How do you do that? I've never seen you with any equipment or mechanism and I'm fascinated."

She stopped, looking across the sitting room at Jake. They were in the Warden's Flat at Montgomerie Hall, talking about the act and doing some forward planning. He wanted to make her an offer to be his regular assistant – at least until he went to America. He had never had a better one – except, maybe, Kate. Naomi was doing bits of magic herself now; but he hadn't expected her to ask about his party piece.

"Oh, that," he replied. "It's a glamour."

"It's a what?" Naomi looked puzzled, no doubt thinking about Marilyn Monroe.

"Glamour," said Jake, "In its old sense. A magic spell, an enchantment, a charm. An effect. You've got to let a man retain a bit of mystery; I can't tell you. Magic Circle and all that."

"A clue," she said, "Just one little clue?"

"I don't know what that could be, I'm afraid." He smiled at her with regret; no way he could tell her – even if he could be sure she'd keep it to herself. "I do want to tell you that you are the very best assistant I've ever had, though," he went on, "And it would be great if you could work for me until I leave for the US. I wish it could be until you graduate but I have been offered a super job over there! Still, until I go…". She looked both pleased and sorry.

"How long will it be?" she asked, "I'm anxious because I don't want to try to get a job as a waitress until I have to-this is much better!"

"I don't know yet," said Jake, "But I'll keep you informed." They raised their glasses, a little hesitatingly, in a toast.

"To us," said Jake, "And a short but rewarding partnership!"

*

The first Sunday of the new term, Whitsunday, was a beautiful day, with warm sunshine and the feeling of a good summer to come. Ben was going to 11am University Service in the University Church of St Salvator in North Street. He was giving religion its last chance. If it didn't do something soon, he was giving up on it and committing to psychosis. He chuckled as he walked across Market Street.

People were already arriving and crowding into the Quadrangle. Ben had decided to do the thing properly and join the Academic Procession; other academics were robing in the upper room at the Head Porter's Lodge. He had brought his hood and gown thrown over his shoulder. He went into the Robing Room and allowed Mr Dodson, the Head Janitor, to hood him formally.

It was very close to kick off at 11 o'clock when Belinda Fleming arrived hurriedly, already wearing the purple gown and soft black Principal's hat. She wasn't wearing any of her many hoods - Ben chuckled that, if she wore all of them, she wouldn't be able to see over the top. The procession formed up to walk across to the chapel cloister, Mr Dodson with the Big Bible at the front and the Chaplain and guest preacher coming at the rear. Academics joined the procession in order of seniority: Ben, himself, found his place about halfway down the column.

As they reached the centre of the chapel, Ben spotted someone he thought he knew in the pew normally reserved for academic wives. She was rather pretty and a wee bit plump, and she had bright silver hair. She was wearing an olive-green suit, with a pale beige blouse. He knew he knew her but couldn't think who she might be. He was listening to the guest preacher's sermon when he realized it was Doctor Latimer, Minnie. He wondered why she was sitting with the academic wives. Who could she be married to?

The rest of the church filled-up with students from the United Colleges of St Salvator's and St Leonard's in scarlet gowns, and those from St Mary's College in black.

✦

Tommy Ridge, a Private Detective

Joanne Critchley, despite being a Religious Correspondent, had access to the full resources of a national newspaper and knew how to use them. She needed to find out more about Lucy Elizabeth "Wisp" Furness and about why her father did not know that his daughter had died almost as soon as she was born. Joanne had never heard of anything like this before.

There seemed little point, at this stage, in going to the medical authorities; they consider confidentiality to be a sacred form of secrecy. She went through her contacts book to find someone who might be able to help. She found Tommy Ridge, an elderly ex-police detective whom the paper sometimes used for delicate investigations. She asked him to pop into her office, soonest.

It was next morning when Tommy managed to get in and, over a cup of strong coffee and a bag of doughnuts, Joanne explained the situation to the detective. As usual, Tommy listened carefully without interruptions until she had finished. Then he asked her just one question:

"Where was the wean born?"

"Her father said it was in the Liverpool School of Tropical Medicine but, when I checked it turned out to be the Liverpool Maternity Hospital."

"OK. That's a bittie odd, but not to worry."

He left, sketching a bow to Joanne. She wouldn't hear from him again until he had something solid to tell her.

*

Felicity arrived at Tubby's flat in Hepburn Gardens at 7pm. He had telephoned her laboratory first thing, offering to give her a run through for her Viva. Jake had already given her one of these and she was feeling as confident as she possibly could, but when her boyfriend, whose own PhD was more recent, had offered, she had given in immediately. She hoped that an overnight stay would also be on offer. She could do with a bit of excitement!

Tubby opened the door from above and she climbed the stairs, meeting him on the landing, having a preparatory cuddle. He still thought she liked sherry and had poured them both a glass. She played with hers as he talked about how she should perform on the day of the defence of her thesis.

"Never forget," he instructed, "That YOU are the expert on this, not them, so they'll only be looking for general impressions at the first level, just to help you settle down. Do you fully understand the scientific method? Of course you do! Have you done all the paperwork for the Ethics Committee and got your permissions in a row? Of course you have. Remember when you went for your appearance before the Ethics Committee – how many of them actually followed what you were saying?"

"Possibly none," she said, "One or two asked the odd relevant question but I doubt any of them really understood. They were all kinds of medics and senior nurses and pharmacists and…there was a minister of some kind in a dog collar…I'm not even sure there was anyone who had much genetics, or appreciation of Parkinson's Disease!"

"I'd get a flip-chart or an overhead projector and get your diagrams done in plenty of time…"

Felicity thought, but didn't say, 'how primitive'. What she did say was that she had a PowerPoint presentation, all ready to go.

"You need to know, though," he said, "That there are academics who absolutely hate PowerPoint, and if you get one – or two – you might have to work way too hard. And don't use it like some do; don't talk through the slides, without elaboration, and then give them handouts which are exactly the same!"

"Oh, no, I won't do that," she said, "I've seen some of the people who do, and it is annoying beyond belief. I'll only use it as a cue and speak to it. And I'm rather good at explanatory diagrams!"

"I'm so glad," said Tubby, "That's such a help. I'm not great at drawing and I think it made it harder than it should have been for me.

"The other thing I want to say is that they want you to pass. It really isn't a contest where you hope your trident is sharp enough and you have remembered your net! It'll be OK. Oh, and you should make up your mind about whether you want your supervisor in the room. He'll be at the back if you do and can't speak, but only you can decide whether you will be more nervous with him there or not. He'll have a view about it, of course. But it's your choice. What's he like, Dr Ellwood?"

"He's fine," she said, "Very nice, helpful, not arrogant. He'll be supporting me."

"OK," said Tubby, "It really will be all right you know."

"I hope it will," she said, gulping to finish the awful sherry.

"I do want to talk to you a bit more about ethics," he said.

Felicity, who had been hoping that the academic advice was over, and they might go into the bedroom, was a little disappointed. He was looking very serious.

"I was thinking," he said, "What we talked about the other day, you know, the ethics of animal experiments?"

"Um," she said, not her favourite subject.

"We talked about mice and rats and apes, didn't we?"

"We did. And we agreed that a lot of animal models are pretty pointless."

"Yes. I was thinking about the right to live and what philosophers say about it. There's lots of material; some people think that a creature only has the right to live if it has the will to live. The Princeton philosopher Peter Singer says that that will requires 'rationality, autonomy, and self-consciousness' – without those it isn't actually a person."

"Do you agree with that, Tubby?" said Felicity, eyes opening wider.

"I'm thinking about it," returns Tubby, "Singer points out that intelligent apes are more real people than morons."

"Um. Define 'morons'. Is he using that argument to protect animals, or to say that 'morons' – whatever he thinks those are - or even, perhaps, disabled people, are not really people at all?"

She is conscious that what she has uttered is peculiar and is not at all sure that Tubby will understand what she's getting at.

"He does say, about severely disabled babies, that when a life is so miserable it is not worth living and it is permissible to give it a lethal injection."

"Is he sure he knows when life is not worth living?"

"Not sure," said Tubby, "I'm still thinking about it.

*

Jake was settling down, in his sitting room at Montgomerie Hall, with the strong intention of writing an extremely well-thought-out question for first year exams. This had been the first time, for many a year, that he had taught a short course in what was advertised as "Make Up Your Mind". He felt that, because of the title, more undergraduates had turned up than would had it been called "Neurology for Idiots", which would have been his preferred title. Still, he found his present task quite hard because he kept flowing over into the question he was simultaneously preparing for Senior Honours. That was, and had to be, much more interesting.

He had just come out of the lavatory when there was a knock at the front door and Minnie and Ben presented themselves, both bright eyed and bushy tailed, despite a matching pair of common colds. He had quite forgotten that he had asked them to come round.

"Tell me more about the child you saw," said Jake, when they were sitting in his living room. "We need to think about that in isolation from the visions, don't you think?"

"I do," said Ben. "There's this thing about getting them mixed up because they were both so weird but you're right to separate them. The child was something which was odd but which I did see. I wasn't hallucinating that, even if I was hallucinating the holy thing. We should think about what it could have been. I'm really sure I saw it!"

Minnie sipped her tea, made a face because the milk was on the turn, and put the cup down on the side table.

"You said it was a wee girl," said Minnie, "And she looked rather strange?"

"A very small head and a large nose," said Ben, "And dressed in just a thin shift. It was cold – one of those beginning of winter days when St Andrews is so empty because the tourists have gone, and the students aren't back yet. There was even a flurry of early snow, not much, but it was raw. I remember that I was wearing my winter overcoat and a woolly scarf. I thought she must be out without her parents' knowing; no one would have sent her out without a coat."

"Could she have been a small adult?" asked Jake. "Not an actual child at all?"

"I suppose she could," said Ben. "I didn't get a really good look because it was moonlight, she wasn't there long, and she punched me in the stomach before she ran away. I daresay she could have been older but with restricted growth…"

"It's just," said Jake, "That your description reminded me of something I've read somewhere. The big nose and small head thing. I'll have to see if I can find it."

Around midnight, Jake found it. A magazine article about temple servants in Pakistan.

"Chua," he said out loud. Ah.

Maya, a Human Being

The spiral stairs opened at the end of a long corridor with doors on either side; eight in all. The far end of the corridor appeared to lead to a well-lit room with an open door. Halfway down the hall there was a small woman on her knees scrubbing the floor, a large pail at her side. The floor was extremely clean; it didn't look like it needed a hands and knees scrub. The woman didn't look up as Felicity took a step towards the first door.

There was a window in the door, shaded on the outside by a canvas blind. As she raised the blind, Felicity realized that the window was reinforced glass, thicker and stronger than usual. Inside the room, she saw a narrow bed; a striped blanket covering a small, huddled shape. There was nothing else in the room and the walls were softly padded.

She felt her already tight stomach tensing. It took a lot of effort for her to walk to the other side of the corridor and raise the blind on the opposite room. This one was padded too but there was no sign of an occupant. Felicity wondered if they were sometimes taken out but, as she speculated on this, there was a sudden movement, and a hideously grinning face came up at her from the other side and squashed itself against the glass.

She couldn't help a stifled scream as she leapt backwards away from the door. The face tried to flatten itself further against the window, its mouth moving as if shouting at her. She didn't know what to do now, leaning – propped, really – against the opposite wall, as far as she could get away from the face.

She tried to take a deep breath and failed miserably. She told herself to calm down and tried again. This time she succeeded in a shuddering breath but, after that, managed a couple which started to calm her. Her heart was still racing, though, as she looked into the third room.

This one wasn't padded and had furniture as well as a single bed. The occupant, who looked like a tiny, elderly woman, was sitting on the side of the bed with her head in her hands. She was wearing a thin grey shift tucked behind her knees, her narrow bony shins, and bare feet on the concrete floor. She was obviously too mired in misery even to look up and notice she was being observed.

Felicity was steady enough now to proceed down the corridor looking into each room as she went. The remainder of the rooms were not padded and some also had rudimentary furniture as well as a bed. Some rooms had a small table and a dining chair, some had a night table or a small drawer unit. None had any form of floor covering or a window onto the outside.

The little scrubbing woman was almost at Felicity's feet now, still washing with a cloth and scrubbing with a big brush. There was a strong smell of disinfectant. As she approached the visitor's legs, she looked up.

Her face was just like the others; what seemed like a huge nose and tiny eyes, her very small head sitting on a spindly small body. Her skin was pale brown, like all the others, and her eyes were very dark. As their eyes met, Felicity felt a jolt of electricity.

In the eyes of this microcephalic woman was a depth she had never seen before, suffering which was beyond belief, beyond repair.

"Can we talk?" asked Felicity, with little hope that this would happen. The woman made to get up. Her legs weren't strong, and Felicity got hold of her arm to help. It was as frail as the wing of a bird. For a moment, Felicity felt her trying to draw away but then she apparently changed her mind and co-operated. The woman took a lead and indicated by pointing that they should go through the door into the last small room before the end of the passageway.

"Is this your room?" she asked, not expecting an answer. The woman looked around the small space and shook her head. She obviously understood speech; whether she could form words was a different thing. She indicated the narrow bed, and she and Felicity sat down on it together.

The woman made a grunt, clearly divided into two different sounds, maybe syllables: "maa-aa". Although she had already called forth Felicity's natural deep empathy, the scientist managed a split second to give a nod to the principle of not making assumptions about other people. She could not see what else she could do in these strange circumstances.

"Maya?" asked Felicity, "Is that your name? Maya? It's a pretty name!" The woman nodded, her small mouth trying to form a smile. "Mine's Felicity. Four syllables, I'm afraid!" The woman moved her mouth, seeming to roll the word around in it, then produced a sound:

"Sss-iss-ee".

Tears formed in Felicity's eyes; Maya was trying so hard to say her impossible name. Moving on, Felicity asked her if she was all right; trying to elicit another impossible reaction. Maya understood only too well, though. She shook her tiny head firmly.

"O-o-o!" Felicity wiped her eyes. and Maya laid her hand on the scientist's forearm. She wants to comfort *me*, thought Felicity, incredulously. This won't do. This won't do at all.

*

Joanne Critchley, waiting for contact from Tommy Ridge, was thinking about the other odd thing which had happened to Ben Furness. It seemed extremely strange, but he clearly believed in it absolutely. It was the juxtaposition with the holy visions which made it appear as if they were connected. Or maybe she was wrong? Maybe there was a connection?

She wondered whom she could call, who might know about something so peculiar. Ben had mentioned his niece, his only relative. What was her name? Chris, she thought, no, Christie. She works at the UN. Incredibly, Joanne got her contact details from the UN website: she was listed as Head of UK Security. A quick 'phone call to her New York office revealed that she was presently in St Andrews: a trawl around the hotels revealed registration at the Royal Hotel. Christabel Furness would be happy to meet Joanne in the bar in the evening. Joanne agreed that that would be super.

*

May Morning is traditional in St Andrews (isn't everything?) and the male members of the Kate Kennedy Klub, and all of them *are* male, leap from the cliffs into the Witches Pool below. It is a very long drop, and it is unspeakably cold. There have been cases of fit young men getting into difficulties with cramp; there is an ambulance standing by.

A small number of fit young men who lived in Montgomerie Hall were going to dive, so their Warden, Dr Jake Ellwood, felt he had to be present, despite the cold and the early hour, when he would have preferred to stay in bed. He privately thought that the divers were nuts: he would rather eat his feet.

It was a beautiful shiny morning though, and it buoyed his spirits, which were somewhat low because of what Felicity had confided when she arrived, extremely upset, in his office yesterday. She had explained the situation out at the Genetic Engineering Laboratory and told him about the chuas. She had been surprised when he called them that; that he already knew.

"Are you involved, then?" she asked, with an expression of dread on her tear-stained face. He was appalled that she might think that and denied it immediately.

"No," he answered, "I certainly am not. I don't know what they think they're doing but I do intend to find out!"

"You don't need to," said Felicity, sadly. "I know all about it."

*

Max Denfrell had had enough. Enough of being spoken to as if he were an idiot American. He was certainly American, and patriotic, but far from an idiot. He had been first in his class, both in Social Anthropology at the University of North Carolina at Charlotte, and in Navy SEAL training at Coronado. He wondered if it was this which was currently trumping his military tendency to obey orders or whether it was the unimpeachable stripe of common humanity he had kept in check for so long.

He was aware that the look on the face of Felicity Malcolm, when she had left the laboratory yesterday, had triggered his treacherous thinking. He had not addressed it consciously, but it had been percolating at the back of his mind through the working night. He had decided he didn't much like this set-up. The work, which he didn't fully understand, seemed alarming and he had failed to find a friendly academic willing to explain it.

Alone, in his miserable flat, he opened his email and set to write his commanding officer, in the States, for a transfer. Anywhere, he wrote, as long as it's not here. He spellchecked it, emailed it to Washington DC. When he had done so, he began to wonder whether he should rather have opted to stay and sabotage the whole horrible thing.

*

Joanne recognized Christabel immediately, from a photograph on Ben's shelves. She had been a little younger when it was taken but there actually seemed very little difference. She was still willowy, very tall, very fair. She had very few wrinkles. Joanne wished she had used the age-renewal cream she had been suckered into buying on Princes Street.

Never mind. Christabel stood up from the easy chair she was occupying, approaching Joanne with a hand stretched to shake. Joanne noticed that it was not a dominant handshake; she wondered if that was contrived for effect. They sat down in a group of chairs and the other woman ordered a large pot of tea and some 'nice' biscuits.

The reporter explained that she had first met Professor Furness after the Dean of Divinity had summoned her, to make sure that, when the papers got hold of Ben's story, they would print something suitable rather than over-the-top florid.

"But," she said, "That was about the strange visions he's been having, not about the odd child he saw last autumn. I wonder what you know about that?" Christabel looked surprised and said that she had expected the journalist to want to talk about Ben's visions: after all, that's what the pieces in the papers had been all about.

"No. I think that this is more interesting," said Joanne. "Partly because I've been severely warned off by someone in authority; a veiled threat but a real one, I felt. Why do you think anyone would feel the need to do that? Not because a middle-aged academic has been having holy visions, I don't think…"

"I don't know anything about that," lied Christabel, as smoothly as she expressed everything else, "I don't know what my uncle's been telling you, but I shouldn't take it too seriously. He's not quite with it, you know. He's on his own and lonely.

"You'd probably find he's spinning a yarn to have something to talk about. You know what these academics are like: if they must no longer strain everything through six layers of abstract reasoning; life is boring, and they must find ways to cope with that. We shouldn't really be surprised."

Joanne left soon after that, Christabel clearly didn't know anything useful. She wondered who did. Then she remembered that Mark Fleming's wife was now Principal of the university. That could be interesting.

Christabel finished her tea and returned to her nice bedroom on the first floor. Raffaella was curled up in the middle of the bed but raised her head when her Mum came in. She gazed at Christie in adoration, but Christie imagined she saw something else too, a bewildered disappointment.

*

It was a few days later when Minnie brought up the story of the Virology Lab where Free and Ben had worked years ago. Felicity had stayed away from asking her about it because it obviously upset her a great deal. This time, it was a beautiful day and Minnie had asked if Felicity would care to go to the Botanic Gardens with her.

They had been walking slowly, because Minnie's arthritis was being troublesome, and admiring the signs of summer. After silence had fallen, Minnie referred Felicity back to their talk about the flaviviruses the other day and started to tell the younger woman more of the story. She was clearly upset because Free had been a good friend, although she didn't, specifically, refer to that.

"Ben and Free were in the laboratory one day," said Minnie, "And the technician who was responsible, hadn't been in to do any cleaning-up. I don't know whether they didn't do it every day, or whether he was sick, or what it was. But he hadn't been in. Ben was irritated because he always liked things as clean as possible, especially any animal cages. He said he would do it himself. He went and got the stuff and got on with it. Free was doing some microscopy on her own bench, looking at samples she'd prepared from mosquitoes they had infected, and making notes. They probably would have done the cleaning together otherwise."

Minnie paused, then told Felicity that Ben had carelessly missed sealing the gap properly between the dirty tank and the clean one into which he was decanting the insects.

"It isn't hard," said Minnie, "But this time a mosquito came through the gap, flew straight over to Free and bit her.

*

It was the day before Felicity's viva that Minnie added the most shocking piece of her story-by-instalments. Ben's wife had been pregnant.

They packed that night and immediately took the train south, went straight to the Liverpool School of Tropical Medicine, which had a specialist research project. Three days later, Free had mild symptoms of Zika, rash, headache, muscle, and joint pains. Not much really. But terrifying because of the pregnancy. She and Ben had both panicked.

"It affects foetuses, doesn't it?" asked Felicity, "I have read something about it…"

"It does," replied Minnie, "Quite dreadfully, apparently. It's microcephaly."

Felicity looked stunned and said, meekly, "Like the chuas?"

Minnie said, "Yes, exactly like the chuas."

*

"What I can't understand," said Jake, "Is why the Catholic church is interested at all. Ben isn't a Catholic; he isn't even a believer. Why are they sending someone?" Martin Reilly looked at him coolly. Amateurs, he thought. He didn't even know if he could be bothered explaining.

"They think they have a monopoly on religious manifestations," he said. "The Congregation for the Causes of the Saints, in the Vatican, is the ultimate expert on this kind of stuff, even though it thinks only devout Roman Catholics can have holy visions - and the stigmata, for that matter.

"And there was that document from the Congregation for the Doctrine of the Faith, that's the Inquisition you know, which said something like the Orthodox church suffered from a 'wound' because it did not recognise the primacy of the Pope. The wound was 'still more profound' in Protestant denominations. They said that it was 'difficult to see how the title of "Church" could possibly be attributed to them'. Roman Catholicism was 'the one true Church of Christ' they said. Not that long ago. They're a bit funny about it."

"Why are we talking about the stigmata?" asked Jake. "No one's got that, have they?"

"Of course not," Reilly breathed in deeply and leaned back in his chair. "It's just

a part of all the general rigmarole; visions, stigmata, miracle healing. Sorry. And then there's weeping statues of the Virgin and all the Saints. All rubbish, of course. But it helps the Simple Faithful". He sighed and groomed his moustache. "I'm fed up of it actually. I wish I'd never got involved."

"Why did you?" asked Jake quite interested to hear the answer.

"Kind of comes with the territory," said Reilly, "Kind of walked into it. I've been lucky really, over the last few years. My predecessor got involved with a very sticky situation involving exorcism," he shuddered extravagantly. "Absolutely ghastly. Makes one wish one had applied for a vacancy in a quiet country kirk. Did you know there's another one?"

"Another what?"

*

Denfrell's meeting with Professor Meredith Williams had quickly turned from a courtesy visit, to explain that the Night

Superintendent had asked for a transfer, to a full-scale row. Denfrell had not intended it to be so; he had expected the Welshman to listen to the little he had to say, accept it and dismiss him. However, Meredith Williams had a nasty temper and had slid easily into a fight. Denfrell determined not to fight him but found the personal insults desperate for response.

"What the bloody hell do you mean, you have asked for a transfer?" Meredith Williams didn't wait for an answer, "I can't have people General Challoner has personally sent to me walking out! You know far too much about the work. It's highly sensitive and secret. Classified. You can't go. I won't let you!"

He was shouting now, up at full volume, red-faced, pop-eyed, out of control.

"Are you too fucking stupid to understand the importance of what I'm doing? Why do you want to go anyway? Can't fucking cut it?"

Denfrell, who had been brought up a Southern Baptist, didn't care for the cursing.

"I don't understand the work," he interrupted, adopting a calm demeanor he wasn't feeling, "But I am very concerned about the people in the Animal House, and in the dormitory. They don't seem to have much of a life. Your experiments... I don't know if you should be..." If it were possible, Meredith Williams's eyes were almost popping out of his balding head.

"They're not fucking people," he screeched, "They're just experimental animals. I created them. They aren't fucking people. They don't have human rights. I can treat them how I want as long as it promotes the fucking work!"

Doctor Gateside, who had heard the furore, had arrived at speed, and put his hand gently on the Professor's twitching arm.

"Calm down, Prof! It's not worth having a stroke for. Why don't you sit down, and I'll make you a nice cup of tea? Mr Denfrell will go downstairs to his office, and you can maybe talk later or something."

He gestured with a tilt of his head that Denfrell should leave the room. Denfrell went, thinking, Limeys and their cups of horrible tea, I can do without it. The security staff, American to an agent, had a proper coffee machine in their room. He went to get some to calm his nerves. The negative reply, complete with more curse-words, about his transfer request, from General Challoner, was already in his inbox.

✦

Sister Honoria, a Nun

Sister Honoria was sitting in the dark when Ben was shown into the convent parlour. He'd been quite surprised to see the convent, never having been inside before. It was just an ordinary though large house at the end of a St Andrews terrace – still it felt, and smelt, like his idea of a convent. He wondered if this could be the odour of sanctity. He supposed not, just the odour of candles and flowers, incense, and beeswax floor polish.

A narrow nun, Sister Philomena, had opened the door and let him in, following an internal phone call to the Mother Superior, who seemed to have a very similar voice. It had, finally, occurred to him to go to the horse's mouth. The custodian of sanctity in St Andrews wasn't the Dean of Divinity, it was Sister Honoria - whom everyone agreed was "rather holy." In the end, Ben knew that only she would be able to help him.

Sister Philomena, leading him into St Cecilia's parlour, flipped on the light and told her sister that Professor Furness was here. Her accent, though matured in England and Scotland for many years, was as liltingly Irish as if she had left Galway yesterday. She indicated a chair near to Honoria and said she'd bring tea. Sister Honoria smelled dry, like old paper. Ben sat down opposite to the nun and wished her a good afternoon.

"Thank you and welcome," responded Sister Honoria, also Irish, "All days are the gift of the good God. What can I do for you, Professor?"

He realized, as he looked into her milky eyes, that she was blind or, at least, so near-sighted that it made no difference. Her back was straight, though, and her voice was crisp and sure.

"I wonder if you can help me," he said. "I have been having what you might call visions, and no one seems to be able to work out what they might be, where they're coming from, or what... So, I thought you might have some idea. I'm not religious you see; I never have been. And now this thing keeps on happening and I have no idea what to do about it."

"What *I* would call visions?" said the nun, "And what might that be, Professor?" He explained to her about the nature of what he had seen, heard, felt, smelled, tasted. He told her it had happened several times over the last year; that he didn't know what it was *for*.

"The voice of science," said the nun, "Always wanting to know what things are *for*; never happy to let things just *be*."

The parlour door opened, and Sister Philomena came in with a tray of tea. She set it down on a coffee table but, instead of retreating, she took a seat and began to pour. Ben, accepting a cup of weary tea he didn't want, allowed his hand to stray towards the plate of elderly-looking biscuits. Before he could take one, he noticed Sister Philomena's pinched but frightening stare and changed his mind. Perhaps they were only for show.

"Sister used to have visions," said Philomena, as if she had never left the room, "In the Old Country, when she was a girl. But they have stopped now, haven't they, Sister?"

Honoria nodded. She had been very young, she said, and very susceptible to suggestion. God had kindly taken them away when she entered the convent.

"I offered them up," she said, "And God took them. Perhaps..." Her voice died away under Sister Philomena's sharp intake of breath. It had not been long after that that Ben found himself back on the street, sweating from the overheated convent. No help there, he thought with a sigh.

He had only been home for about ten minutes when there was a knock at the door and he opened it to a young nun, in the white veil of a novice. He had been told that senior nuns don't wear veils anymore; the sisters he had visited with this afternoon certainly hadn't.

The novice was young and pretty and her voice breathless when she asked if she could speak to him for a moment. He let her in and the high-colour in her cheeks began to subside as she recovered from her rush from the convent. She introduced herself as Sister Mary Catherine and said that Sister Honoria had sent her.

"She told me exactly what to say," she said, quickly, "She made me repeat it so I would get it just right. She said I was to tell you that it doesn't matter who the man is; he has been dead for a long time, and you cannot affect those who have moved on.

"This is about *this* world and there is something only you can do for him. You already know what it is." She stopped and then said that Honoria had also said that her sight had been the sacrifice. For not accepting the gift. Did Ben understand what she meant? Sister Mary Catherine didn't.

Ben indicated that he understood and, as the young nun left, he heard the click of everything falling into place.

✦

Ben's Diary entry 12

It's amazing how much better I'm feeling even though nothing has really changed. What the young sister said, in the message from Sister Honoria, helped me to see that it's the message, not the man, which is important – it doesn't really matter who he is. The only thing to find out is what to do about it. It's a little bit funny to think of it – like assembling the Dirty Dozen or the Magnificent Seven, but I'm nothing like Yul Brynner or whatever that other chap was called…

Still, if my skills are needed. I know other people; with other skills I can call on too.

The first thing, though, is to go and see Principal Fleming, let her know what's going on. I suppose there's a cowardly bit of me that hopes she'll take over and put a stop to it all – then I won't have to do anything. No good. I know, still, that I must do something. But I'm OK with whatever it is emerging as we go along; I'm going to stop trying to force it; that's what has been making me crazy.

◆

Ignatius Craven, the Devil's Advocate

Ben met with the Inquisitor in St Mary's, in a small office off the library. Reilly had thought it was best and, of course, he especially wanted to be there - being the public face of religion in the town. Ben noted that the local Catholic priest whose name, he thought, was Father Doran, was not present.

The Reverend Monsignor Ignatius Craven SJ., of the Society of Jesus, was English and looked very severe in his black suit and Roman collar. He was exceptionally tall and thin, with a large beak of a nose, and neither his scanty hair nor his eyes had any discernable colour. He folded himself onto a straight dining chair, imported for the occasion, and spread out his large, knobby, farmer's hands on his skinny, bony knees.

Ben, who had been sitting waiting in the office for Reilly and the monsignor from Rome for twenty minutes before the appointed time and ten after it, had stood up when they arrived. Only polite. The monsignor, who appeared also to be of no fixed age, began to speak in a deep, sonorous voice. He explained that he had been sent from the Congregation for the Causes of the Saints in the Vatican; that he was the one they called the 'Devil's Advocate'.

"I am," he said, "The one who investigates so-called miracles, visions etc., usually when the alleged holy person has died…" He fixed Ben with his peely-wally eyes, implying it would be better if he had joined those who had had the courtesy to die before his investigation. Reilly, who had perched himself on the edge of another dining chair, was scintillating with excitement.

"The Monsignor," he said, breathlessly, "Spent a lot of time, some years ago, with Padre Pio. He was instrumental in the Beatification of the Padre!"

Ben, who had never heard of Padre Pio, wasn't that impressed. He had vowed, previously, to keep as quiet as possible. He was less concerned, now, with exploring the visions: more with working out what to do about the child.

"You may think," said the monsignor, with an irritated glance at Reilly - who was clearly not one of the faithful and really rather pointless, "That it is strange that I, a Roman Catholic cleric of exceedingly high rank, should come to speak with you, who are not even a Catholic…"

He waited as if for some response from Ben. Receiving none, he went on. "I came, mainly, because I was asked to by Cardinal Quinlan in Glasgow, who was, in turn, alerted by Sister Philomena at the local convent. We also take a lot of notice of the local man in these matters, so I spoke to Father Doran last night for a little background. Father Doran didn't have any; background that is. He's never heard of you, never mind your visions."

He stopped again, as if for some punctuating acknowledgement – but Ben said nothing. He was beginning to think this was going to be easier than he'd thought. He wondered what Jake and Felicity were doing and whether Minnie had recovered from her cold.

"Tell me," said Monsignor Craven, "Why did you not talk to Father Doran about this?" He eyed Reilly again, as if surprised that anyone would discuss religion with him at all.

"Never thought of it," said Ben. "Didn't think it could be anything to do with Catholicism. Why would it be?"

The monsignor drew in his breath in shock and horror. He realized that there was no future in pursuing that line of inquiry.

"Did you ever think," he asked, "That it might not actually be a saint or a real holy vision? That it might be a demon or other diabolic entity, trying to tempt you or make you do wrong? Force you to bring the Church into disrepute?" It was Ben's turn to draw breath in shock and horror.

"Don't be ridiculous!" he said curtly, as he walked out.

✦

Ben's Diary entry 13

Well, he was a funny old bird! The Inquisitor, Reilly said. No, that isn't right. That's the other department he mentioned. Devil's Advocate. Amazing names, I thought, going right back to don't know when. Don't know what either. What a load of hooey. He didn't tell me anything, but I don't think I'll hear from him again. He's decided I'm daft. I could tell. I think he is. Demon indeed!

*

When Ben had left in anger, Reilly tried to turn the conversation around to the young Catholic girl in Divinity who had been telling her fellow students that she'd had a vision of the Virgin Mary under the Holm Oak in St Mary's Quad.

"They all seem to revere her, the other students, that is; think she's terribly holy and that. She apparently goes off into a sort of fugue state every so often. Bleeds from her hands and feet too, I'm told. I have wondered, though, if that might be self-harming…" The monsignor looked, momentarily, like he'd eaten a bad oyster and almost shouted that Reilly should leave that to him:

"The Catholic Church has been looking after its own for two thousand years!"

✦

Mark Fleming, a Petro-Geologist

Mark Fleming was marketing director of Carydon Petrochemicals, a multinational whose UK headquarters was in Charlotte Square, Edinburgh. Joanne met him some years ago when she was a young reporter on the economics beat. She didn't know him well enough just to drop by, but she did it anyway, on the off chance. It happened that she didn't need to negotiate her way through successive walls of secretaries and PAs, because she spotted Mark hanging over the front desk, talking to the woman on the switchboard. As he turned around, Joanne hailed him.

He looked a little older than she remembered but he still had that thick curly dark hair, only a few flecks of silver, and his long, athletic frame. He looked surprised to see her, but only for a moment. Then he was welcoming her and saying he hasn't seen her for years. He introduced her, by her maiden name, to the telephonist, saying that she was an old mate. They were in a small office off the lobby, waiting for refreshments, when he asked her what story, she was following up.

"A peculiar one, actually," she said, and repeated the tale of the goings on in St Andrews in the autumn, and the respected academic who had seen something rather peculiar. It was immediately obvious that Mark had never heard anything about this. He promised to speak to his wife.

*

Minnie began to review the case, with Felicity, as if Ben were her patient rather than a good friend, she thought it was time after so many years. She had made a snap diagnosis when she met him, after a few years away, back in St Andrews, as a newly qualified psychiatrist from Dundee University. She had, of course, applied for a house-officer job at the Royal Liff Psychiatric Hospital, and living in St Andrews was an obvious choice – and she could live in the house left her by her parents.

The old colleagues met in Market Street, and he had not recognised her.

She had been upset, naturally, although not surprised. He fitted all the criteria for a tendency to deal with an indescribable trauma by dissociation. He was utterly absorbed in his work and could use it for distraction; he had had a painful childhood, where he was not fully loved.

He had had an unspeakable shock.

Dissociation can provide an effective defence by protecting the person from helplessness and overwhelming anxiety, maintaining some sense of control. It can screen out some of the many threatening aspects by restricting the fields of consciousness.

She stopped suddenly. She had had as much as she could cope with for now.

*

That night, Belinda came home very late from an important meeting. When, she thought, did all my meetings get important? Unusually, Mark was waiting up, sitting at the kitchen table with a large gin and tonic; not his first either. She kissed his ear and asked him to pour her a large one. There was clearly something wrong and she asked anxiously about the kids.

"No," he says, "Kids're fine, it's something different. Joanne McLaren from *The Scotsman* came to see me today at the office."

He told her what Joanne had said, about the small person, about the "official" phone call telling her to drop an investigation she wasn't making; about their joint suspicion that something unethical was happening in the university.

"I know it isn't my business," he said, "But it's certainly something you should know about. I'm not thinking Joanne's going to drop it easily – and God knows what's going on down there."

"I suppose," said Belinda, "That I should be thinking about protecting the university first, but I have to say that I'm more bothered about whatever it is they're doing. I'll need to look up the project details in my office, so I know what I'm thinking about. Come with me?"

It was easy enough to slip next door to the Principal's Office but another thing altogether to find anything truly informative about the projects going on in the Genetic Engineering Building. The only files Belinda knew about were to do with applying for grants to build it, the search for staff and commissioning notices for the work being done. The remainder of the information was, maybe, lodged with the Science Administration at the North Haugh.

Although Belinda supposedly had access to anything she wanted, any time she wanted it, she felt an urgency to begin on it now. She found several files which were in one of the cabinets in Hazel's office and successively tossed them over to Mark who was sitting at Hazel's desk, checking what they were about.

"It says here," said Mark, as Belinda closed and locked the cabinet and came across the room towards him, "That the Centre will be used for establishing the principles to be used in future genetic engineering projects and developing innovative practical uses for them."

"OK, then," said Belinda, "I think I'll make an unannounced inspection tomorrow. See what they are actually doing. Makes me think I should have kept a closer eye on it."

*

Sitting in his room in the Bute Building, Jake had just finished a talk with one of the undergraduates to whom he was Advisor of Studies. Harry was interested in becoming, eventually, a Forensic Anthropologist, and he was looking at courses which would lead him towards entry on a suitable course after his first degree.

He was a bright lad and Jake liked him very much, he'd had several ideas about what Harry could do in the interim but had also offered to ring a friend of his at the Leverhulme Research Centre for Forensic Science at Dundee University.

Jake was feeling good, satisfied that he had done something useful, until the telephone rang.

"Jake?" said Professor Marlon Biggs, Department Chair and Holder of the Home Office License in Anatomy (known as 'Bigg Boss' in the department), "I need to talk to you about something. When can you come up and see me today?"

Jake's diary was open on his desk, with lectures blocked in yellow highlighter and seminars in green. He should be in the lab this afternoon, but he could skive off for a half hour.

"I'm OK, Prof, if you don't need more than about half an hour," he said, "But I will have to be back in the lab for a bit before 5 o'clock."

"That's fine," said Biggs, "It won't take that long."

Marlon Biggs, the Chair of Medical Sciences

He left the lab, with the Head Technician in charge, and Felicity working at her microscope in the back, and took the stairs two at a time up to Marlon Biggs' office.

The Professor appeared to be waiting outside his room, on the landing. He shook Jake's hand vigorously and warmly invited him in. This wasn't normal behaviour; the Professor was known to be a curmudgeon. He didn't take long to get to the point.

"I want to give you a heads-up," he said, "That the Home Office is thinking about cancelling our Forensics contract and giving another institution our project funding! It came out of the blue, I didn't expect it. It isn't even renewal time. We were granted the project as a pilot for five years; we've only had two and less than half. But, although they didn't say 'we are withdrawing our funding immediately', they did issue some heavy threats!"

"What like?" asked Jake.

"Have we done something wrong or dodgy in some way?" asked Biggs, shuffling papers on the desk.

"No," said Jake, "Definitely not. It's all been going fine. Fewer problems than I anticipated. They gave us the money, we set-up the referrals, we did the work, we did the paperwork, I wrote the report at the end of the first and second years. I have the report for this year, so far, on my computer now.

"As you know from our budget, I've used a proportion of the cash to support my PhD students, Felicity Malcolm and Robert McCrae. I thought everything was on track and I was hoping to get your support to apply for an extension for another three years – or, better, a permanent arrangement!"

"Well, I don't think either of those is going to work out," said the Professor, "They said that they weren't sure that we had carried-out our part of the bargain, that, perhaps, some of our staff weren't properly qualified to do the work, that our reports don't have the correct level of data, worse, that some of our data may be spurious."

"What can I say?" said Jake, "All that is total rubbish. Our staff are very well qualified, aren't they? Felicity and Bob are high quality doctoral candidates, the lab techies have Masters' degrees, we have two postdoc biochemists, a postdoc toxicologist, a forensic chemist, and a Home Office retired forensic pathologist. I don't see how we could be any better qualified!"

"It would seem so," said Biggs, "What about your paperwork? Is it sloppy at all?"

"It is not!" said Jake, "It's especially clear and, in my view at the correct level. It's a joint enterprise between the scientific staff and Mrs Simonson in the office. You know her experience and precision…"

"OK," said Biggs, "I need you to let me have copies of all your paperwork, including the end-of-year reports by tomorrow. And can I have a sample of lab notebooks so I can look at some raw data? By the way, I take it that your data isn't spurious, I know you too well for that."

Jake, feeling that he was being slightly betrayed by his head of department, agreed to provide what he had requested. He felt now that the Professor didn't trust him, or he would have already told the Home Office that there was no need to worry.

It was only when he got back to his own room, that he thought of the American project and realised that, if his reputation suffered because of this, Baker & Dobinsky wouldn't look at him. He'd still need a job though.

*

"Kermit?" said Jake, on the telephone to Spokane, "I haven't heard anything about the new project. I was wondering if there is something the matter?"

Kermit was his usual jovial self.

"No, no," he answered, "Nothing at all. Everything's going fine. You aren't

worried, are you?"

"Just a wee bit," said Jake, "I'm kind of relying on it, you know?"

"Don't worry," said Kermit, "It's all fine. There are a few things to organise. We'll be in touch very shortly. You can trust me, Jake, don't you know that?"

Jake, who really didn't, said that of course he did, and put down the receiver with his mood descending into his cheap trainers.

*

"Oh, yes," said Minnie, continuing to relate her story to Felicity, "It took a couple of meetings in the street and at the Extension Art History class, followed by coffee-shops, before I fully understood, as far as one can understand, what had happened. He started telling me about his wife and daughter, about their lives together, and what had happened to them."

"And it wasn't true?" said Felicity.

"Um. Well, he did borrow a few things," said Minnie, "Like looking after his wife when she was dying. He made her nice wee meals and took her for wee drives. There was an obvious source for that in the way he cared for her when she was pregnant and wasn't very well at all. The only thing was that he transferred it, spatially, from Liverpool to St Andrews."

"I hadn't realised," said Felicity, "That they did that."

"It's a need to plug autobiographical gaps," said Minnie, her voice sad, "To make an organised, consistent story. His many dog stories too; he's really fond of dogs but, somehow, never had any. The pretend ones are a huge source of comfort.

"But I think, now, following seeing that child from Genetic Engineering, he has started to decompensate. The entire edifice is coming down and he is beginning to remember things as they actually happened."

*

There was an unexpected delivery for Jake when he arrived at the Bute, and the janitor handed him a large brown envelope. He hadn't been expecting anything and wondered what it could be. Sitting down at the desk in his room, he opened the envelope and shook out the contents. It proved to be a half dozen photographs, clearly taken in Paris, at one of the clubs where Kermit had taken him after they had seen the sights.

The pictures starred a woman, wearing only a piled-high stack of platinum hair and a dark blue G-string; and a dark-haired man looking stoned. They were in a variety of compromising positions, some of which Jake did not think were achievable. The head was obviously his, but the bodywork resembled nothing he had ever seen in the mirror.

He walked out of the department with no thought of what he should be doing and managed to catch Minnie Latimer at her house. She was the one who had immediately come to mind out of his distress.

"Where can they have come from?" he asked, "And who can be

trying to discredit me? And what for?"

"And so badly," commented Minnie, "It's obviously photoshopped, by someone who wasn't that good at it! It can only have come from someone who knew you were in Paris for the weekend, can't it? And no one here knew…"

"But why would anyone from Baker and Dobinsky want to blackmail me? I'm assuming it's blackmail."

"I expect so," said Minnie, "But why would they want to? Is there anywhere else the photos could have come from?"

"What?" asked Jake, "Someone trying to stop me leaving St Andrews? Why would they?"

"Not the slightest idea. Although we do know someone; well, someones, really, who would like to curb your activities…Prof Williams, Dr Gateside, the Genetic Engineering Americans, all of the above…"

"But wouldn't it be better if they just let me move to the USA?"

"Probably. Unless it's all a con. And there is no job? The other side of blackmail," she said, "Which is bribery…"

"Ah."

"And you will have to wait and see what comes next, won't you? At some stage, someone will ask you to do something – or not do something. There is one thing you need to do, though. Go and tell Marlon Biggs. Now!"

*

It was late on Tuesday night when Christabel arrived back in St

Andrews again. She stopped the taxi at the Genetic Engineering Building, despite the driver's insistence that university departments didn't work through the night. As she rang the bell at the entrance, she wondered who exactly would answer it. It could be Mr Bettany; it could be Mr Denfrell. Or maybe they still used their service ranks; a lot of Americans did. So, Major or Colonel then.

A metal shutter covering a window at the side of the door shot up and she simultaneously heard an American voice with a Southern accent speaking through a communication device. Christie pressed her security service identification up against the glass as she listened to him tell her that the building had been locked down for the night and he had no orders to open it.

"Please open the door," she said, in a highly reasonable voice. "It is necessary for me to speak with you immediately regarding General Challoner's visit on Friday." It took a few minutes but there was obviously no timing protocol which wouldn't open the door until 06.00 tomorrow, which she had half expected.

The door opened as soon as Max Denfrell had checked her security clearance was good. She entered a small anteroom and held out her hand to the shortish, stocky African American in navy blue tracksuit bottoms and a US Navy tee-shirt. He took a step backwards, started to salute, thought better of it, and crisply said:

"Denfrell, Maxim C, Major, ma'am!"

"Major Denfrell," said Christie, "Christabel Furness, British Secret Service. We need to talk. I believe that you had a security breach back in September and Major Florrie had to be relieved?"

"Yes, ma'am. Major Florrie was posted back to Maryland. I arrived soon after Christmas. I have beefed-up security considerably. The entry system, for example, used to have just a door and visitors came straight into the reception area. This room is new, as is the shuttered window. Bullet resistant glass. And superior alarms, of course."

"I've heard it said that one of the experimental animals escaped back then. They caught it though?"

"Yes, ma'am. No damage was done."

"I don't quite know about that Major Denfrell. I understand it was seen by someone."

"Not sure that that's true, ma'am. There's no report of that in the log." He took a step and perched on the edge of an office chair in front of a small computer station. He passed his hand over the computer screen and brought up a logbook/diary. He quickly found the date in last year's fall entries.

"No, ma'am," he said confidently, "As I thought. The entry reads 'Subject 603 recaptured without violence. Restraints applied until return to project. No outside contact. No further concerns.' It's signed by James Florrie, Paul Bettany and A.V.R. Gateside." He looked up at Christabel as if just realizing how tall she was. She looked down at him.

"That isn't the way it happened, Mr Denfrell," she said. "That's what we need to talk about."

*

"I got these," said Jake, "In the post. At my office."

Marlon Biggs looked puzzled as Jake shook the photographs out onto his neat desk.

He picked them up in a bundle and went through them one by one. He looked up at Jake and asked if they were real.

"Well," said Jake, "They're real photos. They look to have been taken in Paris. I was in Paris the weekend before last. I met that woman, although I didn't see her G-String. That is my face; the one with the stoned expression. Fairly sure it isn't my body."

"What am I supposed to think?" asked Biggs, "That you're a bad boy?"

"Wouldn't know. There was no accompanying note. I don't know who sent them, or why. I am mystified."

"And you've come to me because?"

"I thought you should know. In case it blows up into something."

"Suppose it could," said the Professor, "There was that thing in the papers. You know, the one about the biochemist who saw visions of aliens and was a druggie and that…"

"You think it might be attached to that rubbish?" asked Jake, in surprise.

"Might be, I guess. Someone with a grudge against the university?"

"Actually," said Jake, "I am a bit involved in that – not the newspaper coverage, but I know the biochemist – well, mycologist, actually – and he came to me to talk about what he was experiencing. In case I had any insights, as a neuroscientist."

"Ah. D'you think this might be something to do with that? Someone trying to warn you off?"

Jake was even more perplexed. He shook his head; then nodded it.

"Maybe," he said.

*

"There was," said Christabel, "a professor from the Microbiology Department, who happened to see the runaway!"

Denfrell was surprised, both by the fact that someone had seen the subject, and that the logbook was lying to him. He disliked this sort of thing; it undermined his general opinion that the US military was mostly honourable. He needed to maintain this, or he would be unable to continue within the Service.

Having received the refusal to accept his request for transfer, he had not, yet, decided what to do next. This British Secret Service agent, he suddenly thought, might possibly have indicated a way out. He paused, thinking, then said:

"I have a problem, ma'am."

"A problem, Major Denfrell?"

"Affirmative. I am concerned about the work being done here. I don't fully understand it, but I think it may not be entirely ethical…"

"Ethical?"

"Yes, ma'am. I know it is none of my business and I should follow orders. But I am, in the end, responsible for my own co-operation with wrongdoing. That has been established by law, ma'am!" He finished in a hurry, on a slightly triumphant note. His conscience grunted a sound of internal concordance.

Christabel stared at him in amazement. She had realized that there was nothing which could be done in slow-moving, official procedures. Anything like this could be cleared away and/or camouflaged before the authorities could be persuaded there was anything wrong, let alone had obtained necessary proof of evil. If someone, a group of someones, rescued the chuas, however, no one would be able to deny their existence.

She makes an executive decision to explain her idea to Major Denfrell, and to enlist his help.

*

Minnie had arrived at the Bute in a dither because she had met Mavis Dell in South Street and Mavis had told her about Ben's angry outburst the day before.

"And it's the second time!" she'd said, "It happened back in First Term, when he'd stayed in bed, heard me come in, and then didn't recognize me. He was furious both times. He didn't swear at me, he's too much of a gentleman for that, but he did say 'hell' a few times! Which isn't like him..."

"He wasn't violent, though, was he?" asked Minnie.

"No. No, not at all. But he did accuse me of stealing! It was weird. Both times it was the fish fingers in my basket. He shouted at me and asked if I'd taken them from his freezer!"

"Oh, I am sorry," said Minnie, "It's a problem he's got. I do know something about it, and I'll try to help."

"I know that you're a friend of his, Dr Latimer," said Mavis, "That's why I told you. But I have to say that if he does it again, I'll have to leave. I can't do this!"

"You really shouldn't have to," said Minnie, "But thank you for telling me."

She decided to go and see Felicity at work, as she watched the woman walking down the street away from Ben's.

What on earth am I going to do now?

$$\bigstar$$

Mervyn Adams, a Security Man

A large American whose name tag said he was Mervyn Adams opened the heavy metal shutter after three rings on the doorbell. He scowled at the neatly dressed woman in black who was standing there in the light rain and said,

"Yes?"

"Good morning. I am Principal Fleming and I'm here to make an unannounced inspection of your laboratories. Kindly fetch Professor Williams."

"Have you got an appointment?" asked Adams, although she clearly hadn't. "You can't come into the building without one, as well as security clearance from Colonel Bettany." She gave him a steely look. She refused to accept that she didn't have free access to any location in her own university.

"Get Meredith Williams now," she rapped. "Be extremely quick about it!" A stubborn look on his face was followed by a look of confusion, followed by a look of anger, and he closed the door rapidly, leaving the University Principal standing alone outside the building in the rain.

Belinda sheltered under the overhang outside the door, which was little protection against the rain which was falling more heavily now. She looked at her slim gold watch and set herself to wait for fifteen minutes. Then she rang the bell again.

This time, Paul Bettany opened the door. Belinda didn't know him, but she read his name badge, which declared him to be Head of Security. She said good morning and slid her identification out of her handbag. He took it and stood staring up and down, comparing her with her photograph.

It was a normal university identification badge on a lanyard, like everyone else's: it just had "Principal and Vice Chancellor" in the space specified for "position". And the photo was rather better than the usual. She waited for him to admit her. He said um. He opened the door, using both his palm print and retina, and ushered her into the blue and grey lobby, inviting her to sit on a sofa unit by a light wood coffee table. He said that Professor Williams would be down in a few minutes. He did not ask her if she would like a coffee.

It was another half hour before Meredith Williams arrived, puffing, with his teaching gown flying out behind him. He came over to Belinda with a big twinkling smile and outstretched hand.

"Principal Fleming!" he said, grasping her hand rather too firmly, "What can I do for you?" He sounded as if he would be prepared to go to the ends of the earth and back; she had only to command him.

"I like to make the occasional unannounced inspection," said Belinda, "Just to keep up with what's going on in *my* university." She verbally underlined the word 'my'. "I haven't been to see you since I got here from Oxford, so it's beyond time. You'll have to explain everything because I haven't had time to look at your records in admin. I'm a biochemist, though, so you don't need to do it in words of one syllable!"

He offered her coffee, at this late stage, and she refused, saying she wanted to get on with it. He escorted her to the elevator, and they went up to his office. Belinda, who would not have objected to walking up the stairs, was very conscious that Bettany was following them. He had not entered the lift but was visible at the far end of the corridor when they exited onto the first floor. He must have run up the stairs.

Sitting in Meredith Williams's office, Belinda fished her reading glasses from her handbag and put them on. She was very much aware that they made her look fierce, and she knew full well how to use that. She glowered over them at Meredith Williams, who had gone to sit down behind his desk.

"I've come to look at the laboratories, Professor," she said. "Why are we in your office?" Meredith Williams, leaping over her obviously hostile attitude, said that he thought she might like to look at his scrapbook first. He produced the project's Big Red Book from a drawer in his desk and came around to display it to her.

He explained about the chuas, and the project which was curing them in Bradford; he talked, precisely, about the series of six identified genetic faults, locating them on their chromosomes, and how Vic Gateside and his team were manipulating them, how the genetic material had been obtained, first, from Pakistan, then from Bradford; he drew some partial genetic sequences on his whiteboard, with arrows showing where the interventions had to be made.

He talked about the history of the chuas, about temple-gifts and about the myth of head binding. He showed her the happy pictures of the chuas, in Pakistan and in Yorkshire. He was very proud of his work.

"All very good, Professor," said Belinda, "But I need to see the practical side. Please show me the laboratories now."

"Of course," said Meredith Williams, with another brilliant smile. "That's where the real work is done. Come with me and we'll have a look!"

There was no one in the Animal House, except for two medium-sized cages containing actual guineapigs. The cages were sparklingly clean, and the guineapigs were chomping away happily, as far as Belinda could tell. There was a background smell, but it was no more disturbing than in any Animal House she had ever visited.

They went upstairs in the lift again, and, once more, Bettany reappeared in the far distance. The heavy canvas blinds were down over the glass in each door in what Meredith Williams called the "Dormitory Area", but he raised one of them and allowed Belinda to see that there was a small woman sitting on a chair at a child-sized desk, bending over, attending, shortsightedly, to something.

Meredith Williams rapped loudly on the door and opened it without waiting for a response. They entered the room, and the small person did not turn around. Belinda wondered if she was deaf too.

"Oh, hello," said Williams, not using a name, "I've just brought this lady to meet you; to see what you are doing." He raised his voice, as people who don't know better talk to inferiors, and deaf people.

The small head looked up and, although Belinda had seen the photographs and heard the descriptions, she felt a shock at seeing one of the subjects for herself. The head was much smaller than she had picked up from the pictures; the nose seeming much larger.

The woman was colouring-in a simple design of flowers on a sheet of drawing paper. Bright colours were provided by half-a-dozen coloured pencils but their arrangement was wrong; the woman had filled in some of the flower petals in green and the leaves were in various lurid shades.

They went, then, into the laboratories, where a few scientists in lab coats were working at benches containing computers, gene sequencers, and a few pieces of glassware. A fair-haired man Belinda had seen before somewhere, came over to her and greeted her as "Principal Fleming". He said that he had been at the shindig for the South Americans. She recalled his stunning girlfriend, the superb dancer.

He introduced himself as A.V.R. Gateside, "But everybody calls me Tubby." He didn't say why but she didn't take long to catch on. He escorted her to the bench where an older man was working, introducing Jack Redman, who explained what he was doing on the gene sequencer.

All three of them, with Bettany still in discreet attendance, went into the Growing Room with its series of different-sized nutrient tanks. Dr Gateside, with interruptions from Meredith Williams, explained that they used the tanks to grow groups of dividing cells on.

"How far do you take them?" asked Belinda.

"Only as far as the 64-cell stage," said Tubby. "Then we stop them. Can't be seen to be trying to create life, can we? Specially not with the American money. They're all creationists, you see!"

"We aren't, though, are we?"

"No, we aren't!"

*

This time, Tommy brought the pastries, from that nice new cake shop down the street. Joanne immediately appropriated a fudge doughnut. Her sweet tooth was even more severe than that of most Scots. Joanne asked a passing copygirl for coffee, Tommy asked for milky with four sugars.

He seemed a little agitated as he said that he'd been accessing the horse's mouth, twice. He'd been to the Liverpool Maternity Hospital, where he found he slightly knew a receptionist who had been the girlfriend of an old mate. She hadn't had a problem with confidentiality because the information was all so old; she spilled everything in return for a doughnut with chocolate sprinkles.

Then he had travelled down to London, to the Royal College of Psychiatrists. Joanne looked at him with surprise. There was obviously something she didn't yet know. She wouldn't ask him; she would wait.

"Anyway," said Tommy, "I've got a lot of information and I'll get it written up and send you a report in the next few days. However, I thought you might appreciate a verbal; you can pay with doughnuts."

He sipped his coffee and asked if Joanne could let him have a glass of water too; this stuff was a bit harrowing. While she went to get it, he took off his tweed sports jacket and draped it over the back of the chair. When she came back, he seemed to have re-laxed a bit.

"Lucy Elizabeth Furness was born on 4th August 1982 at 16.17hrs in the Intensive Care Unit at the Liverpool Maternity Hospital. There was considerable concern about the mother's health because she had a pre-existing condition, diagnosed by Professor Clement Madison, from the School of Tropical Medicine – that's the connection – who had recommended a termination, which she had refused. The baby was in distress and was delivered by Caesarian Section.

"The child was extremely small; the weight is recorded at 1lb 6oz, pretty well too small to live. They kept her alive in an incubator, with a respirator for just less than fory-eight hours. The mother asked to see her baby and they brought it to her in a blanket; I think it might have already been dead by then."

Tommy stopped for a moment, in difficulty with his notes. He shuffled pages in the notebook before going back to the place he had started reading.

"The House Officer, a young doctor called Ellie Thomas, made a note on the back of a page of the file – where she didn't expect it to be seen. She felt a note needed to be made though none of her superiors did. She wrote: 'The mother pulled back the blanket and looked into the face of the child and then covered it up again. She made no protest as the nurse took it away. I believe the baby had multiple birth defects although I only saw its head, which was of abnormally small size.'

"The death certificate, signed by Dr Ellie Thomas, recorded her death at 15.20hrs on 6ᵗʰ August 1982. Cause of death pneumonia, no deformity mentioned. The mother, who was delirious, was not told she had died until the next day, when she was judged to be more able to cope. The midwife wrote that the mother was calm but had asked them to let her tell her husband herself. That didn't happen because the father had walked into the nursery, on his own, and interrupted them taking away the dead child."

"Oh, God!" said Joanne, "Enough to make anyone lose touch with reality!"

"Yes, absolutely," said Tommy. "Apparently, he went into the waiting room and sat rigidly still and completely silent for three hours, then rushed back into the nursery and started yelling 'What have you done with my daughter?', refusing to believe she had died. Then he left the hospital without going in to see his wife."

"Hard on her," commented Joanne. "You said *two* horses' mouths?"

"Yes, I thought that the father's reaction was peculiar, so I rang someone I know who's a retired GP. I asked him who I should talk to. He told me. So, when I went to London, I got the receptionist at the Royal College of Psychiatrists to swap the telephone number of the main authority on delusions and dissociation for another bag of doughnuts. What a nice girl!"

"The authority?"

"No, the receptionist. But the authority was a nice girl too. She gave me two hours explaining about how these things work; although she did say that it could only be in general, because she hadn't seen the patient in person. The father, that is."

"I see that," said Joanne. "She would have to protect herself."

"Dr Francis said that there are some people who have such an extreme shock that their minds can't cope with it. She said that, as well as the fight or flight mechanism – which is controlled by adrenaline," he checked in his notebook, "There is a third option, especially useful to babies and helpless animals who can't either fly or fight back. The third option is to freeze; become very still or inert – in the hope that the predator won't see you. It's an evolutionary adaptation, apparently."

Tommy took a deep breath and continued, "Some people, perhaps quite a few, they dissociate severely.

"She thought our subject… must have handled his shock in that way and become dissociated. That means that what she called a 'huge existential change' is likely to have happened. He almost became someone else in relation to most of his life.

"His work must have been very strongly ingrained because it was still available to him – to escape into – but anything concerned with his daughter, even his wife, even his location with them, was no longer available as part of his world.

"Before all this happened, Dr Francis reckoned he must have had what she referred to as 'a high level of absorption in his work', and possibly a state of 'high suggestibility'.

What happened after that, in Dr Francis' opinion, was that he undertook what she called 'confabulation' – that apparently means he made some things up to cover the situation he found himself in and which he couldn't understand – because the scaffolding of a big part of his life had been removed.

And then he had to make it somehow indisputable, proof against anyone denying it. It seems to me that he moved, place and house and job, leaving any remaining reminders of his wife and dead child firmly cut out of his past. Amnesia was cultivated and he wouldn't recall any of the real facts."

"What about his wife?" asked Joanne, "What happened to her?"

"Don't know. No trace of Dr Frederica Furness after 9th August 1982, when she was discharged from the Liverpool Maternity Hospital, with a bad scar on her belly and no baby. Did you know John Lennon was born there, at the Liverpool Maternity Hospital?"

*

Belinda couldn't get the small woman she had seen colouring flowers out of her mind. She speculated whether the woman was colour-blind; it didn't occur to her until she was getting into her car to drive back to the office, that she had coloured the plants the wrong way around because she had never seen a real one.

*

Now that Minnie had arrived at the Bute Building, she was even more flustered than she had been talking to Mavis. She identified herself as 'Dr Latimer' and asked the receptionist where Dr Ellwood's laboratory was. She said she needed to speak with Miss Malcolm, one of the doctoral students.

The lab was on the ground-floor and Felicity was working at her computer. It was unaccountably quiet, and the young scientist heard Minnie coming in, turned around and said hello.

"What's the matter?" she asked quickly, noticing the pinkness and flustered-ness.

"Need to talk to you!" said Minnie, breathlessly, "Something's happened!"

Felicity managed to get her to come into the adjoining office, where both doctoral students had desks. Bob was out today, doing something else.

"What happened?" she asked as they sat down on hard lab stools.

"Ben's definitely decompensating!" she said.

"As you predicted," said Felicity, "How do you know? What's happened?"

Minnie was sitting trying to control her breathing. Slowly in. Slowly out. Slowly in. Slowly out. She told Felicity what had happened, what Mavis had said.

"You're sure something is happening to his condition?" said Felicity.

"I am. There have been wee signs before. But the ungovernable temper is a new one. Happily, it didn't lead to any physical violence."

"Could it have?"

"It might."

"Oh, dear."

"There's usually a trigger to decompensation," said Minnie, "And it must have been the microcephalic woman he saw. Would have been odd if it hadn't been. I think he probably knew he'd seen someone like her before, although he didn't have full access to the memory. It was Wisp of course. When he saw them taking her away."

"Oh, my God!" breathed Felicity.

"He went straight into dissociation. I've always known this would happen, decompensation, that's why I tried to support him covertly. I didn't trust anyone else to do it."

"You've been treating him?" said Felicity, feeling a new shock, "Not completely ethical, is it?

"No, it isn't. But what else could I do? We have always been good friends. I saw how much he was suffering because of the tragedy with the child!"

"But it was his mistake caused the infected mosquito to give his wife the virus!" Felicity almost shouted.

Minnie's face crumpled as if she would burst into tears but then she started to speak again.

"You have to separate the means from the objectives, in treatment," she said, "In therapy. And the primary objective is to improve adaptive functioning and help the patient to be more attentive to the present. Anchoring techniques are useful. So, it was I who got Ben to walk so much. I should have realized, though, that he was walking more than I'd expect. All the time. Practically.

"He's lost weight too. I hadn't noticed, my mind too much on the psyche, not the embodiment. Fool."

"Walking helps, then?" said Felicity.

"Um. Very much. You see it's a powerful grounding technique.

You walk, you concentrate on tactile sensations, joint and muscle movement, pressure. You intentionally focus on the sensations of your feet alternately touching the ground. As well as all that, you must negotiate any barriers, trees, fences, and such. You must."

"There's a bit of a crossover with Parkinson's Disease there," said Felicity, "Patients need to try to be aware of the environment they are in and their bodily reactions."

"Posture and other sensations of proprioception come later. Followed by the identification of emotions. It all takes a very long time. And a big commitment."

Minnie sighed.

"It was clear that we couldn't function with the level of relationship he and I had had before. But I could try to be the best friend I could. He liked me, that much was retained or, rather, re-built. Although sometimes, he doesn't recognize me, even now. I've never pushed it, to make him feel he ought to know who I am. I just take what is and make the best of it."

"The therapy mainly happened in the street, then? And in coffee shops and at the Art Class?"

"It did, although I do visit him from time to time, on various pretenses. The big success was the dancing class. He learned to dance for Free."

"Ah," said Felicity.

*

When the Principal had gone, Mervyn Adams, in his blue

264

technician's coat, went back into the Upper Animal House from which he had been excluded during her visit. It had been his job, at Professor Meredith Williams's urgent order, to collect the two cages of guineapigs from the basement operating room, where they usually lived, and place them on the newly scrubbed benches in the Nursery.

There were no experimental animals there; they had all been moved out because they were going to start a new series of experiments next week. The floor had been disinfected and everything else had been cleaned to destruction, Williams had autoclaved the equipment himself. Mervyn usually worked here. He had very little contact, usually, with the guineapigs. He had, to his satisfaction, accomplished the required state of the laboratory between Belinda Fleming introducing herself to him and her meeting the Professor!

Looking around to check that there was no one else coming in through the door, who would see him delaying his return to the Operating Room, Mervyn opened the cage door and grasped the largest of the animals, a long-haired beige female. He put her in his large, practical, pocket while closing the cage door with his other hand. He'd drop her off in the pet shop on his way home in the evening. At least she'd have a chance at a life. Until someone noticed that the levels of livestock were unaccountably going down.

*

Minnie, alone in her sitting-room in the middle of the night, was living through those days once more, the days after Free had contracted the Zika virus. Because Ben had studied for a while at the School of Tropical Medicine, and it was near his home-place anyway, it had been obvious to him that Liverpool was the best place to take his wife after the infected mosquito had bitten her.

Both of them had been aware of the other scientists' work on flaviviruses, had corresponded with Professor Madison and his research team. His and Free's joint panic had subsided a bit when Madison had told them that, although Free's blood was showing the virus, she probably wouldn't be too ill. She was a healthy young woman of 21 and her immune system would be strong. No problems then.

"Unless you're pregnant," said Clement Madison, looking at them over his glasses, "But two hardworking young scientists like you won't be starting a family yet, will you?"

It had proven true that she wouldn't be very ill then; just joint and muscle pain – a few headaches, a transitory rash, although she had been very tired during her pregnancy and Ben had made her lie down a lot. He had spent a lot of time with her, making her nice meals, taking good care of her.

*

Jake was invigilating finals in the Younger Hall; three quarters of the under- graduates were historians of various sorts, Scottish at the front, Modern in the middle, Ancient at the back; the other quarter was from Economics. They all looked very young.

He wandered down the first aisle and up the second, completing his pattern through the hall and returning to the desk in front. It was quiet except for the turning over of papers and a few deep sighs from those who had not got the questions for which they had hoped. There was a girl crying softly in the middle row. Daisy Frayn, his invigilation administrator, looked over at him, waiting for a nod before going over to check on the girl.

Jake checked his pile of extra paper, the box of extra pens and pencils for anyone who hadn't remembered to bring their own and picked up the god-book. He had decided to re-read it right through whilst invigilating. He'd never be able to concentrate on anything new, and he might gain insight; you never know.

*

It was the evening following Belinda's unannounced inspection of the Genetic Engineering Laboratories and she and Mark were reading in bed. It was Mark who had been late this time, having come up from a London meeting; Belinda was reading all the information the university had on the set-up in GE and five years of reports on the specific project in which they were interested.

It was called "Blue Bag" – which neither the Professor nor Dr Gateside had mentioned. She had decided to take the rest of it to bed, to read in comfort and wait for Mark. She had helped their teenage children with homework and persuaded them to eat the lasagne the housekeeper had left for them. Belinda herself was no sparkling cook.

"What are you reading?" Mark asked, taking in the large piles of paper both on their bed and on the floor, where his wife tended to file things, she had finished with, for Hazel or himself to pick up.

"All the stuff about Meredith Williams's work," she said, "And the things about how the lab was commissioned and how we paid for it. All before my time, obviously."

"Any brilliant insights yet?"

"Not a one. I don't particularly like the sound of the work, but it's not illegal and probably not immoral as far as I can see, although there are experimental animals involved."

She leaned back against her pile of pillows, trying to get more comfortable. "I think that's the point actually. You can't really tell anything from all this: it's too obscure and it's couched in flannel, with a sideways touch of the Official Secrets Act. It talks about cures and understanding the genetic basis – all of which is a sales pitch to funders of course. The methodology is a bit vague too. I'm not picking up anything which would be so attractive to the Americans that they'd be sending all those rather large men over to Scotland to attend to security."

"Have you decided what you want to do yet?"

"Not yet. The thing is that I didn't find anything, when I went over there, to give me any reason for alarm. Everything was fine; just as I would have expected it. Too fine. I'll have to have a big think."

Mark put his book down on the bedside table and turned in towards her.

"You probably need quite a lot of sleep, then," he said.

"Not necessarily."

*

When Jake returned from invigilating, a wee brown envelope had been pushed through the letterbox of his flat. He got relatively little mail here; most went to his office. He picked-up the envelope, feeling there was just, perhaps, one sheet of paper, folded, in it.

He opened it. It was a poison-pen letter, straight off television, composed with bits of headlines cut out of magazines. It said:

FORNICATOR!

STOP NOW OR PHOTOS WILL BE ON INTERNET

NO REPUTATION = NO JOB

It was signed "A FRIEND".

*

Jake ran to the department without picking-up his briefcase, clattering straight up the stairs to Marlon Biggs' office. He rapped the door frantically and Marlon opened it right away. He ushered Jake in without speaking; the neuroscientist was out of breath and bending down, clutching his knees.

"I got this," puffed Jake, handing the envelope over, thanking god (if any) for Minnie's advice.

"Ah," said Marlon, unfolding the paper and placing it on his blotter. It did not take long for him to read and digest it.

"Did you bring the photographs with you?" he asked.

"They're downstairs in my room," said Jake.

"Okay," said Marlon, rubbing his hands together, "This is what we do."

He retrieved a piece of printer paper from the shelf behind his desk and, taking a black permanent marker wrote 'DO YOU KNOW WHO TOOK THESE PICTURES?' in large block capitals. He added a note, with his title and degrees, to let a reader know it was official:

"Go down to the front entrance and put the three worst

photographs on the notice-board, with this title under them. Then get Mrs Simonson to upload the other three to the Biology website – tell her I said so - the university administrator will take them down when he sees them, but they'll be OK until they've done their job."

"Which is?" asked Jake.

"Make whoever it is aware that everybody already knows; can't blackmail you if everybody knows. It's not you anyway, is it? Just your head."

Jake was astounded at Marlon Biggs' unsuspected anarchic streak, thanked him, and went to do as he had been told.

*

Christabel dropped round to see her uncle, bringing the little Rafaella with her on a lead. The dog made much of Ben, to whom she had taken a shine. Christabel seemed more relaxed than the other times he'd seen her, and she explained to him that she wasn't going back to New York; that part of her life was over.

"What are you going to do now?" Ben asked, running water into a cereal bowl for the dog and putting it down on the kitchen floor.

"Oh, I don't know," replied Christabel, "I'm going to take some time off and spend it at our new cottage in Surrey. I have plenty of money saved, so I can afford to have a good look around before I commit myself to a new job."

"What kind of qualifications have you?" asked Ben, who had no idea.

"Politics and economics," she said, "But I can do all kinds of

270

surprising things!"

Ben did not doubt it, although he realised that she wasn't going to tell him any of the things he would be surprised by.

"Oh, good," he said, "Good. Good."

"You look a little glum," said Christabel, "Is there anything I can do?"

"Oh, well. I have probably lost my job."

Christabel did a double take and asked why.

"The Chair of the Department. He thinks I'm senile. He suggested early retiral – because I'm not as sharp as I was. I'm to take the rest of term off and think about it. I'm not going to teach again."

"Uncle Ben, I'm so sorry. You love teaching, don't you? Daddy always said you did."

"Um, yes. Still have a book to write, though. Not the end of the world, is it?"

"Have you had any more of those visions recently?" she asked.

"I have," he said, "And I'm going to see the Principal tomorrow. There are things going on here that I don't like the look of. That's what the visions were trying to tell me. I was too stupid to understand. It doesn't matter what was in the visions, whether they were holy or not. It's the message which counts, do you see?"

*

As Ben arrived at the Principal's House in The Scores, Mark Fleming was just coming out of the porch. He knew Ben by sight, from being around the town, and said hello as he passed. He turned as he got to the gate and shouted to Ben that he could find Belinda in her study.

Ben rang the bell and was shown in by a housekeeper in a pinafore. Belinda's study was on the first floor, and he managed the stairs at a run, arriving a wee bit puffed but with his newly reclaimed energy still fizzing out of his finger-ends. A quick knock on the half open door and a hello to the bespectacled blonde at the facing desk.

"Hello, Professor Furness!" said Belinda warmly, "How are you? What can I do for you?" She rose from the chair and came towards him, reaching to grasp his hand and removing her terrifying spectacles.

"I need to talk to you, very seriously," said the mycologist. "I have found something out which you need to know about immediately. I know you will be deeply concerned."

✦

Ben's Diary entry 14

Because I've known Belinda for years, since she was an undergraduate in the department, I suppose I'd already known that she would listen to me as a colleague and, maybe even friend, rather than thinking I was a silly old codger who is imagining things. What I didn't dare hope for was her readiness to get involved personally and not only take steps to stop this evil thing but also to render immediate personal assistance. We're having a meeting at her house tomorrow night. Minnie and me, young Jake and Felicity, and Belinda and Mark.

*

As Felicity walked down the corridor towards the dormitories, accompanied by the largest of the American security staff, Mervyn Adams, she could hear some very peculiar noises; a kind of very loud snuffling, followed by screeching. A high-pitched extended sound, an ululation almost. She asked the corridor in general whatever it could be. Adams showed no reaction, not even a shoulder-shrug, and kept on walking. He opened the door into the sub-corridor, off which were the small rooms where the older subjects lived.

The first one was where she had talked to Maya – she had talked, and Maya had made herself understood by gestures and noises. She didn't have any speech and Felicity wondered whether she was physically capable of it. She rather thought not. The general sense of ownership of the rooms did not appear to be high and, on her previous few visits, Felicity had found different chuas staying there. Odd to have a term for them. Possibly pejorative. She resolved not to use it.

It was an extremely small woman today, her face pressed flat against the glass panel in the door, her arm being held behind her by one of the huge blue-coated "technicians". Felicity, looking past the woman to try to understand what was happening, suddenly saw Tubby, in there, tapping a hypodermic syringe, filled with a straw-coloured liquid, preparing to give an injection.

"Open it up. Now!" she ordered Adams in a voice not to be gainsaid and, to her surprise, he did so. Both the woman and the technician were pushed backwards as Adams' gigantic strength was exerted on the door. This made Tubby move back of his own accord; no way to give the needle.

The woman took the opportunity to wrench herself free of the grasp of the bluecoat and cringed up against the back wall of the room. Now inside what had suddenly morphed, for Felicity, from a room into a cell, Felicity insisted on being told what was happening. Tubby, pale, skinny, and nasty, told her to go away.

"What the hell are you doing?" she asked her lover. "Are you giving her insulin? You can't do that; it'll kill her".

"It's her scheduled time," said Tubby, advancing, with the bluecoat, on the cringing woman, who was now screaming loudly, "And there's something wrong with her anyway – we made an error."

"An ERROR?" Felicity said. "What on earth do you mean, an error?"

"Don't tell me you didn't think of it, Felicity," Tubby said, looking at her with incredulity. "Surely, someone as bright as you should have realized that, if we could cure microcephalism by genetic engineering, we could also cause it?"

Felicity felt her legs begin to tremble. The young man she had thought she knew was transforming before her into the very picture of a mad scientist. "Did you really think that the US Department of Defense would spend billions of dollars on producing a cure for a few pathetic children in Pakistan - or in Yorkshire for that matter? Don't be stupid."

"Did you ever hear of Stalin's boy, Ilya Ivanovich Ivanov and later, Hitler's guys, trying to cross humans with chimpanzees? Didn't work, but if they'd been left alone, it would have eventually. All they had to do was to have our modern ways of deactivating genes – chimpanzees have twenty-four pairs of chromosomes to humans' twenty-three, so they needed to fix that before it would work. Why do you think they wanted to do that, Felicity?" She felt her lip beginning to tremble too.

"Because..." she just managed to get the one word out, her heart wasn't in it: it was somewhere else in the vast pool of poison shock.

"Because," he said, pushing her down onto the bed, "they wanted soldiers who would do as they were told, who would fight to the death. They invented the idea of collateral damage before the Yanks ever thought of it.

"These are small enough to get into places others can't go; they can be violent enough to kill as they are told. And they're surprisingly strong, although not strong enough yet; they aren't intelligent enough to be afraid of much in the first place – and the Prof's sorting that out, he's the natural successor of Walter Freeman. People in the 1950s thought the cortex was the important thing, that's how Freeman came up with lobotomy. These days we know how fear works, too, and the Prof has discovered a technique of whittling down parts of their amygdalae.

"When we get that completely right, they won't have any fear at all... And it doesn't matter how many you sacrifice; they aren't people. They don't know any better than to run into the danger zone, they have no concept of self or of self-preservation. They. Don't. Matter."

Felicity looked up at him, tears running down her cheeks. This was the man she thought she loved; the man she had wanted to spend the rest of her life with. From somewhere, she found a voice. It was surprisingly steady.

"The lobotomy man in the fifties, the one who operated on all those people to control them? What went wrong with that?"

"Ah, I thought you'd never ask. Remember Phineas Gage? Do you recall seeing pictures of him when you started studying brain science? The nineteenth century American railway worker who got a railroad spike through his head. Changed his personality but he could still think even though he'd lost a lot of brain matter. There was a song, by Dan Lindner with a banjo:

"Phineas Gage had a hole in his head,

And ev'ryone knew that he oughta be dead.

Was it fate or blind luck,

Though it never came clear,

Kept keepin' on year after year..."

Felicity's shock was mingled with a horrified feeling that he was going to burst into song. He didn't. Thank God. Tubby kept on going too.

"Some of our chuas have started thinking. Didn't know they could, but we were wrong. It only took one of them to find a sense of self somewhere. Just one. All it takes. Now we have to find a way of containing it. It's a pain in the neck."

"But you can't really believe they don't matter," said Felicity, at last. "They can feel, even if they aren't very intelligent. They're living creatures. You created them, now you're killing them!"

"Euthanasia isn't murder," he said. "And don't forget, if we hadn't built them, they would never have had life at all. Just like raising cows for steak. We created them; we can dispose of them. We must, scientific procedure. You know the protocols with experimental animals!"

He moved towards the chua with his hypo of insulin, causing her to try to make herself even smaller as he did. No self-preservation; no fear? Right.

The chua in the cell was one of those Felicity had seen in the recreation room, a particularly small woman with only one foot, her leg ending in a sort of knobby stump. She cowered at the back of the cell, her strange face showing the great fear she was not supposed to feel.

Felicity's heart felt like lead in her chest, her pity for the woman rising in her gullet in acid. Tubby was holding forth again, about ethics in animal experiments, saying that the experimental subjects were kept clean and fed and even allowed "social contact" every evening after their meal. They had a good life.

"But they aren't *supposed* to develop leadership from within. We didn't forsee that!"

Felicity had been desperately trying to work out how to stop him injecting the chua but she knew he was stronger than her, not even thinking about the bluecoat; that, even if she managed to prevent the injection now, he would do it later anyway. Not having a foot, and being able to feel fear, had condemned the tiny person to death. She couldn't watch; she turned her back as Tubby sank the needle into the chua's stomach. There was a wail which ascended in tone but stopped suddenly.

Felicity collapsed back onto the narrow bed. As the bluecoat picked up the body and removed it, Tubby came to sit down next to Felicity. He began talking again, returning to the gentle (she would have said) sweet tones he'd always used to her previously:

"They really *aren't* real people you know," he said. "They have no memories, no way of reasoning, no comparison to us. We have a right to use them if it helps humanity. Lots of philosophers say so. Some say that memory and consciousness are necessary for a being to be called human, others that you have to have intentions, thoughts and will to be truly human.

"You've said yourself that we don't normally use apes in the lab because they're too intelligent. Our subjects aren't capable of wanting to live or die, they aren't people - they don't matter. What matters is whether it's in the best interests of humanity for them to die."

Between her tears, Felicity said, "Did you learn all that by heart?"

Neil McPhee, a Psychiatrist

Joanne Critchley had telephoned Dr Neil McPhee, a consultant psychiatrist with whom she had spoken when her father was diagnosed with Alzheimer's. He had seemed friendly then, and he spoke in his soft islands accent now. He was, however, very dismissive of Professor Furness's claim to have seen the strange child.

"You know what they can be like," he said. "Lots of them hallucinate, and they tend to be very vivid if the diagnosis is something like Dementia with Lewy Bodies – or even Parkinson's Disease Dementia, although Alzheimer sufferers can hallucinate too – theirs are usually pretty benign. Maybe like your mannie. I daresay an allegedly holy vision can be comforting to some of them."

Joanne took a deep breath.

"I wouldn't have thought he was one of those," she said. "Atheist, scientist. There's some possibility of dissociation too, I don't know much about that…"

"A lot of that stuff is rubbish," he said quite shortly. "Too many people have read garbage about multiple personalities; it's all quite sensational and loopy. I'm really sorry, I have to go now, a clinic…" Joanne felt as if she'd been slapped gently in the face as they took their leave.

Had he actually said "loopy"?

*

It was Wednesday, two days after Jake had pinned the photographs to the department's main noticeboard, when he got the email from Kermit Whittaker saying that the job hadn't worked out and the offer was being withdrawn. Sorry.

Oh, thanks, said Jake to himself. Where am I going to get Kate's Manila money from now?

*

They were all meeting together for the first time, in the conference room, upstairs at the Principal's House. Belinda, of course, was in the chair, and she made it clear that she was speaking for Mark, too. He had to be elsewhere, but they were of one mind on this, and he would do whatever they decided.

Stern, dark, portraits of ancient Principals stared down at the little gathering, meeting to consider something at least as important as anything they themselves had ever considered. The large boardroom table was very dark and reflective as well as way too big for their needs. There were crystal water glasses and two or three jugs full of water to pour into them. The chairs had seats covered with burgundy velvet but were too straight-backed to be comfortable.

Belinda explained that she had found nothing unexpected or worrying when she had inspected the laboratories unannounced, but that the documents she had studied had been vague and obfuscatory. She was not clear from any of this what was happening. She turned to Ben.

"Ben," said Belinda, "Can you update us with what you have come up with?" Ben sat forward on the chair opposite Belinda, next to Minnie, who had her hand on his forearm.

"Of course," said Ben. Jake thought he sounded quite different from the last time they had met. Then, the Prof had seemed much older than his years. And defeated. Bewildered. No idea what to do. Now, he appeared twenty years younger, energetic, focused, determined. He had moved on from the 'holy vision'. That had simply been a prompt and needed no further thought.

"Everything just fell into place," he said. "I'd been thinking it was a hallucination or a vision or some flashback, but I was wrong. It's much simpler than that; straight-forward, scientific. There is a frightful genetic experiment going on in Genetic Engineering, and we have to stop it right now. Before people die." Felicity, who was looking tired and upset, was nodding her head and Jake saw her take a deep breath;

pulling herself together to speak.

"People have already died," she said, in a wobbly voice. "I don't know how many. It could be a lot; the experiment has been going on for six years. God knows how many they've sacrificed in that time!" She stopped to get her breath. "Of course, it depends on what you define as 'people'. Or perhaps it doesn't." Felicity leaned on her elbow, on the table, as if her head was too heavy to hold up.

"I've been in that department quite a bit lately," she said, "Going out with one of the postdocs, and he was quite keen to show off the work he's doing. So, I know my way around. The day before yesterday, I went in to talk to Tubby – he's my boyfriend, *was* my boyfriend until I found him euthanizing one of them. He said it was her time to go, like she was an experimental animal." She stopped, with a sob, "To him, she's expendable and his protocol said her usefulness was over.

"He said something had gone wrong, he thought it was in one of the early manipulations. They should never have developed any sense of self. Theirs is an evolutionary cul-de-sac, just for the purposes of the work."

Jake was delighted that Ben had brought in the Principal, he had the idea that direct action was about to be suggested. Not many Principals were ever involved in direct action, this would be a stunner. He had expected nothing more than trying to persuade her that this experiment should be brought to an abrupt and administrative end. In the last few minutes, he had got the distinct impression that that was not what was going to happen.

"Right," said Belinda, "There are several possibilities of what should happen now done: I can issue a closure notice on Professor

Williams's experiment; I can even close his whole department, I can contact whoever is in charge in America, this General Challoner, I think, and in London for that matter; I can sack Meredith Williams; I can make a report to the police, or even go via the Chief Constable. I can call the newspapers; I can call the Prime Minister. I can get it stopped.

"At least I could if I had any actual evidence of wrongdoing. Which I don't. If I just call the police, there will be nothing to find when they get there…" She paused, moistening her lips. "My sense is that those things are for the future. Something must happen, immediately, to stop what is going on, or there will be very little for any authorities to find."

Minnie was staring at Belinda, as if she couldn't believe what the Principal was saying: Ben was staring as if he couldn't believe his luck. Felicity was crying, Jake searching for a handkerchief he could give her.

Suddenly, the hall door opened noisily, and a different voice spoke. Christabel Furness strode into the room, followed by Max Denfrell. With Christie's pallor and Denfrell's very dark skin, they looked like angels in ebony and ivory emerging from the darkened hall.

"It has to be Friday, we shall need two days for the preparation, otherwise it won't work," said Christabel, her polished English tones, slicing through the room, "If we don't pull off a rescue then, more people will die. Unfortunately, we cannot do the planning in time for it to be tonight. That's the price we'll have to pay. They will have to pay.

"Dr Malcolm, can you make a decent drawing of the building? You said you'd spent some time there…"

She and Denfrell had clearly been listening outside the door.

They each took an empty chair at the table.

Felicity, balling up Jake's handkerchief and stuffing it in her pocket, said that she could. She asked for paper and Belinda produced some pads from the elegant little French desk by the huge window. Felicity sat on the accompanying elegant little French chair and got to work.

"I can be in charge of Logistics," said Christie, "What I'm good at. We'll need transport, for speed and distance, three cars. Not your van, Dr Ellwood, it's too distinctive. There are, as Felicity has said, seven small people in the dormitories, including Maya, who appears to be the spokeswoman. Four in one car and three in the other. They aren't very big, which is helpful.

"The third car will bring those of us who are left in the laboratory back here. I'm assuming, Principal, that you can accommodate everyone here, in some security, until we can find them somewhere else to go?"

"Yes. Plenty of bedrooms here and I can easily have more beds made up. Will they want to share rooms? They might want to be together. Not a problem, anyway. There are plenty of window bars and things – since the Prince lived here while he was a student."

"I shall attend to the security," said Denfrell, speaking from his station by the door, in the deep drawl of the South. He rarely felt the need to elaborate on what he said.

Jake wondered, in his shattering amazement, how on earth he had got involved. Minnie chimed in with her feeling that there would be medical matters needing to be taken care of and she could do that.

"But you are medically qualified, too, aren't you, Jake?" she asked the neuroscientist.

"Well, yes, but I haven't used a stethoscope for 20 years! I think that boat has well sailed. I can do something else!" Ben was looking across at Jake as he said this.

"What am I supposed to do?" Ben all but wailed. "Was seeing her the only thing?"

"We'll need some kind of sedative," said Belinda, "Did I hear something about magic mushrooms?"

*

They talked into the night, plotting what they had to do; what they were competent to do. Jake pointedly asked Ben about magic mushrooms, just what their effects are, what sorts of things happen to the person taking them. Ben said that it was interesting; the effects were pleasant enough but could be very scary sometimes – depending a lot on the individual person.

"Obviously, the dose is crucial. Depending on the body size, percentage fat and metabolic rate. That's more important than how much you take. So, really, it's vital to calculate the dose exactly for each person. It's a complex sum and not one I'd be confident in doing these days. Why are you asking?"

"Basically, I was wondering whether we could use your knowledge of these things to dope the people there and get the – what did we call them, Felicity? – yes, chuas; get the chuas out."

"Not really a question of doping them," said Ben, "That's not one of the effects. They'll not go to sleep. It's not narcotic. What happens is that, although none of the brain-centres are stimulated, you would think they are… Psilocybin damps down the parts of the frontal lobes which process things to do with the sense of self – they can be a bit unpredictable.

"Normally, in the laboratory, we'd give subjects a lot of psychological tests to check that they are mentally stable first: we wouldn't use them as experimental subjects if they weren't because hallucinogens might exacerbate mental illness into psychosis."

"What would it feel like then? If a person who isn't psychotic takes them?" asked Jake.

"Experiences of intense colours and patterns. A lot of people describe feelings of spiritual significance. Which is ironic when you think about it…"

Denfrell spoke from the closed doorway:

"The whole thing is rich in irony."

Americans aren't known for appreciating this. Felicity pointed out that the greater irony was the one about what constitutes personhood.

"Ironic that it's their sense of self which is being damped down," said Denfrell, "Dr Gateside, for one, doesn't think the chuas are people. He said they don't matter; they only exist because he and Professor Williams created them."

No one spoke for a moment.

"It would be difficult to use psilocybin," said Belinda, still a biochemist, and not too distant from her own scientific career. "We don't want to kill anybody or drive them permanently insane. It would mean that we'd have to calculate the dose for each person who's likely to be there. It would take a lot of planning and a lot of time. Do we actually have all that time?"

"We could add a glamour?" said Jake, "Maybe we could use 'shrooms and a glamour?"

Christabel asked whatever the hell that was and asked him to explain.

"It's an effect," said Jake, "How to describe it? Um, well. Originally, the term is from the word 'grammar' in the old sense of learning and erudition, via the Scots 'glamer', but was popularly associated with occult practices. My use is the occult one."

Everyone looked a wee bit shocked by this. Universities don't usually include occult practices in their day-to-day business.

"This would be so that the chuas could 'disappear' without anyone knowing immediately. In other words, it would be an illusion."

"Like Pepper's Ghost?" asked Ben, brightening, "You'll make anyone looking see something that isn't there?"

"Yes."

"Does that sort of thing actually work?" said Felicity.

"It does," said Ben, "It works brilliantly if it's done properly! I've seen Jake do it. It's great!"

"We will, though, need to begin the logistics part earlier than you were thinking, Christabel," said Jake.

"Two things to think about," Christabel rapped. "One, getting the equipment for the effect into the department. Two, getting the mushrooms into the staff. Neither easy."

"Doable, though," said Felicity. "The mushrooms anyway. I've been taking cakes for Tubby and the night staff, after tea. Pure psilocybin's more controllable if it's injected but I don't see how that could be managed. On the other hand, it wouldn't be hard to add a smallish dose of it to the brownies without anyone being able to taste it. It would make them likely to disbelieve their eyes!"

It occurred to Ben that Tubby and the Night Staff could be a sixties pop group, eating hash in chocolate brownies. He suppressed a chuckle. *What is wrong with me? This is serious. Short concentration span.*

"The glamour is harder, though," said Christie. "Doping - sorry, I know - the staff is one thing, and important, but disguising the fact that the chuas have been taken is something quite other. The equipment would be pretty large?" the question addressed to Jake, "And I guess that you will need your maroon van?

"Yes. Or I may be able to borrow a different one from a friend. Better that my well-kent one isn't seen anywhere near the G.E. building."

He took out his mobile phone and rang a number.

"Dave," he said, "Are you busy Friday night? No, I was just wondering if I could borrow your van? You can have mine if you need it. It's important and I don't want it recognized where I'm not supposed to be...yes, of course. You can? Oh, that's great! I owe you one!"

He hung-up the 'phone and said that his mate Dave, a magician

287

living in Crieff, would bring his grey van over Friday afternoon and take Jake's maroon one.

"My new assistant, Naomi, will help me shift the equipment from one van to the other. She won't ask questions, except why she's not going with me. I can handle that."

Felicity looked up from her draughts-woman-ship and said:

"The wee people all congregate in the treatment-slash-recreation room when they've been fed at night, and it isn't that big. So, it wouldn't be like trying to disguise that they've gone from each room..." It was Jake's turn to take his tablet from his pocket and start making calculations. He asked Felicity if she had an idea of the measurements of the treatment room. She stood and walked over to him, presenting a sheet with a meticulous drawing of a room – complete with approximate measurements.

She did, he remembered, have eidetic memory for numbers. How handy was that? He would have to work out the details from scratch, where he'd prefer to see the venue and do the measurements himself, but he could do it. He could trust Felicity's numbers. The time frame would be narrow, though. He asked how long the chuas spent in the treatment room and did they always eat at the same time?

"Yes," said Felicity, "Everything is done by the clock, isn't it?" she looked over at Denfrell, who said, nodding his head:

"They all eat together in the Animal House at 6 precisely, finished by 6.15, then they're marched down the stairs to the dormitory corridor. The treatment room is at the end of it."

Felicity produced a second careful, beautifully drawn, plan

showing the lay-out.

"They stay in there for exactly twenty minutes and then the Night Superintendent – that would be me," said Denfrell, "clears the room, and they go into their cells for the night. We have not a shade more than twenty minutes to get them out and cover-up that they've gone. The mushrooms will help with the staff's perception of that, of course. They won't be seeing at all clearly!"

They looked at one another, wondering whether this was real or just a hallucination they had somehow wandered into, whilst Belinda summed up and Christie gave instructions. Max Denfrell seemed to have his ready worked out.

"Oh," said Jake, "One other thing. An American firm has been trying to blackmail me, or bribe me, or something. They offered me a super job, with excessive financial compensation, then they took me to Paris where they got me drunk, photographed me in several compromising positions with a naked prostitute, and sent me the photos.

"Then they threatened me with exposure if I didn't 'stop it', without saying what 'it' was – although we know, don't we? Thanks to Minnie," he looked over at her, still holding Ben's hand on the other side of the boardroom table, "I'd already told my Department Chair and he recommended putting the photos on the internet and on the department's main noticeboard.

"So, they couldn't threaten you because everybody knew!" said Minnie happily. "My God! Jake," said Ben, "I've said it before, but your life makes mine seem very pedestrian!"

*

Not at all sure that any of them would sleep that night, Jake decided to walk for a while and, on the way, accompanied Minnie and Ben to their respective homes. Having left Ben at South Street, Jake and Minnie walked past Deans Court to the top of North Street.

"Still working on the glamour?" she asked.

"No," said Jake, "Plenty of time for that – and I've performed it recently too. I was just thinking about this job I was going to get that didn't exist and feeling a bit of a fool."

"You couldn't have known," said Minnie, "You are very worthy of such a job, had it been real. It just wasn't this time. Another will come along!"

"Thanks for the comfort," he said, "But I was kind of looking forward to the money. My ex-wife, Kate, wants to do her postgraduate clinical psych practice at an NGO in Manila. I offered her a couple of thousand quid on the promise of the American job."

He looked particularly miserable as he said this, despite the otherwise success of the evening. Minnie's face remained smiling happily as they got to her front door.

"Not to worry," she said, "I have some money my parents left me. Who shall I make the cheque out to?"

Miracles do happen.

*

In the end it was surprisingly easy, from Jake's point of view. Christie and Denfrell, using Dave's van during the night, and the garbage area behind the building, handled the set-up, without his presence, using his magic mirror and sheets of clear glass. The effect was based on Pepper's Ghost, of course, but the reflection through the mirror showed, not a supposed ghost but sufficient suggestion of the presence of seven chuas, added to the reflective panel by the clever little hands of Felicity Malcolm. Ben had stolen the mushrooms from young John Malley's reference supply in his lab, and delivered them to Felicity.

The most difficult part was how they were going to enter the locked down building. Max Denfrell had said that he would handle that, that they did not need to worry about it.

*

In the small kitchen of her shared flat in North Street, Felicity adds the finely powdered magic mushrooms to the flour she will use in the chocolate nut brownies, beloved of both Tubby and the assorted Americans on night duty. She always bakes the same number, reflecting the number of people on duty.

There are never any abstentions, there are always eight – one for Tubby, one for each of the five security men on rotation, one for Denfrell, another for Tubby, because he is greedy. He has never had to worry about putting on weight. This time she knows there will be one left – because Denfrell won't be having one. She wonders who will eat it. Felicity lets them cool in the tin and then gets them out onto a cooling rack. They'll go into her airtight dancing polar bear cake tin when they are quite cold.

*

Max Denfrell is a qualified locksmith but his expertise in that area is not going to help him in this situation, as he sits, thinking, in one of the horrid chairs in his horrid flat with a drawing pad on his knee. He is, in a way, hoist on his own petard, having beefed up the security system. However, there are ways to overcome it; he well knows its weak spots and the places where it might, potentially, malfunction.

The inside doors are easy; all locked of course, but his personal keycard will open them all. He'd had it cloned as soon as it had been issued, as his training demanded. For some reason he had postponed putting old-fashioned but efficient bolts on the inside of all the doors. That won't happen until next week. If at all.

The outside door is an obvious problem. The automatic alarm is connected to both the security lounge and his own office and, unless the entry protocols, of a palm-print and retinal scan, are immediately engaged, a klaxon sounds all over the building and an entry-proof shutter immediately slides up from the channel in the floor to cover the back of the main door. The American company which had installed all his new measures had said it was state of the art impenetrable. Denfrell reflects on this and works out how he can disarm it in fifteen seconds.

The extra lockdown protocols are easy to subvert. He simply won't carry-out the lockdown.

*

Felicity takes care of the opening of the Treatment Room, using Denfrell's cloned keycard. There are only seven chuas in the dormitories, including Maya, and that will be quite enough to accommodate in Belinda's house until other arrangements can be made. This is the least clear portion of the plan; everything else has been double-checked to destruction.

Minnie has joined Felicity to try and reassure the small people; Maya is helping too, by being there in her silent way, letting them know that they are safe with these big people. Because Felicity has been seen around the department, with Tubby, although they are still wary, they maybe perceive that she holds transferred authority.

They come out of the recreation room, with Maya carrying the smallest girl, at the back, wary in case of stragglers. Mark's car, driven by Jake, as well as the one they have borrowed from Belinda, and Ben's elderly Morris Minor are parked right outside the building. Everyone rushes towards them, and Christie and Felicity help the chuas into their seats, whilst Denfrell, Ben, and Minnie walk swiftly back into the building to check on the stoned.

It is Jake's task to await the return of Ben and Minnie: Denfrell isn't coming. Jake is clenching his fists on the steering wheel, wishing they'd come and realizing that their timing is out by eight minutes. He debates whether he should go in – but the plan doesn't allow for that. He waits.

*

Inside the building, Minnie has already checked that Meredith Williams is starting to babble nonsensically about periwinkle cars being broken, lying on one of the lobby sofas: he is very obviously stoned. He is expected to be non-functional for at least another five or six minutes and then, probably, will spend a few minutes wishing the effect wasn't fading.

Minnie counts his radial pulse at seventy-nine, not bad for such a driven man, and goes on to a very large security man, lying on the floor outside the door to the Animal House staircase. He is well under and asleep, having consumed two brownies, but she can feel his pulse and counts it at sixty-four: very healthy.

The only other person, apart from security staff, for whom Ben and Denfrell have taken responsibility, is Tubby Gateside, who seems, oddly, to be unconscious where he has fallen, draped from the top of the separate back stairs to the Animal House to the sixth and seventh steps; looking as serene as Felicity had said he always does, the top step serving as a pillow.

Tubby is lying at an awkward angle for Minnie to feel his pulse from above; his right wrist under him and his left hand lying against the metal stair-rail, as if he is about to grasp it. She climbs, slow with arthritic pain, down several steps and manages to rearrange him sufficiently to put the bell of her stethoscope over his heart (Felicity says he doesn't have one).

There is a steady beat, but it is very slow. She straightens to look him in the face and places her hand on his brow. He is quite pale but, as she doesn't know him, she has no idea whether this is normal for him. His forehead is dry and warm, no sweat, no sign of any agitation. His brown eyes open slowly, with a joyous twinkle.

"Hello!" he says.

*

At last, after twelve minutes have passed and nothing has happened, Jake lets himself in through the metal door. It has been held open by an old-fashioned wooden wedge which Max Denfrell brought with him. He'd said the door would automatically lock and re-engage the palm and retinal scans with nothing to hold it and would not stay open by itself. Jake replaces the wedge on the pencil mark, exactly where it had been.

He can see comparatively little with just the security lights on in the foyer. There is a large American lying on the floor by the door, where he had been moved by Denfrell after collapsing in the doorway. There is no sign of the Night Superintendent or Minnie or Ben. They should have been out by now. Where the hell are they?

Jake has memorized the layout of the whole building from Felicity's drawings and knows that the main part of the action would have taken place in the recreation room and dormitories in the basement below. He also knows that there is no lift to get down there. The stairs to the basement are at the extreme right of the first floor, leading only downwards. He walks quickly towards the single door and through it.

The door swings open at his touch and Jake passes through into a darkened space with the metal staircase immediately outside it. He steps down the top few steps, and then, not seeing anyone, runs down the remainder.

Arriving on a landing with two doors ahead, and still following Felicity's map, he opens the (left hand) door into a warm dark corridor with more doors on each side. There is no one to be seen.

Gazing into the glass panel in each door, he sees nothing and arrives quickly at the door of the Recreation/Treatment Room at the end. The glamour does not seem to be in place; the mirror is broken. Jake opens the door slowly.

As his eyes grow accustomed to the low light level, he sees four figures sitting, shrouded in darkness, on lab stools at the far end of the room. Two people are very close together on the stools and two are separate; not only from the others but from one another.

Suddenly, a fluorescent tube, activated by movement, comes on, flooding the room with bleached white light. Jake sees that the two figures sitting together are Minnie and Ben; the others are Max Denfrell and Tubby Gateside, facing each other, each of them holding a gun.

Tubby's Smith and Wesson .38 is aimed at Minnie, Denfrell's Beretta M9 at Tubby. It is a stand-off from a spy thriller.

"Over here," says Tubby, voice cracking with unaccustomed strain. "Get with the old folk."

Jake does exactly as he is told, sitting on the vacant stool next to Minnie. She gives him a sick look. She is very pale and trembling. She gives him her left hand; the other is clutched in Ben's. Denfrell is not looking at them, his cold eyes are locked on Tubby.

"Now," says Tubby, "What am I supposed to do with you? Just keep you here till Challoner arrives. Well, that's too long, obviously."

He keeps his gaze on the three as he fishes a mobile 'phone out of his pants pocket and clicks on a speed dial number. It appears to have been picked up immediately at the other end.

"Bettany," he says, "It's me. I'm waiting for you to come over here but seem to have acquired some hostages. Or something."

There is silence, though obviously not on the other end; Tubby goes a little pink around the gills and looks as if he is about to splutter in reply to some unearned profanity. Eventually, he clicks the 'phone off without speaking again, and replaces it in his pocket.

*

Felicity, driving Ben's beige Morris Minor, arrived in front of the Principal's House ahead of Belinda's British Racing Green S-type Jaguar, driven, too fast, by Christabel Furness.

The Principal and Mark were standing in the porch; both hurried into the pathway and helped the small people to disembark and took them into the house. Christie surrendered command to Belinda and checked that both cars were locked. She stayed outside to wait for the others.

In the Principal's Reception Room, a fire had been lit against the chill of the night after a warm day. The chuas, even though they have not encountered fire before, were not afraid but showed they were quite capable of some rapid learning, following Maya in going towards it and the big floor cushions in front of the hearth.

Belinda invited them all to sit down. She gazed at her guests in some amazement, realizing that taking a verbal head count towards serving tea or coffee would not work. Instead, she and Mark departed for the kitchen to contrive suitable refreshments. Neither really had any idea what they should be.

Maya was communicating with Felicity by sign language; she is good at making herself understood. Felicity immediately grasped that something to drink is needed and told the chua that the need will be met straight away. Christie was trying to make herself understood to the male chua; the one who seemed the most reserved. She was trying to get him to tell her if they needed anything else. She was failing.

*

Nothing seems to have happened for a long time. Ben realizes he is starting to fidget on his high stool; he had quite forgotten that lab stools were so hard. That's something which hasn't changed, he thinks with an interior chuckle, before the fact that he is not in a position to chuckle hits home.

Minnie looks weary, worried, and scared. No wonder. But she has control of herself. Ben looks at Jake. The magician is perched on his lab stool with his legs wound around the spindles. Ben can almost see the cogs of his quicksilver mind clicking over – trying to decide what he can do. Ben wonders if time is running slowly for everyone or just for him.

The two young men with the guns, whom he couldn't have named in a quiz, are still locked on their respective targets: the black man, unwaveringly, on the white man, the white man pointing at Minnie. Neither seem to be having timing problems; they are not getting tired like Ben.

He wonders if Minnie is as exhausted as him; poor dear has had a busy time lately. He feels a glow of warm appreciation for her. After this he'll ask her out for a meal, as a reward for being stalwart. She is fun, anyway. A sharp, frozen blade of feeling pierces his chest as the thought occurs that they will likely not get out of here alive.

*

It all happens at once, as everyone is waiting for something. The door slams into the wall as a policeman in a flak jacket comes through very fast, and there are two shots within the room, almost together: almost blending.

There is a smell of smoke in the small space. A groan. A thump as two men hit the floor in synchrony. Denfrell strides over to Tubby Gateside, bends down, a sickening crack as he pulls Tubby's trigger finger backwards to break it at the proximal joint.

Someone starts screaming.

*

Minnie eventually realised that the screams were hers. Through the chaos in the room, she could see that Ben had fallen with one of the shots, the postdoc, Gateside, was it, with the other? The shots could not have been simultaneous but were sufficiently close together for it not to matter. She wondered why Mr Denfrell had broken Gateside's finger. Then realized that it was so, in the unlikely event of the postdoc not being dead, he would not be able to shoot at anyone else.

Then, slowly, she dared to swivel her mind around to contemplate Ben, who was lying, face-down, on the floor, with blood all over the back of his head. She cannot think, unbearable pain and shock are the only things she has left.

She lurched over to kneel and pick-up Ben's hand. She began screaming anew.

*

They had taken Ben to Ninewells Hospital immediately. He was still alive but the paramedics, arriving straight after the police had broken in, were doubtful he'd even make it across the river. Tubby Gateside had been shot in the heart by Max Denfrell, who was not trained to wound.

The bullet from Tubby's gun had entered Ben's left frontal lobe

299

and exited, in a blaze of glory, from the back of his head. Minnie, still holding his hand, had gone with him in the ambulance, with the siren on and lights flashing. The police arrested Denfrell, as well as Professor Meredith Williams, whom they encountered on the way out, and who appeared to be drunk.

*

There wasn't much time, she knew that only too well. She had practiced something like this over and over, especially as the dissociation seemed to be resolving and Ben was starting to decompensate on various levels.

She had known that this was how it would be at the end. He couldn't talk, she knew that, and probably couldn't even have understood her had he been conscious. And he wasn't. Unlikely he would be again. She had never stopped talking to him, through the years, though, reminding him of their early times, reminding him of all they meant to each other. Of how they had lost Wisp, like she had done for so long, subtly, every time the occasion allowed.

"I've loved you so much," she said, "There's never been anyone like you. I've always been there, you know, even when you didn't know me; meeting in the street and you believing I was your doctor. It was always worth it; the only thing I could do to help you after our baby died and you couldn't bear it. You had to get away from everything, even me. I couldn't tell you; I don't know what would have happened in your mind then – it could have broken completely.

"I've always been a one-man woman, Ben. Just like my mother was. You used to know that, even when we first met. I hoped for a long, lovely life together…"

Impossibly, Ben's eyes flickered open. He gazed at her, almost crouched over him, looking at him with her wonderful wise eyes. "Free!" he murmured on the rattling out-breath, as the heart monitor started to screech.

*

END

Printed in Great Britain
by Amazon